treacherous

ALEX GRAYSON
MELISSA TOPPEN

Treacherous

Cover Design by Melissa Gill Designs. Interior Formatting by Alex Grayson. Editing by Rose David Editing.

chapter one

RYLEE

"rylee, if you don't get downstairs you're going to be late." My mother's voice rings through the closed door of my bedroom, a soft knock following.

Late. I roll my eyes, wishing I could do more than be late—like maybe skip this whole day all together. It's the day I've been dreading since I found out that her and Paul were getting married and we would be moving in with him.

It's not something any teenage girl wants to hear. That with a mere five months left of her senior year, she will have to leave all her friends and everything she loves to live with a man she barely knows and his intolerable son.

Yay me.

"Rylee. Did you hear me?" Mom knocks again.

"I heard you," I call back, trying really hard to keep the irritation from my voice. This isn't Mom's fault.

Well, I guess technically it is, but how could I fault her for going after a chance to be happy? I can't expect her to pass up on love because it's inconvenient for me. Besides, in a few short months I will be leaving all this behind for college anyway.

"Well, chip chop then. You don't want to make a bad first impression," she practically sings.

She is way too chipper for this early in the morning.

"Earth to Rylee. Come in Rylee," Savannah says, reminding me there's a phone pressed to my ear.

"Sorry, Mom was talking to me. What were you saying?"

"I was just saying how bad Bristol is gonna suck without you. You basically left me high and dry with no warning," she playfully jabs—though she's not wrong. When I'd left for winter break I'd thought I'd be back after the New Year. At that time I had no idea I would never grace the halls of Bristol High again. "Who am I going to bitch to in between classes?" she chatters on. "Who's going to tell me when I have food stuck in my teeth, or that my makeup is smudged? Who's going to keep me from throwing myself at Jonah every chance I get? Because you know I have zero restraint without you."

Savannah has been my best friend since kindergarten, and up to this point, we've pretty much never been apart. And while yes, thirty miles of separation isn't the end of the world, especially since we both have cars, it feels like she's an entire world away.

"Don't be dramatic. You still have Jane and Sarah," I remind her.

"Jane and Sarah aren't you."

"Well, it could be worse. You could be walking into a school where the only person you know is your stepbrother who's made it painfully clear he doesn't like you and treats you like an intruder in your new home."

"Still hasn't gotten any better, huh?" she asks, already knowing about the growing list of issues I have had with Oliver since we moved in last week.

"He walked past me in the family room yesterday and didn't sneer at me. That has to count for something, right?" I groan audibly.

"Baby steps," she reassures me lightheartedly. "Besides, if I know you, and I think I do, he won't be the only person you know for long. You'll probably have replaced me by the end of the day. Everyone loves you."

"One, I could never replace you—I've tried," I tease. "And two, not everyone loves me. Clearly." I tack on the last part with an eye roll.

"Don't let him get to you. Just do you and you'll be fine. I know it."

"Thanks." I blow out a shaky breath.

"And if you need me to come over there and beat his ass for you, I totally will."

"Don't tempt me." I chuckle, the thought of tiny little Savannah scratching Oliver's eyes out flashes through my mind.

"Well, it's a standing offer. I'm here if you need me."

"I'll keep that in mind," I say, figuring I need to wrap this up and get going. "I better go. Mom will kill me if I'm late for my first day of school."

"Okay. You'll call me right after?"

"I will."

"Love you, Ry."

"Love you, too." I end the call, turning toward the floor length mirror that adorns my closet door. I run a hand through my thick brown hair, wishing it had been more cooperative this morning.

Honestly, I look terrible. My eyes are all swollen and puffy from lack of sleep. I was so nervous about today that I tossed and turned all night and not even my favorite concealer could hide the evidence of my sleepless night.

My gaze travels down to my pale pink top and dark skinny jeans that I partnered with my favorite pair of brown booties. It took me hours to settle on an outfit, and I still feel uncomfortable, which is very unlike me.

I'm not used to being so unsure of myself, but this entire situation has really thrown me. It had all happened so fast. One day I'm living a normal happy life, looking forward to spending senior year with my friends and doing all the fun things that entails. The next, my mom and Paul are eloping in Fiji, and my entire world gets turned upside down. I've barely had time to wrap my head around it, and now here I am, facing my first day at a new school where none of my friends will be.

Blowing out a puff of air, I turn away from my reflection and head toward the door, grabbing my book bag on the way out. I drop my cell into the front pocket before sliding the strap over my shoulder. Opening my bedroom door, I pause when Oliver opens his at the exact moment as I step into the hall. As if moving wasn't bad enough, I got stuck with quite possibly the worst stepbrother in history. He hates that Mom and I are here.

Before he can say anything snarky, I quickly turn and take off down the stairs, heading in the direction of the kitchen.

If they had moved in with us, I wouldn't be forced to have a bedroom directly across from a person who hates me for reasons that are completely out of my control. I can't help that his parents divorced, or that his dad remarried within a year. None of that has anything to do with me. But I think it's safe to say he doesn't see it that way. Either that, or he's taking it out on me because he knows he can't take it out on my mom, or his dad for that matter. Not if he wants to maintain free access to his father's money.

Unfortunately, Mom thought Paul's house was the more logical choice. Good school, a nice neighborhood, and closer to the hospital where she performs most of her surgeries. I get it, but it certainly doesn't make the pill any easier to swallow.

I walk through the foyer and down a long hallway, dropping my book bag right inside the door of the kitchen.

"There she is." Paul looks up from his laptop and smiles, his freshly pressed suit perfectly fitted to his broad shoulders.

At least he's *nice to me.*

"Good morning." I force a smile and head toward the refrigerator to grab some orange juice. I still feel so weird being here. I know it's my home now, but I can't help but feel on edge and uneasy, like I'm walking on eggshells all of the time.

"Excited for your first day?" he asks.

"I guess." I shrug, my back to him as I retrieve a glass from the cabinet.

"She'll be great." My shoulders tense at the sound of Oliver's voice. I know he's only saying that because he wants his father to believe he's playing nice, but I don't miss the hint of something dark in his tone.

"Of course she will," Paul agrees.

I turn right as mom enters the kitchen; her slender frame somewhat hidden beneath unflattering scrubs—her dark hair pulled back in a ponytail.

"Surgery today?" I ask, knowing that's the only time Mom wears scrubs to work.

She nods, taking the seat next to Paul where a cup of coffee is already waiting for her. This makes me smile, despite my sour mood. Paul really is good to Mom. Truthfully, it's the only thing that makes any of this worth it—seeing the smile that slides across her face as she sits down next to her new husband.

"Glioblastoma," she tells me, taking a sip of her coffee.

I nod before taking a long drink of my juice, ignoring Oliver who settles in next to me, shoving half a banana into his mouth in one bite.

Growing up with a neurosurgeon for a mom, I've picked up on a few things over the years. Not that I really know what removing a glioblastoma actually entails, but I at least know what type of tumor it is.

"Now remember, I won't be home until late tonight, and Paul is working on a big case, so he will probably be at the office most of the evening. You'll have to fend for yourself for dinner."

I swear, sometimes she treats me like I'm still ten rather than almost eighteen. I resist the urge to point out that I know how to feed myself.

"No problem." I nod.

"There's a list of menus in the top drawer over there." Paul points toward the massive island in the center of the large eat in kitchen. "You and Oliver can order in if you want."

"Got it." I nod again.

"And don't forget that you need to call your father today," Mom chimes in.

Just the mention of my dad has a tight knot forming in my chest. I love my dad, don't get me wrong, but we don't have the closest relationship these days. Growing up, I was always a daddy's girl. But when he and mom divorced, everything changed. I'm lucky if I get to see him once every few months, with him being busy with his new family and all.

I try to remind myself that I'm happy for him, but it's hard to push past the bitterness I feel about the entire situation. Before he met Cynthia, his world revolved around me. After? Well, let's just say he found other people to spend his time with. Mainly his new wife and their now five-year-old twin daughters.

"I'll see what I can do," I tell her, finishing off my juice before setting my empty glass in the sink.

"They're leaving for their cruise in the morning, and I know he'd love to hear about how your first day went before they leave."

How could I forget—*insert sarcasm.* The *family* cruise that I wasn't invited to go on with them.

I bite my tongue and hold back saying what I really want to say—that he probably doesn't even remember that today is my first day at a new school. Mom tries so hard to be the bridge between my father and me. Sometimes I want to shake her and tell her to open her big brown eyes and see what's really going on. Dad may love me in his own way, but he stopped caring about my life a long time ago.

"Okay," I grumble out in agreement. I can always tell her I called but he didn't answer if she asks later. "I'll see you tonight when you get home." I turn, preparing to leave.

"Where are you going?" She stops me before I can even take a step.

"School?" I throw her a questioning look.

"You haven't eaten." She gestures to the plate of pastries and bowl of fruit sitting on the table.

"I'm not really hungry. I'll grab something from the cafeteria at school if I need to." She gives me a look of disapproval but doesn't say anything more on the subject.

"Oliver is riding with you today," Paul interjects, gesturing to his son. My stomach instantly drops.

"What? Why? What's wrong with your car?" My gaze slides to my stepbrother, and I internally cringe. Oliver isn't a bad looking guy. Honestly, he looks just like his father, only in a younger form. He's tall and thin with sandy blond hair, hazel eyes, and perfectly straight white teeth. He's the epitome of a pretty boy. But I know what lies beneath the designer clothes and that perfectly put together exterior of his and it's not a heart of gold.

"I'm having it painted."

"But it's a brand-new car."

"And?" He lets the question hang there for a long moment.

Wow, okay then.

"But I'm good." He directs his attention back to his father. "Z is giving me a ride."

On that note, I turn and snag my book bag off the floor, not wanting to press my luck. "Well, I really should get going. Good luck on your surgery today," I tell Mom, throwing up a half wave as I exit the kitchen, snagging my jacket off the coat rack on my way.

"Have a good first day," she calls after me as I make my way to the front door. Tugging it open, I nearly jump out of my skin when I almost collide with the tall frame standing directly on the other side.

"Whoa," he starts, taking a small step back, my sudden appearance surprising him as much as his did me.

"Sorry." I blink upward.

The instant my eyes hit his face my jaw goes slack. He's… he's… he's… *Gorgeous.* That's the only word I can come up with, but it doesn't seem to do him justice.

Holy hell.

Dark messy hair, square jawline, full lips. I swear, by the time I make it to his eyes I can feel the sweat forming at the nape of my neck. Crisp blue eyes—the kind of blue that makes you feel like you're standing on the beach with the ocean waves crashing around your feet. He blinks, his thick lashes touching the tops of his cheeks and I realize I'm openly gawking.

"You must be Oliver's friend," I stutter, feeling heat creep across my cheeks.

"Zayden." He nods.

So this is Z?

"I'm…." I start to introduce myself but stop when his gaze darts behind me.

"Hey, man." Oliver's voice startles me seconds before he brushes past me in the doorway. "You could have texted that you were here."

"Yeah, left my phone at home. You ready?" His eyes sweep to mine for one more brief moment before he turns, but he doesn't say anything. Doesn't ask my name or say that it was nice to meet me. *Nothing*. It's like I wasn't even standing here.

And even though his lack of interest bothers me, I can't stop myself from watching the way his back and shoulders flex as he walks away, the material of his dark jacket stretching against his lean, but muscular frame. I can't help it. He's *that* good looking.

Oliver nods as he follows after his friend, stopping at the bottom of the front porch steps before turning to give me the fakest smile I think I've ever seen. "Have a great first day, *sis*," he mocks, his voice dripping with sarcasm.

I bite back the urge to give a retort. Not like it would do me any good. Talking to Oliver is like talking to a brick wall. I get zero reaction from him. It's like he doesn't find me worthy of conversing with if it doesn't involve spouting off little insults whenever he has the chance.

It's been eight months since my mom and his dad started dating, but I can count on one hand how many times Oliver and I have actually spent time together. Whenever Paul would come over to our house, Oliver never came with him, and he made it clear to me the very first night we all had dinner together that he was not okay with his dad dating my mom, which automatically made me public enemy number one. I wish I could have been a fly on the wall when he found out that his dad and my mom eloped while they were vacationing in Fiji the week before Christmas.

I wait until Oliver and Zayden disappear inside the black truck parked in front of the house before heading for my red Audi in the driveway. It was a sixteenth birthday present from my mom. She bought it used, but it still looks new. Unlike Paul does for Oliver, my mother does not just hand me the best of everything. Don't get me wrong, I've definitely grown up with some of the finer things in life, but Mom has never spoiled me or bought me expensive things just because I wanted them. I bet Paul has never told Oliver no a day in his life. Then again, being one of the top attorneys in the great state of Washington, it's not like he doesn't have the money to spare.

Pulling open the driver's side door, I toss my book bag into the passenger seat and slide on my jacket before climbing inside, my earlier nerves returning full force. I consider calling Savannah again, fearing I'm at risk of fleeing the scene, but decide against it. She's no doubt headed for school herself, and even if she did answer, what can she really say that she hasn't already?

So, I do the one thing I always do whenever I feel anxious or upset. I start the car, pull my phone out of my bag, scroll through my music playlist until I find what I'm looking for, and crank up the speakers—smiling to myself when "Shake it Off" by Taylor Swift starts playing.

I don't know what it is about this song that instantly brightens my mood, but it works every single time. Put on a little T. Swift and all is right with the world again.

chapter two

ZAYDEN

"i hate that bitch," Oliver growls before throwing a handful of Red Hots into his mouth, chomping down on them.

I glance at him out the side of my aviators. "What's the deal with her, anyway?"

His eyes narrow into slits and pure hatred mars his face. Oliver doesn't like many people, and you have to earn it to get on his good side, but this is different than his normal dislike of someone. His usual MO is to pretend they don't exist. He not only hates this girl, but despises her.

He tosses the empty box on the dash and stretches out in his seat. "You know what's up with her. Her and her money-grubbing mother are squatting in my house. Probably stealing the silver and draining as much as they can from our bank accounts while they do it. Fuck my dad for marrying her and letting them come live with us."

"Come on, man." I side-eye the rearview mirror and switch lanes. "It's more than that. They have money of their own. They don't need yours."

"They may have money, but not like my old man does. People like them… they can never have enough." I feel his eyes on me. "Why the hell are you defending them?"

I grit my teeth, my fingers cramping around the steering wheel. An image of thick, luscious brown hair and startled dark-brown eyes comes to mind. Along with it is the addicting scent of roses and the remembered warmth radiating off her body. Despite her having lived there for a couple of weeks already, this morning was my first glimpse of her. Oliver's new sister is hot as fuck, and it pisses me off. Someone as cunning as her has no business encompassing such a sweet package.

"You know me better than that, Oliver," I grunt, anger making the words come out harsh.

"Dad's only been divorced for a year. The fucking ink isn't even dry on the papers. The last thing he needs is some hussy moving into my mother's house. And my new *sister*,"—he sneers— "will think she can get anything and everything she wants. Spoiled brat."

"Like *you* always get everything?" The corner of my mouth tips up as I smirk.

"Fuck off," he grumbles. His phone chimes, and he tilts to the side to pull it from his back pocket. "Terri says her party's still on for this weekend. You in?"

Goddamn parties. I hate them because their mostly filled with sluts from school, wannabes, jocks, and rich pricks. I only go because Oliver wants me there. He says it's good to show face. Whatever the hell *that* means.

"Yeah. I'll be there." I flip the blinker and pull into the school parking lot. "But I can't stay long. Dad has a midnight shift, so I have to watch Danielle."

Dad is a janitor at the hospital. The pay is shit, but between his checks and what I make at Benny's Auto Repair, we make do. We did better when mom was still around. But the bitch had to run off with the rich asshole she worked for, leaving Dad and me behind to take care of Danielle. Not that I'm complaining about watching out for my little sister. I'd do anything for her.

"How is little Dani?"

I don't answer until I've parked and gotten out of my truck. "The doctors are worried the pneumonia will come back. They've got her on a strong round of antibiotics to try and stave it off."

Thinking about the struggle Danielle's faced her whole life darkens my mood. I snatch my backpack from my truck and slam the door shut, grinding my molars when the loose window rattles and drops down a couple of inches.

I meet Oliver at the tail gate.

"That's shit. Any word on if she got approved for the transplant list?"

"Insurance company denied her again. Said her case isn't serious enough."

Fucking insurance companies and pharmaceuticals. No doubt if it was their loved ones suffering from emphysema, no matter how mild or severe the case, they'd worm their way to the top of the transplant list faster than a whore drops her panties when she sees a twenty-dollar bill. All rich people are the same.

Entitled, greedy, and with the mentality that the world owes them whatever the hell they want.

Oliver falls into step beside me as we make our way up to the school. “My offer still stands to ask my dad—”

“No.” I cut him off before he can finish. “You know I appreciate the offer, but we’ll figure it out on our own. We always do.”

Oliver and his father are a select few who are loaded that I can stand to be around. Oliver and I have been friends since elementary school, before the spoils of riches made him jaded. He and his father have both offered several times to pay for Danielle’s treatments and medicine, but I refuse to take the help of others. Being in debt to the wealthy, even if it is the father of my best friend, is something I’ll never let happen.

I plan to stop by Hart’s on the way home and talk to him about booking me for a few extra fights.

“If anything happens, you know my dad will take care of it,” he adds.

I sidestep a guy before he barrels into me, trying to catch a flying football. “Watch it, asshole,” I growl. He turns to face me, an angry scowl in place, but the look quickly dies when he sees me.

“Shit, Zayden. I didn’t see you there. Sorry, man.”

I ignore his apology and step through the school doors. Brandon’s one of the rich pricks I *don’t* like being around. Especially after he got pulled over for almost hitting an elderly woman while driving drunk, and having his father, who happens to be a judge, get him off on the charges. It’s people like him the world needs less of.

“Tiffany’s supposed to be at the party this weekend,” Oliver comments when we come to a stop at my locker. "You gonna finally hit it? She's been jonesing after you for a while."

Tiffany's been after my dick since last year. Ever since I banged Sylvia, one of her friends, and she let loose the size of my cock and how well I can use it. Tiffany's a pretty girl, but I've got no real interest in her. Of course, I don't need to be interested in a girl to bang her; so long as she looks good and isn't a clinger, I'm usually down. I've let her suck me off a couple of times and it was only mediocre at best. Her fucking teeth almost scraped my dick raw the first time, but I let her have another go, thinking it was from excitement that had her so enthusiastic. Time number two wasn't any better. She won't be getting a third chance. At least not with her mouth.

"Maybe," I answer noncommittedly. It's been a few weeks since I've felt a warm pussy. Maybe I'll give that part of her anatomy a chance.

"Pattie's coming, too. And she's bringing her double D cousin. Remember last time—" He stops abruptly. "Motherfucker."

I turn at Oliver's harsh mutter and spot his stepsister come through the doors. And what do you fucking know. My dick takes notice, too.

She looks around the crowded hallway. Seconds later, her eyes widen and she jerks forward when the closing door pops her in the ass. She drops a couple of books and almost falls on her prettily made up face. She releases a yelp and every pair of eyes move to her. Laughter fills the hallway, including mine and Oliver's.

Matters get worse when the door opens again and she's shoved to the side. "Get outta the way," Kassandra shrieks.

I reluctantly give her credit when she doesn't bow down to the resident mean girl. She glares daggers at the girl's back and looks like she might chase after her. Eventually, she rolls her eyes, bends, and scoops up the books she dropped.

"Kassandra should have pushed the bitch harder," Oliver states, pulling my attention back to him.

"You don't think that's a bit much?" I shove my backpack in my locker.

"Fuck no. She needs to learn from the get-go that she's a nobody here." He pulls out a small box of Red Hots from his pocket and tips it to his lips. The guy is obsessed with the candy. "I gotta hit my locker. I'll see you later."

"Later."

I turn back to my locker and snatch out my chemistry book. As I'm reaching for my calculus book, I feel her at my side.

"Hi."

I glance over, already knowing who it is. Deep brown eyes stare back at me. Thick brown hair falls over her slender shoulders in soft waves. And that damn fresh scent of roses hits me square in the chest.

I grunt. Not really a hello, but not altogether ignoring her either. I turn back and grab my calculus book, then slam my locker shut. It bangs loudly, and I don't miss her flinch.

"My name's Rylee," she states, her voice sounding way too soft and alluring. "In case you were wondering. We never got a chance to really introduce ourselves earlier."

Rylee.

I already know her name because Oliver's bitched about her enough that it's seared into my brain.

"This is my locker," she continues like I'm standing here being the pillar of a listening ear.

Apparently, the girl wants to talk, so I turn and face her, leaning against my locker. I lift a brow and regard her.

"So?"

A frown line appears between her eyes. "Just trying to make polite conversation. You know, since we'll be locker neighbors."

"I don't like conversation."

"What?" She frowns. "How can you not like conversation?"

I lean in closer, ignoring her rose scent, and say in a low but rude tone, "Because I don't like talking."

She scoffs and flips her hair over her shoulder. Whatever the hell shampoo she uses smells too fucking good for comfort. "That's dumb. We're having a conversation right now."

I stand from my perch against the lockers and look down at her. "Only because you won't shut up."

Her eyes widen, showing off the little specks of gold hidden in their brown depths, but before she has a chance to open her mouth, I turn and walk away, ready to be out of her presence.

"Wait!" she calls, and I release a sigh of annoyance. Why can't the girl get a fucking clue?

I keep walking, but a moment later, she's back at my side. "I, uh...." She turns to the side to avoid getting rammed by a couple of seniors. "I was wondering if I could get your help. I have Mrs. Daily first period. Could you tell me which direction to go?"

"No."

I feel her confusion, along with her heated stare. "No? No you won't help me, or no you don't know which way to go?"

"Either. Both. Take your pick." I stop and turn to face her. "I'm not your goddamn guide, okay? I've got no desire to be your friend. And by the end of the day, your locker will be somewhere away from mine. So, find someone else to be your lap dog, and steer clear of me."

I don't wait for her response, as I continue on my way to chemistry, which also happens to be Mrs. Daily's class.

"Asshole!" she yells at my back.

I flip her off over my shoulder.

Fuck Rylee and her mesmerizing scent.

chapter three

RYLEE

Well, if the first half of my day is any indication on how the rest of the school year is going to go, I'm in for some rough days ahead. After the complete blow off I got from Zayden this morning, things only got worse. I got lost trying to find my first class and ended up showing up nearly five minutes after the last bell. As if it weren't hard enough being the new girl, having to walk through a room full of strangers with every eye trained on you put the icing on the cake. And to make matters worse, the jerk who refused to help me find my first period class was actually *in* my first period class.

I didn't have better luck with second period, but by third I was starting to get a feel for the building.

Gripping my lunch tray with both hands, I look out over the crowded cafeteria, trying to find a place to sit. Finally spotting an empty round table in the far corner, I cross the room with my eyes trained directly ahead.

I'm not a shy person by any means, and I typically make friends pretty easily, but this is a whole new situation for me. Truthfully, I'm just trying to feel my way through it and find some footing.

Sliding down into one of the chairs, I sit my tray in front of me and twist the cap off my water. Laughter from a few feet away draws my attention, and I look to the right to see Zayden sitting on top of the lunch table like he's some sort of king and the table is his throne. I guess that makes all the people in front of him his loyal subjects. Guessing by how he seems to be the center of everyone's focus, I might have hit the nail on the head.

He's leaning forward, elbows on his knees as he surveys the crowd. Oliver and a few others are grouped around him, laughing and talking.

Even though I don't want to look, I can't seem to tear my eyes away. The way his messy hair hangs across his forehead. The broadness of his shoulders. The sliver of tanned skin peeking out where his shirt has ridden up in the back. I lick my lips, my mouth suddenly parched.

"Hey there." I'm pulled out of my trance by a male voice.

I blink as I look up to the stranger.

"Hi," I stutter, the smirk on his face enough to tell me I've been caught staring.

"Are you by chance Rylee?" He plays the name on his lips like he's trying to figure out if he remembers it correctly. He slides down into the seat across from me without asking if I mind—which I don't.

"I am." I survey the guy in one quick sweep. Average height. Average build. Nice smile. Cute dimple. Blonde hair that's slicked back from his face, giving him a Leonardo DiCaprio vibe. All in all, I'd say he's pretty good looking. Not as good looking as some people, my eyes dart to Zayden before coming back to the boy sitting in front of me, but still quite handsome.

"My friend Chloe said there was a new girl in her French class today. When I saw you sitting over here all by yourself, I assumed it must be you." He adjusts in his seat. "I'm Charles, by the way. But most of my friends call me Pierce."

"Your last name?" I guess.

"Pretty unoriginal, I know. But it started in grade school and sort of stuck." He shrugs, pulling the top off of his yogurt.

"Well, it's nice to meet you, Charles." I offer him a friendly smile, turning my attention to my food, untouched on the tray in front of me.

"Pierce," he corrects.

"Right. Pierce." I nod, my smile spreading.

I didn't realize how much I needed this. The human interaction. Actually talking to someone who wasn't either growling at me or glaring at me like they wanted to take my head off in one quick swipe.

"So, I see you've noticed Zayden." He looks to the side and my gaze immediately follows.

God, why does he have to be so good looking?

My stomach knots thinking about the way he treated me this morning. Guess it's safe to say Oliver has gotten to him. Not that I expected anything different. Well, I didn't expect him to be quite so hateful, but I certainly never betted on any of Oliver's friends actually liking me.

"Noticed him, was blown off by him, called him an asshole." I blow out a breath and turn my gaze back to Pierce.

"Wait, you called Zayden Michaels an asshole?" He snorts out a laugh. "And you're still sitting here to tell me about it?"

"Am I missing something?" I hit him with a confused look.

"Let's just say Zayden kind of rules the roost around here. Not many people can talk back to him and get away with it. If it's not him doing the dirty work, it's one of his minions. They're all assholes." He loosely gestures around the room. "But, you're still in one piece, so I guess that's something."

"I guess," I halfheartedly agree, picking up a breadstick from my plate before ripping a piece off and popping it into my mouth. I have zero appetite, but considering I haven't eaten anything since dinner yesterday, I know I need to force a little something down.

"Too bad he's such a dick. It's a shame really." He glances back at Zayden almost longingly.

"You're gay." It's a statement, not a question.

"Bi, actually. I appreciate both sexes equally." He turns back to me and hits me with a flirty smile.

"You're charming, I'll give you that." I wave my breadstick at him.

"So, what's your story?" he asks as I pop another piece of bread into my mouth, finally starting to relax a little.

I finish chewing before answering. "No story. At least not an interesting one."

"How did you end up at Parkview?" He picks up his plastic spoon and jabs it into his cup of yogurt.

"My mom remarried."

"Where did you go to school before?"

"Bristol." I take a long pull of water.

"No shit? I have a friend that goes to Bristol. Sarah Jennings. Do you know her?" The sound of the familiar name sends a warm sensation through my limbs, bringing back a small piece of home.

"Sarah Jennings is one of my closest friends." The smile on my face is completely unforced for the first time all day. "How do you know her?"

"We dated over the summer a couple of years ago. It didn't work out, but we've stayed in touch."

"Wait." I hold up my hand, starting to piece together the puzzle. "You're *the* Charles? The one she met at the fair the summer between freshman and sophomore year?" Sarah talked about this guy all summer—though she never called him Pierce that I can remember. She hyped him up to the point that Savannah, Jane, and I had started to believe she had made him up. No guy was *that* perfect. Our suspicions only grew when they conveniently broke up right before school started and not a single person ever met him.

"The one and only," he boasts.

I immediately make a mental note that I need to call Sarah and apologize for giving her crap about this guy all those years ago.

"I'm not going to lie to you, we all thought she made you up," I admit. "You know, she still has that stupid stuffed turtle you won her on the balloon dart game," I tell him, laughter dancing around my words. I purposely leave out the fact that up until today, I believed she had won it herself or conned one of the workers into giving it to her for free. Sarah has a way of getting what she wants.

"I know, she makes me say hi to the damn thing every time we FaceTime." He chuckles.

"What a small world."

"That it is," he agrees. "Wait, so if you went to Bristol…." he trails off. It's now his turn to put the pieces together. "Are you Oliver's new stepsister?"

"The one and only," I repeat his words back to him. "Though if you've heard of me, that can't be a good thing."

"I heard whisperings that his dad remarried and that he had a new stepsister. I just didn't realize you were the same age as him. I was envisioning some cute little girl with pink cheeks and pigtails."

"Sorry to disappoint," I tease.

"Oh honey, I'm not even a little disappointed." He makes a spectacle of checking me out. While normally I would feel a little put off by his forwardness, there's something so comical and endearing about the way he looks at me that makes me want to laugh rather than wrap my arms around myself to shield my body from his wandering eyes.

"Do you think you could hook me up with your brother? I mean, I've been on a girl kick recently, but I'm feeling like it's time to switch things up." He winks playfully at me.

"One, he's not my brother. And two, I'm pretty sure you'd have more luck than I would, considering the guy hates my guts." My brow furrows. "Besides, I don't think he swings for your team."

"Damn shame, too." He grins, and I realize that he's trying to lighten the mood.

I'm really liking this guy already. My heart warms at the thought. I think I might have just found my first friend.

"Nah, you're too good for him. He's a narcissistic asshole. Trust me, stay as far away from that one as you can."

"I don't have a death sentence," he jokes. "But he sure is pretty to look at."

"I guess if you like the pretty boy type." I shrug, realizing Pierce is also what I would consider a pretty boy.

"What's wrong with a pretty boy?" He arches a brow and gestures to himself.

"I just meant…." I stutter out.

"Relax, Rylee." He laughs. "I'm only messing with you. And don't worry. I know exactly who Oliver Conley is, and other than appreciating his good looks, I know to stay far, *far* away. His group is not too accepting of my lifestyle."

"Well screw them," I almost shout, angry that anyone could judge someone based on who they're attracted to.

"Amen to that." He holds up his juice and gestures to my water. It takes me a minute to realize what he's doing before I quickly grab the bottle. "To new friends." He smiles, his dimple popping out on his right cheek.

"To new friends." I tap my bottle against his, feeling more at ease than I have in weeks.

We spend the rest of the lunch period chit chatting about nothing of any real importance. We laugh and joke and by the end of the half hour you would think we had been friends forever.

He walked me to my sixth period class and we exchanged numbers before he had to take off to get to his own. Feeling more comfortable, there's a small skip in my step as I make my way into English. Unfortunately, my good mood instantly disappears when I spot Zayden sitting in the back of the classroom.

Great.

The lighthearted feeling that had flowed through me only moments ago is instantly replaced with a heavy dread in the pit of my stomach. And here I was beginning to think that this day might actually end on a high note.

I swiftly force my eyes in another direction, holding my head high as I make my way to an empty seat at the front of the class. I dig into my bag for a notebook and pencil, sliding them onto my desk right as the teacher enters the classroom.

Because this is my first day, and I'm starting each class over four months behind, I've spent most of the day taking notes of the things I need to catch up on. Luckily, a lot of things they are teaching are the same at Bristol, so it hasn't been too overwhelming up to this point.

Mr. McHenry takes a seat behind a large brown desk that bares the marks of use. Straightening his posture, his eyes go directly to me as the class starts to fall silent.

"It appears we have a new student with us today," Mr. McHenry starts, and my stomach doubles over on itself into a fury of nerves. I hate being the center of everyone's focus. So far, I'd been lucky and no other teacher had even commented on the fact that there was a new student in attendance. "Miss Harper, I believe." He waits for my confirmation before continuing, "Why don't you stand up and tell us a couple things about yourself."

The knots in my stomach tighten, and my knees tremble slightly as I stand. I'm not sure what's worse, having to stand up in front of a room full of complete strangers or the fact that I have to stand up in front of *him*.

"I'm Rylee," I say, throwing in an awkward wave as my eyes stay glued to the teacher.

"Why don't you turn around and address the room, Rylee?" he offers, gesturing to the classmates behind me.

If looks could kill, poor Mr. McHenry would be laying in a heap on the floor right now. But, being the good student that I am, I do as I'm told, looking anywhere but at the ocean blue eyes I know are watching me. I can feel the heat of his stare like a match being held too close to my face.

"Hi, I'm Rylee," I start again, my gaze bouncing around the classroom full of strangers. "I'm eighteen years old. And I just transferred from Bristol High." Thinking that is enough, I start to turn back around, but Mr. McHenry stops me in my tracks.

"What's something you can tell us that will help us get to know you a little better?"

I take a sharp breath in through my nose and let it out through my mouth, trying to appear confident and collected when I feel anything but.

"Um...," I stutter out, trying to come up with something to say. "I love old TV shows like *I Love Lucy* and *Bewitched*, and I have a serious girl crush on Taylor Swift."

A few giggles sound around the room, and I fear that maybe they don't understand my humor. But then a red-headed girl at the back of the class pumps her fist in the air and says, "Preach girl," making me relax a little.

"I plan to attend Seattle University in the fall, pre-med, and my favorite kind of ice cream is rocky road." I make the mistake of looking at the one person I'm trying to avoid looking at. Our eyes lock, and I swear I lose all sense of my surroundings. Everything fades to the background. Everything but the way my heart pounds heavily in my chest and my breathing comes in short quick spurts like my lungs can't figure out how to pull in a proper breath.

I can't read his expression. A mixture of amusement and anger dance behind those brilliant eyes of his, but I can't figure out which one is more prominent. All I know for sure is that Zayden Michaels is one intimidating guy. And for whatever reason, I'm intrigued.

The sound of chair legs scratching against the tile floor snaps me back to the present, and I turn to see Mr. McHenry stand.

"Thank you for that, Miss Harper." He nods, and I quickly move to reclaim my seat. "Now, as I told you all before winter break, our next assignment will be breaking down the difference between novel and film. Each of you had the opportunity to nominate a title for consideration. After much discussion with the school board, we settled on a title we feel is both current to today's youth and appropriate for classroom discussion. Anyone want to guess what it might be?" He looks around the room.

"*Fifty Shades*," a student calls, and the room breaks into soft murmurs and laughter.

"You wish, Miss Tenley." He shakes his head, sliding the square rimmed glasses from his face. "Someone else care to make a guess." He holds up his hand before the girl can speak again. "Someone other than Miss Tenley." He smiles.

"*Harry Potter*?" one student guesses.

"*The Notebook*?" says another.

"You're getting warmer. Anyone else?"

"*Twilight*?" another girl asks hopefully.

"Ding. Ding. Ding." Mr. McHenry claps his hands together. The room becomes a flurry of groans and eye rolls.

"Of course it's freaking *Twilight*." The guy next to me slouches in his seat. "You realize that only girls like that stuff, right, Mr. M? I mean, come on. The dude sparkles in the sun light. Whatever happened to vampires bursting into flames?"

"Seriously, *Twilight* is like so ten years ago," the girl behind him whines. "Why can't we do something more current?"

"Yeah, like *Fifty Shades*," the same girl as before interjects and a few people laugh.

"Everyone had a chance to nominate a title, and this is the one we decided on. If you have a problem with that, too bad."

There are a few more grumbles that eventually die off as the teacher continues, "So, your assignment for this quarter will be to both read the book as well as watch the movie. After which time you will write a five-page essay on the difference between the book and the movie, and how those differences may have changed how certain characters were perceived, as well as the overall feel of the story." He holds up his finger, telling the class he isn't done yet. "But, this isn't a solo assignment. While one person may see things one way, someone else may see them another, and that class, is the beauty of art. It can mean one thing to you and something entirely different to another person. Essays are due on my desk four weeks from today, at which time we will split you off into teams of four where you will discuss the different points of each of your essays. Then, you will write a ten-page essay, which will include the five pages already written in your initial essay and five more pages covering the points made from other team members, and how their opinions may have altered your overall view of the story. Now, so that there are no surprises, I've already randomly assigned your teams. Rylee," he turns his attention to me, "since you were just added to this class over break, you will be included in the last group on the page, which only has three members," he says, handing me a stack of papers before proceeding to the first student in every row and handing them a similar stack. "Take one and pass them back."

I do as he says, snagging the top copy before turning around and passing the remaining papers to the person behind me. I scroll the list of names, finally landing on the last group where only three names are listed—knowing this will be my group.

My heart nearly jumps clean out of my chest when my eyes land on the last name on the list. Zayden Michaels.... You have got to be kidding me. Of all the people, of course I would be partnered with one of only two people in this school who I know doesn't like me. If his actions this morning didn't make that perfectly clear, the way he glares at me at the end of class certainly puts any hope I had to rest.

Yep, he definitely hates me.

Awesome.

chapter four

ZAYDEN

using my fists. I slam through the doors leading outside, my anger and raised blood pressure making me twitch. Fuck Mrs. Miller and the high horse she thinks she rides on. I've got one chance to get into the University of Washington, and it sure as hell isn't with money. An academic scholarship is my only way in, which means I have to keep my GPA at 4.0. Mrs. Miller knows this. But the bitch gave me a C halfway through the school year because "*my essay wasn't strong enough*". Which is utter bullshit. She just didn't understand what the fuck I wrote because it went over her head. Now I've got to work twice as hard to get my grade back up before the end of the school year.

I stalk the sidewalk that leads to the parking lot. Students clear a path when they see the dark look on my face. It's a good thing, too, because I'm not sure I could curve the need to plow my fist through someone's face if they were to get in my way. I bare my teeth at some pansy-dressed sophomore that has the balls to look me in the eye. His face pales and he spins around, scurrying away like a coward.

Once I reach my truck, I open the side door and throw my books inside. I look over and spot Rylee standing at her bright ass red car. My molars grind when I notice Charles Pierce standing behind her, looking over her shoulder at something she's showing him on her phone. They both laugh, and it irritates me further.

I'd noticed the two of them in the lunchroom earlier, huddled up all buddy-buddy. I also felt Rylee's eyes on me several times. We won't talk about how my body betrayed itself each time it happened. Fucking cock has a mind of its own all of a sudden.

I slam the door closed so hard it echoes across the lot, gaining Rylee's and Charles' attention. I let both see the ire in my eyes. Rylee pinches her lips shut, and going by the daggers she shoots at me with her eyes, the feeling is mutual.

Good. I certainly don't need her assuming we're going to be friends or some shit. Even if Oliver didn't hate her, I know her type, and I don't want a damn thing to do with her. Doesn't matter if my dick thinks she's pretty to look at and weeps at the thought of her surrounding him.

My eyes move to Charles and the smirk curving up one corner of his mouth as he stares back at me. Up until recently, I thought he was an okay guy. Fourth richest family in the county, but he doesn't feel the need to flaunt it like most people do. Right now, though, I want to rearrange his face for him

Dismissing the two, I spin away and climb into my truck. Oliver sent a message earlier saying he had a ride home with a girl. By ride, he meant stopping by her house, getting his dick wet, then informing her she owed him a lift home.

My truck turns over on the third try. Fucking starter. It's needed to be replaced for a couple of weeks, but I was hoping it would last until my next fight.

A few minutes later, I pull up to a medium sized, nondescript building that houses a massive illegal fighting ring in the basement. The ground level, if you can believe it, is a comic bookstore. I didn't even know those existed anymore until a couple of years ago. Oliver and I were walking home, having just left a friend's house, when we saw a man barreling out of the building. A big, bald, black dude was chasing him, but the guy was younger and faster. He ran into me, and when I tried to steady him, he threw a punch, clocking me in the jaw. After that, I saw red, swung, and knocked his ass to the ground.

Come to find out, the guy had taken cash out of the register when the owner, Gentry Hart, turned his back. Hart was the guy chasing him. He brought Oliver and me back into the shop when he saw my knuckles were busted from where I hit the guy in the teeth. After washing my hand and pouring alcohol on it, we sat and talked with Hart for over an hour. We came back a few times because Hart was laid back and cool to be around. When evenings came, he always made us leave, saying he had business to attend to. One night, when I was there by myself, Hart showed me what his "business" was. I'll never forget the first fight I saw in that basement. Or the cash that exchanged hands.

Earlier that day, we had found out that the medicine Danielle takes increased in cost exponentially, but dad's hours had decreased. The insurance premiums at dad's job are high, so he was forced to take the lowest form of benefits, which doesn't include prescription coverage.

As I'd watched flesh meet flesh, blood spew from mouths, and bones break, I knew what I needed to do. Hart was firmly against my joining the ring, but I was adamant. I swallowed my pride and told him my situation and about Danielle's illness. After what felt like hours, in which time my nerves were banging around in my chest, he reluctantly agreed; but only after stating he was starting me out slow and putting me against the lightest opponents. Now I'm his best fighter and go up against some of the best in the area.

I pocket my keys and approach the building, the *Hart's Comics* sign looking down at me. Some bluesy shit is playing on the overhead speakers when I walk through the door. Behind the counter I spot Hart and head toward him. Leaning against the counter, I cross my arms over my chest and wait for him to finish with his customer. Surprisingly, the comic business, or rather, this particular one, is quite lucrative. Who knew comics were still so popular?

"Hey, Z. How's it going?" he asks after his customer walks away.

I touch my knuckles to his.

"Same shit as always." I stand to my full height and get down to business. "You got any fights for me?"

He runs his hand over his bald head a couple of times. "Might have somethin' next week. Still waiting on a call from Boz."

I nod. "I need you to find me more. I need as much cash as I can get."

His hairy brows dip down, showing his concern. "You in some kind of trouble, boy?" he asks, his voice gruff.

"The doctors want to put Danielle on the transplant list, but the insurance company is refusing to pay for it. Claims her case isn't dire enough."

"Stupid fuckin' insurance companies. They've all got God complexes. Bastards. Every single one of 'em."

"You'll get no disagreement from me." I take a deep breath, hold it in for a moment, and let it out slow. "It's getting worse, Hart. Sometimes she can't breathe on her own."

It scares the shit out of me when she has a bad episode. And they're happening more and more.

"Shit, kid, I'm sorry to hear that," he mumbles sympathetically. "That precious girl doesn't deserve this lot in life."

I couldn't agree with him more. There isn't another person I know who's more caring and loving as Danielle. She's like the perfect blend of all things good. Nothing like her big brother, that's for sure.

"Think you can hook me up?" I ask.

His brows pucker, making the lines by his eyes more pronounced. "Can't promise anything, but I'll see what I can do."

I tip my chin up. "Thanks. I owe you."

His frown turns into a scowl. "You don't owe me shit. Besides, the more you win, the more money goes in my pocket," he finishes with a smirk.

I chuckle and slap him on his massive back. "I see why you keep me around. Bread and butter."

"It sure as shit ain't for your conversation skills," he snarks good-naturedly.

I take no offense to his statement. I'm not much of a talker, never have been. In the beginning, when Oliver and I would visit, it was mostly Hart talking to us, Oliver jabbing about something that happened at school, or us helping him around the store. I'd always wondered why he kept letting us come around, but now I think it's because we remind him what it was like to be young again. Hart never married or had kids. Other than the fighters he employs, he's been alone.

"In all seriousness," he continues, his tone turning somber. "You're a good boy, Zayden, with a good head on your shoulders."

"Thanks, Hart. That means a lot coming from you."

A boy in his young teens approaches the counter carrying a couple of comics. I tap my knuckles against the glass display case, turning to leave. "I'm headed out. Call if you hear anything."

"You got it. And bring that sister of yours by sometime! It's been too long since I've seen her!" he yells as I walk out the door.

I toss a wave over my shoulder, letting him know I'll bring Danielle for a visit. I glance at my watch and curse. I've got twenty minutes to get home before dad has to leave for work. Luckily, my truck starts on the first try.

I pull in the driveway with five minutes to spare. At the youthful age of nine, along with her illness, Danielle can't be left alone.

I shove through the front door, drop my keys and books on the kitchen counter, and grab a glass to fill with water. I'm halfway through draining my second glass when dad walks into the kitchen.

"How was school?" he asks, snatching up his own keys and shoving them into his pocket. He walks to the fridge and pulls out a brown paper bag that I know contains his dinner.

"Fine," I grunt, spinning to set the glass in the sink. I step to the side so he can reach the spigot, then lean back against the counter and cross my arms. "Mrs. Miller gave me a C on my base 12 math paper."

He pauses filling up his big half-gallon water bottle. "You deserve it?"

"Hell no, I didn't deserve it."

"Watch the language," he warns, keeping his head forward, but slanting his eyes toward me. "And Mrs. Miller must feel like you did. You take it up with her?"

I jerk my chin up.

"She gonna give you a chance to make it up?"

"She's letting me redo the paper." Which is fucking stupid. The paper was good the first time. The assignment was to discover an unconventional method of doing math and convince the reader why that system is better. It's not my fault the base twelve math model is so obscure and over her head. She's a twelfth-grade Calculus teacher, for fuck's sake.

"Then make sure you do it right this time," he states, like I'm not giving it my all already. Next time, I'll dumb it down a notch. Then maybe Mrs. Miller will understand the shit I write.

"You still off Saturday?"

"As of right now, yes." He twists the lid on the jug, grabs his lunch, and begins to leave the kitchen. "I'll let you know if it changes."

As much as dad needs the hours at work, it's better if he's not called in. I'll make more money in one night of fighting than he'll make in one week. Of course, he doesn't know about my weekly fights, and he won't be learning about them anytime soon.

I follow him to the front door.

"I've already given Danielle her medicine, so it's just dinner you need to take care of."

"Got it."

I close the door and head to Danielle's room. She's lying on her bed with her favorite stuffed elephant pressed up against her side as she reads a book. Since I bought her the stuffed animal on one of our zoo excursions, she clings to it like it's a lifeline.

I stay in the doorway for several seconds and look at her. She's pale today, and her oxygen mask is sitting on her chest, ready to use when she needs it. Today hasn't been a good day.

Her long brown hair is twisted into some weird braid and is draped over her pillow. Her eyes fly over the page before she flips to another.

I walk into the room. "Hey, Dani. How's my girl?"

Her eyes light up when she sees me, and she gifts me with a smile. My heart hurts when I see the dark spots under her eyes. She must have slept like shit last night. She's usually still asleep when I leave in the mornings. Last year was her last year in school, switching to home schooling because she missed so many days.

"I'm okay." Her chest rises and falls slowly as she puts the book down on her stomach.

"You get all of your assignments done for the day?"

She wrinkles her cute little nose. "Yeah. That science test was hard though, so I don't know how well I did."

Her breathing is a bit faster now, as if just saying those few words has taken their toll. She lifts the mask to her face to give herself a little oxygen boost. I sit on the side of her bed and grab the end of her braid, giving it a gentle tug.

"Nah. I'm sure you aced it." I smile. Danielle is extremely smart. "Dad said he gave you your medicine already." She nods. "What sounds good for dinner?"

She pulls the mask away and narrows her eyes, her lips puckering in thought. A cheeky grin appears on her face. "How about… mint chocolate chip ice cream?"

I chuckle and tug her braid again. "Nice try. How about I throw us some chicken and home fries on the grill and we eat it out back?"

"Then mint chocolate chip ice cream?" she asks, her eyes sparkling hopefully.

There's no way I could deny her. "Then mint chocolate ice cream."

"Deal!"

"Meet me in the kitchen. You can sit and peel the potatoes."

Leaning down, I press a kiss to her forehead before leaving her room. A lot of guys my age despise their younger siblings, calling them nuisances, and would resent them if they were forced to watch them instead of being able to hang out with friends. I've never felt that way toward Danielle. I enjoy being around her. Some would say that was born out of pity and obligation. Those people, I'd like to punch their noses through their skulls.

Danielle is special on so many levels. I've never felt resentment toward her or felt her illness was a burden. She's my baby sister, and I'd do damn near anything for her.

I pull the chicken out of the freezer and grab a bowl, filling it with potatoes. Snatching a potato peeler from the silverware drawer, I carry it and the bowl to the eat-in kitchen table.

I glance up with a smile when Danielle slowly walks into the room, wheeling her oxygen tank behind her.

My planned evening may not be on the typical teen guy's wish list, but damn if I'm not looking forward to spending it with my little sister.

chapter five

RYLEE

"it's friday!" Pierce sings as he skips up next to me on the sidewalk.

"Thank goodness." I sigh. This week has been even more challenging than I had anticipated, but I feel like it's getting a little easier with each day that passes.

"Got any plans for the weekend?"

"That would imply that I actually have friends." I turn in the direction of my locker and Pierce follows me.

"Um, hello! What am I—chopped liver?" He knocks his shoulder into mine.

"Sorry, I didn't mean…." I pause. "It's just, well, you're the only *actual* friend I've made this week. I swear people think I have some contagious disease. No one will talk to me. Like what the heck?"

"Well I know just the solution. Come to a party with me tonight."

"And that's the solution how?"

"I can introduce you to some of my friends and it will give you a chance to socialize outside of school. Come on. It will be fun."

"And where is this party?"

"Terri's house."

"And Terri is?"

"She's who's throwing the party, that's who." He pauses. "Don't worry. Her parties are usually pretty good, and you'll be there with me so it's guaranteed to be a good time."

"I'll think about it," I promise, not really sure if I'm in the partying mood.

"No thinking. You're going," he tells me matter of fact.

"You're really quite pushy when you want to be." I smile up at him.

"I know." He chuckles.

My steps falter when I turn the corner and find Zayden at his locker.

He'd said something the first day about my locker being next to his and how it wouldn't be for long, but clearly he doesn't have the power he thinks he does, because it's still my locker.

"He looks even more brooding today than usual." Pierce follows my line of sight just as Oliver slides up next to Zayden. "If I had to guess, I'd say right there is your friend roadblock." He gestures to the two of them.

"What do you mean?"

"I warned you about them and their minions. If Zayden's got a problem with you then most of the school will, too. Even if they personally don't have a problem with you, they won't go anywhere near you if it means putting themselves in the line of fire."

"But I haven't done anything to him." My temper flares in my voice.

"No, but his best friend has declared you public enemy number one, and that's enough to put you on the list."

"Freaking Oliver," I groan. "As if he doesn't make me miserable enough at home, now he's going to ruin what's left of my senior year."

"Just keep your head up. I'm sure as time goes on they'll get bored. Give it a few weeks. You'll be old news before you know it."

"Walk over there with me?" I look up at him pleadingly.

"Fine, but if I end up with a broken nose, your ass is paying for the plastic surgery to fix it," he teases, looping his arm through mine.

"Deal."

We reach my locker right as Zayden is closing his. When he turns and catches sight of us, his nostrils flare. I have half a mind to ask him what the hell his problem is, but given his reputation, I figure it's better to kill him with kindness instead.

"Good morning." I smile at him as I slide in front of my locker.

"Why the fuck are you so chipper this morning?" Oliver sneers at me, his gaze going to where Pierce is standing behind me. "And what the fuck are you looking at?"

"Just waiting for my friend." Pierce holds his hands up in front of himself as if to say *I don't want any trouble.*

"I didn't know you had any friends." His gaze cuts back to me. "I guess I shouldn't be surprised you'd sink your claws into this one. Like mother like daughter, right?"

"What are you talking about?" I try to keep my voice even.

"You know exactly what I'm talking about." An evil grin tugs at the corners of his mouth.

"Actually, I don't. And you know what, I don't really care either. Whatever issues you've got with your dad and my mom, take it up with him. As for me, stay out of my way, and I'll stay out of yours."

"Or maybe I'll just remove you altogether."

"I'd like to see you try," I challenge, refusing to back down. I've never shied away from confrontation, and I'm not about to start now. I've been trying to play nice for my mom's sake, but that doesn't mean I'm going to let this jackass walk all over me for sport.

"You have no idea the shit I can rain down on you."

"Save your threats for someone who's actually scared of you." I give him a smile that reads *fuck you* before starting to work on the combination for my locker. I can feel the anger radiating off of him, but rather than frighten me, it makes me smile. I'm glad I've gotten under his skin. Serves him right.

I pull on the lock after entering the combination, but it doesn't open. Figuring I've entered it wrong; I spin the dial and start again. When it doesn't work a second time, I start to feel like maybe something is up.

"Trouble with your lock?" Oliver smiles, emptying a few Red Hot candies into his hand before popping them into his mouth.

"What did you do?" I glare at him.

"Me?" He chews slowly and then swallows. "I didn't do anything."

"Bullshit. What did you do?" I repeat, trying the lock one more time.

Nothing.

My gaze jumps from Oliver to Zayden. During this entire altercation he hasn't spoken a word. Our eyes meet and a little bit of my resolve disintegrates. God, why does he have to be so good looking? Why does he have to be friends with my sadistic stepbrother? And why does he have to look at me like he can't decide if he wants to murder me and throw me in a dumpster, or push me up against his locker and shut me up with his mouth? My vote would go to the latter.

"Did you do this?" I ask, pointing at my locker angrily.

"You can just go to the office during your free period and have someone cut the lock off and give you a new one," Pierce says from behind me. "It's probably broken or something," he offers, but I think we both know that's not the case.

"You know what, you're right." I adjust my bag on my shoulder. "Nothing that can't be taken care of." I glare between Oliver and Zayden before plastering on the biggest, fakest smile I can muster. "Have an awesome day," I say to the both of them, squaring my shoulders as I turn and quickly walk away.

"That was crazy. I think I just saw smoke come out of Oliver's ears." Pierce follows me toward first period. "I don't think anyone has ever talked to him the way you just did."

"Serves him right. Jerk."

"Aren't you a little worried though?" We slow to a stop outside of my classroom.

"Why would I be worried?"

"You're new here so I don't expect you to understand the gravity of the situation, but Oliver tends to take things to the extreme, and I've never heard him make a threat that he didn't deliver on. The guy is a real piece of work. You might want to think about sleeping with one eye open—that's all I'm saying."

"Oliver is harmless."

"That's debatable. But I know for sure Zayden isn't." He narrows his eyes at me. "If Oliver wants to retaliate, he'll use his friend to do it. I'm just saying, keep your head up and your eyes open."

"Thanks for the advice." I blow out a breath, wondering if my inability to keep my mouth shut is finally going to come back to bite me.

"Whatever happens, I got your back." He drops an arm over my shoulder and pulls me to him, giving me a tight little squeeze. "Anyway, I gotta go. I'll meet up with you at lunch."

"Okay, sounds good." I give him a little wave before turning to head inside the classroom.

I take the seat closest to the door at the front of the room and place my book bag on the floor next to my chair. Pulling out my planner and a notebook, I flip it open and scribble today's date at the top—figuring if I don't have my book I should at least take notes.

My head is down as I write, when something bumps into my chair hard enough to cause the legs to skid a couple of inches before everything on my desk crashes to the floor. Stunned and a little caught off guard, I look up to see Zayden straightening back up like he had tripped or something.

"My bad," he says sarcastically, trying to imply that it was an accident when we all know it was most definitely on purpose.

My gut instinct is to lash out and tell him where he can stick his 'my bad', but then I remember my earlier thought. *Kill him with kindness.*

"Oh no problem." I smile up at him. "I've been known to be rather clumsy myself." I lean down and pick up my stuff off the floor. By the time I turn back, Zayden has claimed his usual seat at the back of the class.

Knocking my stuff on the floor—really? How original. I roll my eyes as I settle back into my chair.

If he thinks that's all it's going to take to send me running and crying, he's got another thing coming. I don't scare that easy.

---

lunch has become my favorite part of the day. Obviously because it's the only period I share with Pierce. Five days and I've managed to land a whopping *one* friend. Then again, he's an awesome guy, so I guess in that sense I'm pretty lucky. I'd rather have one good friend than dozens of sorta friends.

He isn't at our table yet when I arrive, so I slide into my usual seat and tear open the bag of Doritos I got for lunch. I've just shoved one of the cheesy chips into my mouth, when a group of three girls approach my table.

I recognize one from Math. Tiffany, I think. She's one of those perfectly polished girls. You know the kind—perfect makeup, highlighted blonde hair, sparkly manicured fingers and toes. Couple that with her obvious love of fashion and all things trendy and you get the stereotypical mean girl. Which makes her two friends, who are both equally as pretty and yet somehow not, her minions.

"Hey, Rylee." She slides down into the chair across from me, her friends taking the seats on either side of her.

"Hi." I clear my throat, having swallowed my chip too early, causing it to lodge on its way down.

"So, the girls and I were wondering if maybe you wanted to go shopping after school." She wipes a crumb off the table in front of her, her nose crinkling in disgust.

"We know you're new and all, so we thought maybe we could show you around town. Show you all the best places to shop and stuff. It will totally be fun," the brunette on her right chimes in.

"So much fun," the other brunette on her left tacks on.

I feel like I'm being punked. It's like I stepped onto the set of another *Mean Girls* movie. I'm waiting for one of them to tell me that I have to wear pink on Wednesday's.

"I appreciate the offer, but I have a lot of schoolwork to catch up on. You know, first week and all." I make the first excuse I can think of. Do I want to make more friends? Of course I do. Do I want friends like these girls? Hell no. I've known girls like these my whole life. Every school has them.

"Oh, we totally get it." Tiffany smiles. "Maybe another time?"

"Sure. Absolutely," I readily agree.

"Awesome."

I watch her gaze lock onto something behind me, but before I can turn and look, I feel something cold and thick hit the top of my head and slowly trickle through my hair.

What the…?

I run a hand over the top of my head, feeling the thick mess of what I now realize is a milkshake. The three mean girls point and laugh and it doesn't take long for several more sets of eyes to come my way—curious to know what's going on.

I feel heat flood my cheeks as I turn, locking eyes with another girl I recognize from math class—another friend of Tiffany's.

"Oops." She laughs, looking from me to the empty cup in her hand and then back to me.

"What the fuck, Amber?" I hear Pierce before I see him. He slides up next to me and quickly pulls me to my feet. "Come on." He grabs my hand and tugs me through the cafeteria, people laughing and pointing as we pass them.

My heart is hammering a million miles a minute, and I'm a thousand percent sure that my face is beat red. I can feel the heat creeping up my neck and spreading across my cheeks.

I still haven't processed what actually happened when Pierce pulls me into the closest restroom and leads me to the sink. I'm too confused and upset to point out that he's a guy in the girl's restroom. I think it's kind of irrelevant at this point in time.

When I catch sight of my reflection in the mirror as Pierce flips on the water, tears instantly fill my eyes. There's milkshake everywhere. In my hair, on my shirt, dripping down my forehead.

"What the hell happened out there?" Pierce asks, guiding me forward to try to rinse some of the sugary liquid from my hair.

"I don't know," I answer honestly. "Tiffany and her friends came over to invite me to go shopping with them. Next thing I know, some girl is dumping a milkshake on my head."

"Fucking Tiffany." He scrubs his hand over my scalp, water splashing me in the face as he does. "I should have known Oliver and Zayden would recruit the mean girl squad."

"You think they did this?" I ask, standing up abruptly, causing water to drain down my back and over my shoulders.

"I don't think. I know. Why else would Devens purposely stop me right before I got to the cafeteria to talk about some bullshit class I took two years ago? Because he knew I would know something was up the second those girls sat down at the table."

"Oh my God." The words are lost to the pounding in my ears.

"Come here." He guides me back down, continuing to rinse my hair out.

It takes nearly twenty minutes to get the milkshake out of my hair, and even then, there's still parts that are clumped together and knotted—the pitfall of having extremely thick hair. My shirt is disgusting, covered in water and melted ice cream. And my face isn't much better. My eyes are puffy and red, and even though I told myself I wouldn't cry, within five minutes of being in the bathroom with Pierce tears started to pour. I couldn't help it. I was humiliated in front of nearly the entire senior class. But once the embarrassment had passed, all I was left with was anger.

"I'm going to murder him," I tell Pierce as he follows me out of the bathroom. "I mean, straight suffocate him with a pillow in his sleep—dead."

"Slow down there, killer. Don't go offing anyone just yet." Pierce laughs, wrapping his fingers around my hand.

Oliver and Zayden pick that exact moment to come around the corner, and while every single instinct I have is screaming *attack,* I freeze, rooted to the spot like someone super glued my feet to the floor.

"Nice hair." Oliver smiles. "You know, you're supposed to drink the milkshake, right?"

Zayden chokes on a laugh, giving me a quick once over. I've never wanted to punch someone in the face as badly as I do at this very moment.

"Let's go," Pierce says, tightening his grip on my hand.

"You're right." I let out a heavy breath. "They aren't worth it."

"They aren't worth it," Oliver mocks as we step around them. "See you at home, *sis*," he calls as we make our way toward the rear entrance of the school where my car is parked.

"You want me to come with you?" Pierce offers, walking me to my car.

"No, there's no reason for you to get in trouble for missing class. I'm just going to go home and take a very long shower. Maybe I'll put some tacks in Oliver's bed while I'm at it."

"Maybe you shouldn't poke the bear."

"Maybe they shouldn't have poked *me*." I unlock my car and tear the door open, tossing my book bag onto the passenger seat, before turning back to my friend. "Thank you for today. Had you not shown up when you did…." I trail off, knowing it would likely have ended up a lot worse.

"Don't mention it." He pulls me to his chest and gives me a hug. "And don't worry about the party tonight. Maybe we can just get together later this weekend and hang out. Grab some dinner and go see a movie. What do you say?"

"Are Oliver and Zayden going to be at the party?" I ask, stepping out of his embrace.

"That's very likely."

"Then we're going."

"You sure?" He gives me a questioning look.

"If I run away and hide, they win. I'm not going to let them win."

"You have the biggest balls I've ever seen. Figuratively speaking of course." He smiles. "Either that, or you have a death wish."

"Let's go with the big balls theory." I laugh, not sure how I'm so calm after the ordeal in the cafeteria. "You mind picking me up?"

"It'd be my pleasure. Text me your address, and I'll let you know what time I'll be there."

"Sounds good." I slide into the driver's seat and close the door, rolling down the window the instant the engine purrs to life.

"Be safe on your way home and try not to kill anyone before this evening."

"I'll do my best." I smile up at him as I pop the car into drive.

Thank God for Pierce. He's one of those people you can't help but love. The kind of person you're instantly drawn to. Good looking. Funny. Sweet. I honestly don't know what I would have done without him this past week. He has been a bright light in an otherwise dark room.

On the drive home, I replay the events of the day over in my head. Starting with the altercation this morning, to Zayden shoving all my stuff off my desk, before ending with the milkshake fiasco. Well, at least I can say that my first week at the new school wasn't boring.

I give myself a silent applaud for how well I'm handling all of this. Okay, I was a serious mess earlier, but I'm better now. I didn't punch anyone or claw their eyes out, and I managed to slip out of the building before anything else could happen—so there's that.

My thoughts drift back to Zayden. Oliver I understand. Well, I don't really understand, but I guess I kind of do. He blames me for his dad's actions because I'm the only person he can take it out on. *Fine.* It's not okay, but whatever. But Zayden? I can't help but wonder what he stands to gain from any of this. Is he really a bad guy, or is there something driving his actions—something behind the scenes that I'm not privy to?

I've dealt with assholes before. Jerks. Bullies. You name it, I've crossed paths with them all at one point or another. And while Zayden definitely rocks the bad boy persona, he doesn't strike me as someone who would orchestrate a milkshake being poured on someone's head.

Then again, maybe that's just what I'm telling myself because that's what I want to believe. I'm just not sure why that is.

chapter six

ZAYDEN

tipping the red solo cup to my lips, I drain the rest of my beer. I lean back against the bar and cross my arms over my chest as I scan the room. We're all packed in here like a bunch of fucking sardines. Over half of the junior and senior class is here. How the hell anyone could think this is fun is beyond me.

I spot Oliver with his face buried in the neck of some chick he has pressed against the wall. I'm assuming it's Patty, judging by the girl with huge tits at his back. His hips press against Patty's, while her cousin, Double D, grinds against his ass. It's disgusting to watch. But that's Oliver for you. He's all about having a good time and making the girls happy.

Moving my eyes away from the threesome waiting to happen, I continue my perusal around the room. It's full of music, laughter, rich drunk girls vying for attention, and asshole guys who give it to them—

whether they're sober enough to receive it or not. These parties are always the same.

Her overwhelmingly scent hits me seconds before I feel her tits press against my side, her hand going to my lower stomach.

"Hey, Z baby," Tiffany purrs in my ear.

I grit my teeth and fight the urge to rub said ear against my shoulder to wipe away the hot and wet breath she left behind. Instead, I turn and face her.

"How's it going, Tiffany?"

Her red lips tip up, revealing a set of bright as fuck teeth. "Much better now that I've found you."

"That so?" I ask, offering my signature smirk.

She inches her hand down until the tip of her fingers tuck into the waistband of my jeans. My dick twitches, but that's about it, only mildly curious.

"It sure is." She smiles bigger as her eyes grow hooded. "You wanna dance?"

I look out across the room. There's hardly any walking room, let alone enough space to dance.

I glance back at Tiffany. "Maybe some other time."

She pouts, and it makes her look ridiculous with her plump lips sticking out even more. Tiffany's a smokin' hot chick with long blonde hair, stunning blue eyes, and a killer body any guy would give his left nut to fuck. The package is nice, but the contents inside are questionable.

Of course, that questionable nature sure as hell comes in handy sometimes. I smirk when an image of Rylee with milkshake running down her face and hair comes to mind.

My smirk dies a sudden death when I remember seeing her as she left the bathroom with Charles. Her face was red, and while some of it was from her anger directed at Oliver and me, I knew some was from crying. I have no fucking clue why the thought of her crying bothers me. Whatever the reason may be, I shove that shit to the back of my mind. People like Rylee don't deserve my sympathy.

Tiffany sidles up closer to me, practically melding her breasts into my side. "You wanna head upstairs then?"

I put some thought into it. Her teeth may be a bitch to deal with, but I bet her pussy would feel like heaven. Even so, by the lack of blood *not* rushing to my dick, *he* doesn't appear to be that interested. Which lines up with the head between my shoulders, too. The thought is only slightly interesting. It surely isn't as appealing as sandwiching myself between a certain pair of legs that belong to a girl with luscious brown hair and deceiving brown eyes.

"Not tonight."

Someone catches my eye, causing me to glance up. I mutter a silent curse and grit my teeth when she comes completely into view. My dick instantly hardens when I see what she's wearing. A tight black leather skirt that's entirely too short—if she bends over, there's no doubt she'll be flashing ass cheeks to half the school population—a silky light-blue shirt that hangs so far off one shoulder that the top of one breast is showing, and a pair of black fuck-me heels. Her hair is loosely swept up off her shoulders in some complicated bun, and her face is made up in some type of smoky look. It's not over the top—it actually looks fucking hot—but it's not the natural look she normally uses.

Tiffany reasserts herself back into my thoughts when her fingers creep lower into my jeans, trying her best to get to my junk. I grab her wrist and yank her hand out. My expression is hard when I look down at her. My anger isn't directed at her—it's not her fault Rylee Harper decided to show up here. Unfortunately, Tiffany is closer to me than Rylee is.

"I know you fucking heard me, Tiffany. I said, not tonight." The words come out harsh, and I should probably feel remorse when hurt appears on her face, but I don't. Tiffany is just like all the other girls in this room. They think if they push hard enough, show enough tit, grind their pussies against places they wish to visit, they'll finally get their way. Most guys here will give in, but I'm not most guys.

I let go of her wrist and leave her behind. My steps are long and purposeful as I stalk toward Rylee. I'm only a few feet away when I notice Charles at her side, which only heightens my anger. But what really pisses me off is the red Solo cup in her hand.

I don't stop my pursuit until I'm right in front of her. Her eyes widen in surprise before they quickly narrow into slits.

I bend over so my face is right in hers. "What the fuck are you doing here?" I growl over the loud music.

I have to admit, even if only to myself, I admire her bravery when she doesn't back down or flinch at my tone.

"Not that it's any of your business, but I'm here to let loose and party," she answers, her tone matching the ire in mine.

"I highly doubt Terri invited you." I sneer and rake my eyes up and down her body.

I know for a fact Terri wouldn't have invited Rylee. She knows of Oliver's distaste for his new stepsister. She also knows there would be consequences if she went against him by inviting her.

"The word around school was the party was an open invite to everyone."

"Everyone except *you*."

She scoffs, unphased by the blatant rejection of her. "Well then, she should have been more specific."

"No one wants you here, Rylee. Get the fuck out and go home."

"To hell with you, Zayden. I don't see anyone else telling me to leave." She looks around the room before bringing her eyes back to me. Mirth plays in their depths. "It seems to me you're the only one that has a problem with me being here."

With that, she spins on her high heel, grabs a startled Charles' hand, and stalks away.

Boiling rage starts in my gut and sends lava through my veins. The bitch just won't catch a clue. But she will.

I look around and find Oliver in the same spot as before. Except, instead of being immersed with Patty and her cousin, his face is hard as he watches Rylee and Charles cross into the center of the room and start dancing. My rage intensifies when she throws one arm around his shoulder and grinds down on his leg that's between hers. She laughs and tips the cup to her lips, swallowing down half the contents.

I glance back at Oliver and find his eyes on me. I tip my chin at him, and he detangles himself from his entourage and walks off.

I leave Oliver to do whatever he plans to do and make my way over to Rylee and Charles.

I don't give them time to notice me before I snatch Rylee by the wrist and drag her behind me. She digs in her heels, but it doesn't stop me.

"What are you doing, Zayden?" she screeches. "Let me go."

When I don't comply, she yanks her wrist away from my grip so hard I know a mark will be left behind.

I spin around and grit out, "Outside. Now."

"No."

I step closer. "Either you go outside with me willingly, or I'll toss you over my shoulder. Either way, you're going. I need to talk to you."

Pretty Boy Charles moves to her side, stepping slightly in front of her. "Just calm the hell down, Z."

"Back the fuck up, Charles," I warn. "This isn't your business."

Although he doesn't back down, I see the wariness in his eyes. "Rylee's my friend, so it is my business. She's not going anywhere with you."

I get in his face, ready to plow my fist into his jaw, when Rylee steps between us. She puts a hand on both of our chests and shoves us away from each other. The party around us quiets down several decimals and the dance floor begins to clear.

"That's enough," Rylee inserts with a firm voice. She turns to Charles. "I'll be okay. I'm just going to step outside to see what he wants. I'll be back in a minute."

He looks at her with concern. "You don't have to." He narrows his eyes at me. "This prick can go fuck himself."

I wouldn't call Charles a pussy—he normally stays in the background—but I've seen him face off with a couple guys before. He's just never done it to anyone in the crowds I run with. Even so, he's a hell of a lot smaller than I am, and brave as fuck to stand up to me. I'd hate to fuck up his pretty face, but if he doesn't calm his shit that's exactly what I'll do.

"I know I don't *have* to, but I'm going to." She smiles, but even I can tell it's forced. "Why don't you grab us another drink while you wait."

The muscles in his jaw bunch as he grinds his teeth. His eyes flicker from Rylee to me, then back to Rylee. "Fine. But all I'm giving you is five minutes. That's it, Rylee."

If it wasn't so ludicrous to think he could actually take me, I'd laugh in his face. Man points to him for being willing to have his ass handed to him.

Rylee turns to me, and the look in her eyes would scare the shit out of most grown men. To me, it's just amusing. I bare my teeth in a faux smile and hold my arm out toward the front door. "Lead the way."

She huffs as she stomps away, and fuck if my eyes don't go straight down to watch her ass move with attitude. My cock stiffens, and I mentally berate the traitor as I follow her.

Get with the program, you prick. We don't like her.

Once we're out in the yard where only a few stragglers are scattered about, she spins to face me. She opens her mouth, surely to berate me, but I hold up my finger. I turn to the couple who were making out against a tree, but now have swiveled toward us, their dazed eyes darting between Rylee and me.

"Leave," I snarl, and they scurry away.

The next thing I know, I have a finger poking my chest. "What was so important you threatened to drag me out here?" she asks, practically shooting fire from her eyes.

I get right to the point. "Where did you get your drink?"

She takes a step back, her brows dipping. She looks at the cup in her hand, then back at me. "What?" Her tone is incredulous and a bit confused.

I release a sigh and rub my forehead. “Your drink, Rylee. Who gave it to you?”

She blinks a couple of times, still looking baffled. “I don’t know. Some guy at the door was handing them out.”

I tip my head up and grind my molars together. How the hell could this woman be so fucking stupid? When I look back down, she has the cup to her lips. I dart forward and snatch it from her hands, spilling some of the liquid on the ground between us, before I toss the cup to the side.

“What the hell is your problem?” she growls, balling her little fists by her side like she’s dying to launch them at me.

“You are,” I answer heatedly. “You don’t take drinks from people you don’t fucking know and trust. Unless you’re asking to be roofied and forced to do shit you won’t remember tomorrow, but you’ll damn sure feel.”

Her eyes widen in shock and the red on her face from her anger melts away, leaving her pale. She looks around for a moment before bringing her eyes back to me. “That really happens at these things?”

I barely refrain from rolling my eyes. “Yes.”

“Oh.” Her eyes drop to the ground between us.

“If you insist on being here, you only take drinks from Charles. Got it?”

She lifts her head and shame is written in her features. The look quickly morphs into curiosity. “Why do you care anyway?”

I scoff. “I don’t care what happens to you.” The lie rolls off my tongue easily. I may not like the bitch, but I wouldn’t want any woman to be taken advantage of. That shit is not how I roll. “But if something does, every guy in there will be a suspect. I don't need that shit in my life."

Her lips tighten in irritation. "Maybe next time you can warn me without being a dick."

"Don't count on it, sugar."

"Whatever," she mutters and walks away, leaving me out on the lawn.

I take a minute to compose myself. Why the hell does that girl have to be so maddening? Why can't my body get the memo that I don't want her? And why the fuck does the thought of someone drugging her and fucking her unconscious body send a murderous rage through me? I'd be pissed if that happened to any girl but knowing it could happen to Rylee makes me feel unhinged. Knowing she carelessly put herself in danger makes me want to slap some sense into her.

Blowing out a harsh breath to reign in my mounting temper, I go back inside. My eyes immediately try to find her, but she's nowhere to be found. A crackling sound comes over the speaker, and I turn to face the front of the room. Oliver is on the coffee table, microphone in hand.

"Hello, all you Parkview fuckers!" he yells, and receives a chorus of hoots and hollers. "As some of you already know, I gained a sister over the winter break." He grins mischievously as he looks out across the room. "I realized I haven't properly introduced you all to my new lovely sibling. How very rude of me."

His eyes stop somewhere behind me, and I glance over my shoulder. Rylee is standing with Charles at her side, her glacial stare pinned on Oliver.

Oliver points his finger in her direction, and all eyes narrow in on her.

"There she is. Why don't you come on up here, Rylee, and meet your fellow classmates?" When she doesn't make a move to do what he asked, but instead flips him the middle finger, Oliver pouts dramatically.

"Spoilsport," he jeers into the microphone. "Anyway, to help you all get to know Rylee a little better, because you know, I'm helpful like that, I figured I'd give you a few fun facts about her."

Murmurs and snickers reverberate throughout the room. Everyone knows Rylee isn't liked by Oliver; therefore, this isn't some attempt to gain her friends. He's putting on a show. I lean against the wall to watch.

"Fact number one." He holds up his pointer finger. "When Rylee laughs hard, she farts."

Raucous laughter erupts in the room. People bend over and actually clutch their stomachs and wipe their eyes.

Not waiting for it to die down, Oliver holds up another finger.

"Fact number two. She sings in the shower, and let's just say, she won't be winning any awards anytime soon."

More laughter ensues. I glance at her over my shoulder. Her face is red, and if it were possible, there'd be steam coming from her ears. I grin at her discomfort and face forward again.

"Fact number three," he states, holding up a third finger. "She stalks her ex on Instagram. Like, come on, chick, he dumped your ass for a reason. Get over it already."

He lifts his pinky finger. "Number four is she talks to herself in the bathroom. Like full blown conversations and shit."

A sinister smile creeps over Oliver's face, and I'm sure the last one will be the kicker. He holds up his hand, indicating all five fingers.

"Before I give the last fun fact, I feel I should give out a bit of advice to my dear sister." His dancing eyes meet hers. "You should really learn to lock the bathroom door." His gaze sweeps across the room once more. "Apparently, my amorous sister here likes to use the showerhead for more than just washing her body. And if you're wondering guys, *yes*, she does make the "O" face."

I swivel around as the peals of laughter in the room ramp up several degrees. I barely catch sight of Rylee running out the back door with Charles hot on her heels. Several emotions race through my head at once; guilt and remorse at the forefront.

I never expected Oliver would take it this far. I'm all for embarrassing the girl, and the first four "facts" I was okay with. But that last one was too personal, even for my standards. I don't know if everything he said was true, but from the small glimpse I got of Rylee's face as she ran away, my guess would be yes. At least to that last one.

Which begs the question; why the fuck was Oliver in the bathroom while she was in the shower? The other question is, why do I want to pummel his face in for witnessing it?

Pissed off at myself for letting Oliver take things too far and wanting to get the fuck out of this place, I leave the living room and head out the same door Rylee escaped from. I forego telling Oliver I'm leaving, because I'm not sure I could hold back the desire to wrap my hands around his throat at the moment. I glance around the backyard, not surprised when I don't see Rylee or Charles. I toss the idea around in my head to go to her house to check on her, but I'm sure I'm the last person she wants to see.

I climb in my truck. Thank fuck it starts right away.

It takes me twenty minutes to get home, but I don't go in immediately. I sit in my truck and try to assuage my guilt over what happened tonight.

In the end, I know there's only one thing I can do.

chapter seven

RYLEE

"Well, that was an absolute nightmare." Pierce sighs, pulling to a stop next to the curb in front of my house.

"Yeah, that's one way to put it." I try to force a smile, but it feels too heavy and instantly falls.

"Oliver's a dick."

"You know what?" I shuffle my feet against the floorboard. "I don't even care about what he said. Most of it wasn't true. What bothers me is that everyone just bought what he was selling without even reading the label. It's so frustrating."

"Welcome to Parkview. It's been this way as long as I can remember."

"But why? What is it about him that has everyone eating out of the palm of his hand?"

"Well," Pierce throws me an apologetic look, "he's good looking, rich, and he's best friends with Zayden. I know none of that should matter, but to most of the brainless asshats we go to school with, it's all that matters."

"You're not in on it, right?" I hate that the question even comes out, but with everything else that's happened I feel suspicious of everything and everyone.

"Wait, what?" He draws back like I smacked him right across the face.

"I'm sorry. I know you don't deserve to have me asking such questions, but if you think about it, it would totally make sense. Oliver recruits one of his friends to get close to me. It's his kill shot."

"His what?" He seems so confused that I almost feel sorry for him.

"Kill shot. You know, he stabs me several times before finally delivering the fatal blow."

"And you think I'm the fatal blow?"

"No," I answer honestly. "But it feels like something he would do."

"I'm not sure if I should be pissed that you're accusing me of working with Oliver or amused." A smile plays on his lips. "Look, I've been around Oliver enough to know he's not the kind of people I need in my life. Besides, are you forgetting the part where I also like men? Have you met Oliver? Do I strike you as the kind of person *he* would hang out with?"

"Probably not," I admit. "God, I'm sorry. You've been nothing short of amazing and here I am questioning your motives."

"You've had one hell of a week, so I'm going to give you a free pass this time," he tells me, taking this way better than I would have if the roles were reversed. "But the next time I might not be so easy on you," he playfully warns.

"You really are something special, Charles Pierce."

"Now that's something we can both agree on."

We both laugh, and despite everything that's gone on today, there's nothing forced or fake about it.

"I'm sorry about tonight. I should never have insisted on going. I walked into the lion's den and they feasted, just like I knew they would. I guess I thought maybe there were some decent people mixed in with all the assholes."

"Oh, there are. You'll just be hard pressed to see any of them stand against Zayden or Oliver," he says. "Speaking of which, what the fuck did Z want earlier?" he asks, reminding me that I never got the chance to tell him. Oliver made sure of that.

"He yelled at me for drinking." I laugh at the absurdity of it now, though at the time I was too confused to really process it all.

"Come again?" Pierce seems as confused as I had felt.

"He told me that I was going to be roofied, and that I shouldn't drink anything that I didn't pour myself or got from you. He was being so mean about it and yet, I couldn't help but feel like for whatever reason, he was looking out for me. It was really weird." I shake my head.

"I wouldn't have let that happen. Jared is a buddy of mine and he would never slip something into someone's drink. Not saying that it's never happened, but I knew the drink was safe." He thinks on it for a moment. "But what I don't get is why he felt the need to say anything to begin with. Unless…." A slow smile tugs at his lips.

"Unless?" I ask impatiently when he doesn't finish his thought right away.

"Unless he has a thing for you."

I stare at him for a long moment, trying to gauge if he's being serious. When he gives me no indication to prove otherwise, I immediately burst into laughter. And not just a little laugh either. No, this is stomach cramping, can't catch my breath kind of laugh.

"You can't be serious," I manage through my hysterics.

"I'm just saying, maybe he does. You're beautiful, funny, witty, and you don't take his shit—which is probably a first for him."

"Zayden Michaels does *not* have a thing for me," I reassure him, my laughter dying off. "And even if he did, I wouldn't give that asshole the time of day," I quickly add, hoping Pierce doesn't see through the lie.

I know it's crazy. I should hate Zayden. I should, but I don't. I've never been so intrigued by someone before. It's like the meaner he is to me, the more curious I become. And in some sick way I like the attention. Because even if it's negative attention, it shows he's thinking about me.

Okay, I think I've officially lost my mind.

"I wouldn't be so sure." Pierce reaches across the console and tips my chin. "You didn't see the way he was looking at you tonight. Nice touch by the way." His eyes scan my outfit.

"I figured if I was going to be humiliated, might as well look good doing it." I shrug, looking down at the revealing outfit that I normally wouldn't be caught dead in. I'd be lying if I said I didn't pick it out with Zayden in mind.

"Well, you definitely succeeded. Even if our first outing was a huge bust, the night did have some high points."

"It did?" I arch a brow at him.

"I got to walk into a packed party with the hottest girl in school on my arm." He grins. "I think we turned more heads than just Zayden's."

"Anyone's head in particular you were aiming to turn?" I probe for information. So far Pierce has been pretty secretive about his love life.

"Maybe." He kneads his bottom lip between his teeth.

"That's all I get? Maybe?" I playfully swat his leg.

"Her name is Chelsea. I told you I've been on a girl kick as of late. We have Spanish together, and even though I've attempted to flirt, she's either really shy or isn't interested. After tonight, I think it's the former. Which just means I need to up my game."

"And how do you plan to do that?"

"Well, rumor has it she's going to be at Hart's tomorrow night. Thinking I might make an appearance."

"What's Harts?"

"Hart's Comics."

"Wait, she's going to be at a comic bookstore?" I question, fighting the urge to poke fun at him.

"Well, not exactly."

"What do you mean, not exactly?"

"Hart's isn't *just* a comic store. He also has a fight ring in the basement."

"Wait, what?"

"It's a pretty hot hang out, if you can get in. There's only room enough for so many people, so they typically turn a lot away at the door."

"Are we talking like *Fight Club*?" I reference the movie I've seen more times than I care to admit.

"Not exactly, but yeah, you're getting the picture. It's an underground fighting ring. It pulls in a pretty big crowd. Some people go to watch the fight, but most have money on the line."

"So, they're taking bets?"

He nods. "You'd be surprised how much money circulates that place, especially when some of the better-known fighters are there." He pauses like he's about to say more but changes his mind.

"How does something like this take place? Clearly it's illegal."

"Hart, the guy who runs the place, has a buddy at the local PD. Not sure on their arrangement, but he keeps the cops off Hart's back, and in return, Hart takes care of him—financially speaking."

"So he pays him off?"

"I guess that's one way to put it."

"And how do you know all this?"

"Same way everyone does—word of mouth. I've been there a few times. Pay enough attention and you can piece together how it all works pretty quick."

"How freaking cool. I didn't know things like that actually existed."

"You wouldn't want to maybe go, would you?"

"Are you serious? Hell yes, I would!" I say a little too enthusiastically. "But…." I pause. "I hate that I even have to ask this."

"Yes, Zayden and Oliver will likely be there. But," he quickly continues. "there are so many people there that it's unlikely they will have any clue you're in attendance. Besides, you can't let them scare you into hiding. Isn't that what you said earlier?"

"I don't know. Two nights in a row might be pressing my luck."

"Or, maybe it will show them that they can't break you."

I consider his words.

"I'm in," I finally agree.

"The first fight starts at nine. We'll want to be there by seven if we want any shot of getting inside."

"Pick me up at six-thirty?" I reach for the door handle.

"It's a date." He nods, his dimple making an appearance as he smiles.

"Rylee and Charles take on the world—take two," I tell him, pushing open the door.

"Let's just hope it goes better than take one." He chuckles.

I step out of the car and turn to lean against the open door. "Just one question. What does one wear to an underground fight club?" Just saying the words makes me smile.

"Ripped jeans and a sexy top." His eyes dip to my heels. "And those shoes." He smiles. "Definitely those shoes."

"Casual, but sexy. Got it." I step back to shut the door.

"See you at six-thirty."

"See you then." I give him a small wave before swinging the door closed.

Pierce waits until I make it inside before driving away. I lock the door behind myself and turn, taking the stairs two at a time on the way up to my bedroom. When I reach the last step I nearly fall on my face when my heel catches and sends me off balance. Luckily I'm able to catch myself on the railing.

Straightening back up, I feel a slight twinge in my wrist. Holding it up for closer inspection, I see a light bruise has formed, five unmistakable fingerprints marring my wrist and lower forearm.

My mind darts back to the party when Zayden grabbed me. At the time, it didn't hurt. I definitely never suspected it would bruise. Then again, my adrenaline was pumping so hard I doubt I would have felt much of anything. I doubt me jerking my arm away helped matters. That's probably why I bruised. I'd pulled so hard I damn near dislocated my shoulder.

Sliding my heels off, I snag them off the floor and continue to my room, but when I reach my door, I hesitate. Turning around, I stare at Oliver's door for a solid minute, the wheels slowly turning.

Two can play at his game. I drop my things right inside my room and quietly slip across the hall. His room is dark when I step inside. And quiet. It feels almost too quiet.

I almost chicken out.

Almost….

Taking a deep breath, I flip the switch that powers his bedside lamp, causing a soft light to flood through the room. Other than looking through his open door, I've never actually been in here. It feels wrong on more levels than one. How would I feel if he did this to me?

I think back to the "fun fact introduction" and my resolve thickens. If he can spy on me in the bathroom, then why the hell should I feel bad about snooping in his room?

I start with his nightstand. Pulling open all three drawers, I rummage through an assortment of junk, magazines, and unused condoms—gross—before dropping to my knees to look under the bed…. Nothing.

I go for the closet next, a little surprised by his organization skills. Everything is separated into storage bins, labeled and stacked on shelves that hang above his clothing inside the massive walk in.

Scanning the handwritten labels, I stop on one that says *pictures*, hoping to find some incriminating photos or something I can use to deliver a little well-deserved payback. Pushing up on my tiptoes, I manage to pull the bin down, holding it against my chest as I make my way back into his room. Crossing to his desk, I set the container down and pop off the lid, pulling out a handful of pictures.

A lot of the ones on top are family photos—pictures of Oliver with his mom and dad. Some are old, some more recent. All in all they look like the all-American, happy family.

I don't know what happened between his parents, or why they divorced. It's not something I thought to ask. I just assumed it was for the same reason most couples separate—because they no longer love each other or one cheated.

I think about that for a moment, a gut curdling realization settling in my stomach. Is that why Oliver hates me and my mom so much? Did his dad cheat on his mom? Was my mom the other woman?

There's no way… Mom would never knowingly break up a family. At least, I don't think she would….

Shaking off the thought, I continue rummaging through the pictures. I find several of Oliver with various girls. One after the other, it's like every picture has a different face. How many girlfriends has this guy had?

I pause when I come across one of him and Zayden. They're sitting in the back of a pickup truck, legs dangling over the open bed, fishing poles propped up next to them. They are both smiling at the camera. I would guess them between maybe twelve or thirteen in the photo. Both look so innocent and carefree that I hardly recognize either of them.

I hone in on Zayden. Even the younger version of him is breathtaking. His messy dark hair, those incredible eyes, but it's the smile that really draws me in. I've seen him smile, not at me of course, but I've never seen him smile like he is in this picture.

The sound of the front door shutting causes me to jump, and I end up knocking the tub of pictures off the desk. They go sliding across the slick hardwood in every direction.

Shit. Shit. Shit.

I lean down and frantically pick them up, sure that I'm about to be caught at any moment. Throwing the lid haphazardly back on top, I sprint to the closet and quickly return it to where I found it.

My heart is pounding a million beats per second as I exit the bedroom, flipping off the light before quietly closing the door behind me. I've just turned the knob to my own room when Oliver appears at the top of the stairs. If he has any indication that I was in his room, he doesn't lead on. Then again, it could be due to the fact he's a bit preoccupied at the moment—given the red head hanging on his arm.

"I thought you'd be face down crying in your pillow by now," he sneers, causing the girl next to him to giggle.

"Sorry to disappoint you, *brother,* but per usual, you're wrong."

"Guess I'm not trying hard enough." A wicked smile tugs at the corners of his mouth.

"What you did tonight was low, even for you, but there's something you're failing to realize."

"And what's that?"

"That eventually I'm going to start pushing back. And I have a feeling you're not going to like what that means for you."

"Is that a threat?" he spits, his tone murderous.

"Keep up this little charade of yours and find out," I challenge, turning my attention to the girl on his arm. "And just so you know, he won't call you tomorrow. But by all means, go spread your legs for him. When you end up with an STD, you can't say he didn't give you anything for your trouble." With that, I spin on my heel and disappear inside my room.

Pressing my back to the door, I have to cover my mouth with my hand to conceal the laughter that bubbles from my throat.

Damn that felt good. Almost too good. And while my snooping was cut short before I could find anything to use against him, that doesn't mean I'm giving up. I meant what I said. If he keeps pushing, I'm going to push back. And that goes for Zayden, too. He may not have been the one feeding the lies, but he's just as guilty as Oliver.

Our earlier altercation comes back to the forefront of my mind, and just like when it was happening, it only serves to confuse me further. He's cruel, there's no question about that, but not in the same way Oliver is. Oliver's goal is to hurt people; whereas Zayden seems like he only wants everyone to fear him.

There's just something about him. Something that tells me there's a lot more to Zayden Michaels than what he lets people see—something beyond the tough guy exterior. And if I want any chance of coming out of this on the other side still standing, I have to know what that is.

chapter eight

ZAYDEN

i pull up to the back entrance of Hart's just before nine and shut off the engine. My hands grip the steering wheel so tight my knuckles turn white. Pulling in a deep breath, I let it out slow. The adrenaline rushing through my body has me twitchy and my muscles tight. This is how it always is right before a fight. Hyped up on endorphins with the need to do some damage coursing through me.

Giving my head a shake, I open my door and get out of my truck. The bright light over the back door of Hart's flickers. Just beyond the reach of the beam, Oliver stands with his back against the brick wall, waiting for me. I haven't seen him since last night, when we both took part in humiliating his sister.

Anger at the both of us along with a twinge of guilt lead the way as I walk toward him.

"You ready for tonight?" he asks, stepping away from the wall.

"Yes," I grunt. I bang the side of my fist against the rusted metal door and wait for Bruce to answer.

Oliver tosses a handful of Red Hots into his mouth and chews as he talks. "Where'd you go last night? Thought you said you didn't have to leave until eleven."

"I dipped out early."

The door swings open and one of the guys Hart uses for security on fight nights greets us. I tap my knuckles against his.

"How's it going, Bruce?"

Oliver and I step inside before he closes and locks the door behind us.

"Busy. Got a full house tonight."

I nod, having seen the long line of cars lining the street. More people means more money will be exchanging hands tonight, and if I have it my way, more money lining my pockets later.

We leave Bruce and walk down the dim hallway that leads to the stairs to the basement. It's quiet for now, but as soon as I open the door, the loud ruckus from below will beat against the walls.

"Tiffany was looking for you last night after you left," he remarks, the box of candy rattling as he dumps more of the shit into his mouth.

Irritation has my scalp prickling. "Tiffany needs to back the hell off. I told her last night I wasn't interested."

"She looked pretty bummed when she couldn't find you."

"She'll get over it."

We come to a stop at the basement door. Instead of opening it, I turn to my best friend. But before I can say anything, he continues, "Did you see Rylee's fucking face after my little stunt?" Unadulterated delight illuminates Oliver's face. "It was pure fucking genius on my part, if I do say so myself." He smirks.

A mental image of hoisting him up by his neck and bashing him against the wall filters through my mind. I could blame it on the adrenaline flowing through my veins from the impending fight, but something tells me it's more than that. I just don't know if I want to know what that *more* is.

"That last part was uncalled for," I state, shoving my hands into the pockets of my gym shorts.

"What?" His eyebrows raise. "The part about her in the shower? That was the *best* part."

"No, asshole, it wasn't," I growl, anger making my words harsher than I intended. "That shit is fucking wrong on all levels."

His eyes narrow in suspicion. "What the hell is up with you, Z?"

"Nothing," I mutter, taking a deep breath to calm my rising temper.

I don't blame him for his suspicion. I've got no right to be angry over something like this. Especially since it's Rylee. But I can't get the image of Oliver watching her during such a private moment from my mind.

"Why were you in the bathroom while she was showering anyway?" I keep my tone as level as possible.

He shrugs and his features smooth out. "It was by accident. She was in there a long time, so I stepped in to grab my razor so I could shave in one of the other bathrooms. She made a small noise, and I unconsciously glanced in the mirror. The shower is frosted, so I couldn't see her, but there was no mistaking from her silhouette what she was doing." His grin is cocky. "Obviously, the part about her "o" face was a little something I added."

His answer doesn't appease me. He may not have seen her body, but he still witnessed her getting off. Maybe not intentionally, but he shouldn't have gone into the bathroom in the first place. He could have fucking waited like a normal person.

I ignore my body's reaction to finding out that Rylee actually did get herself off in the shower, and Oliver had witnessed it. I was hoping it was just a lie he'd formulated—I could have forgotten about it. But knowing that it's true, that she touches herself, has probably delved her fingers between her pussy lips until she was soaking wet and gasping, will play fucking havoc on my body.

I clench my teeth so hard my jaw hurts. The door bangs against the wall when I thrust it open. Laughter and jeers assault my ears as I stomp down the stairs and across the short hallway leading to the big, open room. It's fucking jam-packed.

I push past the hands grabbing at me and ignore the screams trying to get my attention. I spot Hart talking to a guy in the corner, and that's where I head, Oliver following my lead. A couple of his security guys stand off to the side, their attention focused on the crowd.

Hart steps away from the guy he's talking to and leans in close to my ear. "It's fucking hopping tonight and the pot is high. The guy you're against is a crazy motherfucker, so watch your back, but make it quick."

I jerk my chin up in acknowledgement.

Hart's eyes move to Oliver. "When he's done, get his ass out of here. Brett warned they've got a bust tonight nearby. I don't want to take any chances of them coming this way."

Brett Willock is one of the cops Hart pays to keep the police department's prying eyes off this place. As long as the fighters don't kill each other, he turns a blind eye and intercepts any suspicions when necessary. Hart's had this place going for close to ten years, and so far it's worked out for him. There have been a few close calls, but it's usually kept under wraps.

"I'll be back," Oliver hollers, and walks off to a brunette that's been trying to get his attention since we made our way down.

I leave Hart and head over to the chained off area used as the makeshift fighting ring. When I catch sight of a mess of thick brown hair I do a double take, thinking my eyes are playing tricks on me, but my second glance confirms what I don't fucking need right now. At least tonight she's dressed more appropriately in a white shirt and a pair of ripped jeans—or that's what I think until I see the ripped fabric of her fitted tee, showing off small slivers of her perfectly tanned stomach.

Irritation burns in my gut as I change directions and stalk toward Rylee and Charles. Rylee's mouth is practically hanging from its hinges as she gawks at the huge crowd around her. If I thought her being at the party last night was bad, this is ten times worse. The atmosphere here can get hostile; it's the last place she needs to be.

She swivels her head in my direction. At first her eyes widen in surprise, but they soon narrow when she sees the expression on my face.

I grab her by the upper arm and drag her with me until we reach the hallway. When I pivot to face her, I notice Charles has followed. *Good.* I'll need him to get her ass out of here.

"You need to leave," I say, just loud enough for her to hear over the crowd's screams.

She pulls out of my grasp and crosses her arms over her chest, cocking her hip like a fucking diva or something.

"You seem to say that to me a lot," she snarks, increasing my irritation. "And I'll tell you the same thing as last night, I'll leave when I want to, not when you tell me to."

"And how did last night work out for you?" I ask, baring my teeth.

Pink tinges her cheeks, and for a moment I think she's going to relent. Instead, the girl shows her balls and glares at me. "You and Oliver can fuck off. It'll take more than that to make me bow down in defeat."

"It's not safe for you here," I grit between my teeth.

Reaching out, I grab her wrist, ready to haul her ass out and dump her on the sidewalk. She tries to hide it, but I notice the wince before she can. Guilt hits my stomach like dead weight when I look down and see the bruise around the flesh of her small wrist.

"Fuck," I hiss.

The light in the hallway is shit, so I lift her arm and examine the purplish-blue marks marring her otherwise flawless skin. Hatred at myself bleeds into my system. Except for a few palm prints on the asses of girls I've fucked who like that sort of rough shit, I've never left a mark on a girl before. I can beat the shit out of a man without blinking an eye, but the thought of physically hurting a girl, *this girl*, has bile threatening to come up.

"I'm sorry," I choke the words out past dry lips. "I shouldn't have grabbed you like that last night."

I lift my eyes and meet hers. She has her head tilted to the side, her gaze curious and no longer filled with animosity.

"It's no big deal. I bruise easily."

"Doesn't matter. It shouldn't have happened."

I still have one hand wrapped around her bicep with her wrist resting in my other palm. My thumb traces light circles over the injured skin. I have an instinctive need to lower my head and press a kiss over the mark, like a parent does a child. Only, my thoughts are nowhere near innocent.

"Last night…." I stop to clear my throat and try again. "Oliver took shit too far last night." Her throat bobs when she swallows. "What he said… about what he saw in the bathroom, that was private and should have never left the walls of that bathroom."

She dips her head in embarrassment, her entire face turning red. She should never be ashamed of something so natural. Everybody on this side of puberty experiments, whether they admit it or not. And there's not a damn thing wrong with it.

I let go of her arm and take a step back.

"Will you please consider leaving?" I ask instead of insisting or forcing the issue. I'm no longer in the mood to fight with her.

"I don't understand why you want me to leave so badly, but if you're worried it's not safe, don't. I'll be fine. I can take care of myself." She looks over at Charles, who's silently watching our exchange with an expression I can't decipher. "I have Pierce with me."

I release a tired sigh and scrub a hand over the back of my head. I pin Charles with a fierce look. "You stay by her side the entire time. I mean it, Charles. You gotta piss, you hold that shit until you're both out of here. I'm holding you responsible for her. Got it?"

He steps forward and throws an arm over her shoulders. I don't know why that pisses me off, but it does. "I'm glued to her side for the duration of the night."

"Once the fight's over, you both need to leave. The cops are in the neighborhood tonight, so everyone might need to make a quick getaway. People tend to freak out and trample without regard for others."

Once I have their word that they'll leave immediately afterward, I give them both a tight nod. My gaze lingers on Rylee for a second longer, before I spin around and leave them in the hallway. Oliver's already in the chained off area, looking around the crowd for me, when I step over the chain.

"Where'd you go?" he asks over the deafening noise.

"Nowhere." I'm not telling him Rylee's here because I don't want to set him off. I'm sure he'll see her eventually. Rylee is the type of person who stands out in any crowd she's in.

I turn and eye my opponent, Luis Garcia. He's half Mexican and half American. His looks must come from his Mexican side, while his build is American. He's stacked upon stacked with bulging muscles, and he has to be several inches taller than me. His long inky black hair is pulled back into a folded over ponytail against his bulky neck. To most men, he'd be intimidating and imposing, but to me, he's just another guy who will be eating the concrete beneath our feet before the night is over.

One side of his mouth tips up in amusement and he lifts his chin at me. I turn my back to him and my eyes instantly land on the girl who's standing just beyond the barrier that holds the crowd back. True to his word, Charles is pressed against her side.

With the crowd becoming frantic and the shouting getting louder by the second, I hold her gaze as I reach over my shoulder, grip the back of my shirt, and pull it over my head.

Her mouth parts open and her tongue darts out to lick along the bottom lip. Her eyes roam over the dips and valleys of the muscles on my torso. Her slim shoulders rise and fall faster than normal. I'm sure if I had a closer view, her pupils would be dilated, too.

She's fucking turned on by looking at me. I smirk, and her blush is back in full force.

Hart steps into the makeshift ring and begins to announce Luis and me, before doing a quick review of the rules. I don't pay attention—I've heard it all before. Instead I keep my eyes planted firmly on Rylee. Oliver claps me on the back and says something in my ear that I don't hear before going to one of the corners. I sense Luis approaching me, but I still keep looking at the girl who's taking up entirely way too much of my attention. She doesn't look away either. We're both ensnared by whatever fucking spell that has us captivated.

I don't know what it is, but something shifted inside us both when I held her wrist in that darkened hallway.

Her eyes turn into saucers a split second before I feel the wind of Luis' approaching fist. I duck just in time to miss his punch. He staggers from the momentum, surprise evident in his eyes when he misses. He doesn't realize that just because my attention may have been on someone other than him, I still tracked his every movement.

Jerking my gaze away from Rylee, I spin around and land an uppercut to the bottom of Luis' chin.

chapter nine

RYLEE

What the hell?

What the *actual* hell?

I watch Zayden go blow for blow with a man nearly double his size—though he delivers a lot more blows than he receives. I'm entranced by his every move—enthralled by his brute strength and speed.

Suddenly it all makes sense.

Why he has this untouchable persona.

Why people follow him like he's some sort of God.

Why everyone is afraid of him—even the jocks.

As Zayden's competitor crumbles to the floor, he climbs on top of him and continues to land punch after punch to the man's face. His nose splits and blood pours down his cheek, onto the floor below.

Seeing him like this, watching him unleash his rage on another person shouldn't impress me. Hell, it should probably scare me. But it doesn't. I'm in awe.

I've never been one to like violence, but when I was little my dad would always watch MMA fighting, and I kind of fell in love with the sport, which is why I was so excited when Pierce told me about the underground fighting ring. Granted, this is definitely more like two people fighting in the street than the fights I'm used to watching, but it's still cool.

The crowd roars, feeding off the energy. It's so loud that Hart blows the horn three times before Zayden hears it and halts his assault on the man who is now nearly unconscious on the floor.

Coming here tonight, I didn't know Zayden would be one of the fighters—a little detail I think Pierce intentionally left out. When I watched him step into that ring, I think my heart stopped for a moment. I don't know if I was more nervous or scared. Now I see that my concern was misplaced. It should have been the other guy I was worried about, not Zayden.

Sweat trickles down his muscular torso as he stands, shoving a hand through his hair to push the messy locks out of his face. I can't look away. If I thought he was gorgeous with his clothes on, it's nothing compared to how he looks with them off. His body is absolutely insane.

"Come on." Pierce tugs on my arm. Reluctantly looking away from Zayden, I peer up at my friend. "We need to bounce."

"Why?"

He leans down and speaks directly into my ear—the noise of the crowd making it hard to hear anything beyond their cheers. "Because I told Zayden I'd get you out of here directly after the fight."

"Since when do you do Zayden's bidding?" I draw back, not trying to hide my frustration.

"I don't. But when I feel like he's actually looking out for you, I'm going to listen. You heard what he said about the cops."

I groan, tempted to stomp my feet like a spoiled child trying to get my way.

"Fine," I cave, knowing my mom would kill me if she found out I came here tonight—a trip to the police station in the back of a cop car *might* tip her off. Taking Pierce's hand, he turns and pulls me through the crowd. I try to catch one more glimpse of Zayden, but the amount of people packed inside the small space makes it difficult to see anything once we've started moving.

Pierce waits until we step out into the cold night air before speaking again. "I know what you're thinking. You don't want anything to do with that. I promise."

"Anything to do with what?" I don't have to play oblivious; I really don't know what he's talking about.

I pick up speed, having trouble keeping up with his long strides as we make our way away from Hart's. There are several people hanging out outside, despite the fact that it's January. I guess they figured if they couldn't get in they'd wait outside to find out the outcome.

"Zayden." His eyes slide to me. "You don't want anything to do with him. I know the kind of girls he goes for. Trust me when I say you're not *that* kind of girl."

"Is that your way of telling me I'm not pretty enough?" I find myself becoming mildly offended.

"Yeah, right." He snorts. "You're an easy ten out of ten." His eyes do a quick side sweep of me to get his point across. "What you look like is not the hiccup."

"Then what is?"

I don't even know why I care. It's not like I plan on making a play for Zayden. Why would I? The man has made my life a living hell this past week.

"Let's just say that Zayden tends to like girls with a little more *experience.*" He puts the words in air quotes.

"Huh?"

"You know." He gives me a look that says I can't be that dense. "As in sexually. Guys like Zayden have certain expectations from the girls they spend time with. And more often than not, that's all they're interested in."

"How do you know I'm not that kind of girl?" I ask, crossing my arms in front of my chest in an effort to warm myself. We'd decided to leave our jackets in the car so we wouldn't have to hold them. At the moment, I'm regretting that decision.

"Because I have eyes," he tells me knowingly, dropping an arm over my shoulder and pulling me against his side when he notices me shivering.

The warmth of his body is enough to take the edge off, and I welcome it whole heartedly.

"I've messed around with guys before," I say grumpily.

"Messed around how? Because if you haven't taken it in every hole at least once, refer to my previous statement—you don't want anything to do with that."

"Okay well, I haven't—but I've done other things. And who said I want anything to do with *that* to begin with?"

"Like what?" he questions, snagging his keys out of his pocket as we get close to his car.

"Huh?" I'm not sure which part of my statement he's referring to.

"What kind of things have you done?"

"I don't know." Heat flood my cheeks. I've never been one to talk to guys about this kind of stuff—no matter who that guy is.

"You don't know?" He quirks a brow as he unlocks the car and pulls open the passenger door for me.

"I mean, me and my ex-boyfriend participated in some pretty heavy petting," I admit, not really sure how else to describe it.

"Heavy petting?" Laughter bubbles from his throat as he shuts the door and crosses to the driver's side. Sliding inside, he's still chuckling as he jams the key into the ignition and turns it over—immediately flipping on the heat. "Heavy petting," he repeats. "It's even worse than I thought. Have you even had an orgasm before?"

"Were you not at the party last night? I'm pretty sure you already know the answer to that," I say, sliding on my jacket before latching my seatbelt.

"Wait." He does a double take. "The shower thing was true?"

"Well, what do you expect? I'm eighteen and have never had sex. I have to get relief somehow."

"Good point." He chuckles. "I knew you weren't a girl who sleeps around, but I figured you had at least had sex before. A girl who looks like you—I'm sure there's never been a shortage of options. So what's the hold up?"

"There's no hold up. It's not like I haven't wanted to. It's just never felt right, ya know?" I blow out a breath.

"I get it. There's no shame in holding onto your virtue for as long as you can. I know I wish I had."

"How many people have you slept with?" I ask.

I'm curious about Pierce's lifestyle but didn't want to come right out and ask unprompted. This seems like a pretty good time to ask.

"Guys or girls?" He smirks, pulling his car onto the road.

"Shut up!" I smack his arm playfully. "You've been with both?"

"Um, how else would I know that I like both?" He chuckles.

"Good point, I guess." I relax back into the seat. "So, how many of each then?"

"Two guys, six girls."

"Eight people?" I gape at him.

"Don't look at me like that. Eight people isn't that many. Especially considering on two occasions they were threesomes."

"Two people at once." I choke on the words.

"Lord, you really are innocent. From that mouth of yours I never would have guessed."

"What's wrong with my mouth?" I ask. "Wait a minute. Don't you dare change the subject. I need more information, like right now."

"Pretty sure it will take me longer than the car ride to your house to give you all the details." He smiles at me. "How about I fill you in another time?"

"Seriously? You're going to leave me hanging like that?"

"I think you should try making it past second base before I share. I might traumatize you or something."

"Now I'm even more curious," I whine.

"Maybe that's my goal." He wrinkles his nose playfully.

"You're mean." I huff, crossing my arms in front of myself.

"I know someone else who's mean, yet you still spent the last several minutes drooling over him."

"Drooling? I was not drooling."

"Sure you weren't," he says sarcastically. "Look, I'm not judging. I was drooling a little, too."

"He's good looking, I'll give him that. But he's also mean, and bossy and, and, *and*, an asshole." I push the last part out, not able to think of the word I was trying to say.

"Let me ask you something—the guys you've dated before, how would you describe them?"

"What do you mean?"

"Like, were they nice guys? Pretty boys?"

"Well, I've only ever had one serious boyfriend, but yes, I'd say he was a nice guy."

"And yet you didn't want to sleep with him?"

"I wanted to."

"But you said it never felt right. Did you ever think of why that is?"

"What are you getting at?" I ask, not really following.

"Maybe you have a thing for guys that are assholes. Hence, the drooling."

"I was not drooling." I land a playful punch to his bicep.

"It also doesn't hurt that Zayden seems to have a sweet spot for you."

"What?" I practically spring out of my seat.

"You heard me. Don't think I missed the way he was looking at you earlier. Or the way you were looking at him, for that matter. Not to mention the fact that Zayden is not the type of guy that apologizes. *Ever*."

"Well he needed to apologize. Look what he did to me!" I hold up my hand, gesturing to the bruises that wrap around my lower forearm that are hidden beneath my jacket sleeve.

"That's not the point. I've gone to school with Zayden since kindergarten, and I've seen him do some pretty messed up crap, but what I've never seen him do is apologize for it afterward."

I ponder this for a moment, my earlier exchange with Zayden coming to the forefront of my mind. The way he looked at me when he examined my arm—his expression a mix of anger and regret. It really did seem like he felt bad, which was a complete contradiction to how he's treated me thus far.

"He's weirdly protective of you, too," he continues. "First, he got angry with you for drinking at the party last night when you didn't know who made the drink. Then he was pissed you were at the fight, because he said it wasn't safe. I don't think I've ever encountered that side of Zayden before."

"But then he purposely screws with me at school. He's protective when it's convenient for him, but he sure has no problem hurting me either. There's plenty of proof in his actions this past week."

"You're not wrong there." He slows to a stop outside of my house and kills the engine. "But maybe he's doing that to keep you at bay."

"Why would he want to keep me at bay?" I ask before we both answer in unison. "Oliver."

I drop my head back on the headrest and blow out a puff of air.

"I really have no idea why my stepbrother hates me so much."

"Maybe you should ask him."

"I've tried. Well, sort of. He has no interest in having an actual conversation with me."

"Then maybe you should make him."

"Not sure I could even if I tried. And honestly, at this point, I'm not sure I want to know. I just need to get through the rest of the school year, and then I'm gone. Bye, bye Oliver and all his bullshit."

"There, see, just focus on the end goal."

"I'm trying, but when you're forced to live with a person who torments you daily, the end goal seems like a lifetime away."

"I get that. But hey, at least you have me." He grins.

"This is true," I agree, glancing at the clock on my phone. "It's still early. Do you want to come in and hang out?" I gesture to the large, brick house set back several feet from the road.

"Your parents won't care?"

"My mom is at the hospital. She got called into an emergency surgery shortly before you picked me up. She won't be home until really late. And Paul doesn't care. Oliver has a different girl over every other day and he never says a word. I dare him to say something to me for having a friend over. Even if that friend is a very handsome guy." I wink at him.

"Careful now. You know I'm not gay, right? And I've already told you that you're an easy ten out of ten. Keep paying me compliments, and I might get the wrong impression." He smiles and from the playfulness of his expression I know he's just messing with me.

From the first moment Pierce sat down at my lunch table there was this unspoken, mutual thing between us. It's like we both knew that we were destined to be *just* friends.

"You're ridiculous," I tell him, throwing the door open. "Are you coming or not?" I ask as I get out of the car.

"Fine, but if you suggest braiding each other's hair or painting nails, I'm out. I may like boys but that doesn't mean I'm a girl."

"Noted." I laugh, shutting the door as Pierce climbs out of the car.

He's still standing in the open car door when a black truck comes barreling down the road, whipping into the driveway seconds later.

"On second thought." Pierce throws me a sideways glance. "Maybe I'll take a raincheck," he says, looking toward the truck.

"You can't leave me here with him. Oliver's not even here," I hiss over the top of the car.

"No, but he will be. If Zayden is here, Oliver will be right behind him. I love you, but I'm not trying to paint a massive target on my back."

"Fine," I huff. "Wimp."

"Just go lock yourself in your room. You'll be safe in there." He laughs.

"How do you know? Maybe they'll break in and suffocate me while I sleep."

"Really?" He snorts. "I never took you for the dramatic type."

"Dramatic? You're the one running away."

"Touché." He laughs. "But I'm still leaving."

"I hate you," I spit good-naturedly, giving him the best evil glare I can muster.

"Shut up. You love me. Now get your ass inside before Oliver gets here. The last thing you want is to be caught outside in the dark with the two of them."

"Gee, thanks for the warning." I tighten my jacket around myself and take a step back.

"Text me in the morning and let me know you're still alive," he jokes.

"Nope, I'm gonna make you sweat it out until Monday," I fire back.

"That's the mouth I was talking about." He points at me, reminding me of his comment earlier. "You just can't help yourself."

I stick my tongue out and flip him the middle finger, his laughter dancing through the cool night air as he slips back inside the car. Not waiting to watch him leave, I turn and make a beeline for the front door.

Unfortunately, I don't make it there fast enough. Zayden intercepts me on the front porch.

I'm momentarily frozen by the sight of him. He has the gym shorts on that he was wearing during the fight, but his torso is covered by a black hoodie. His hair is disheveled and still appears to be slightly damp with sweat. In the dim porch lighting, I can see a bruise that's formed just below his left eye.

"Oliver isn't here," I blurt before he can say anything.

"Yeah, I know." He blows out a breath. "I actually came to see you." He shoves his hands into the front pocket of his sweatshirt.

"Me?" I croak, my voice suddenly hoarse.

"Can we talk for a minute?"

I want to say no. I want to turn my nose up and walk inside without even considering the idea. But when I see the look on his face everything shifts.

chapter ten

ZAYDEN

i take a step back from Rylee and fist my hands at my side. This was a mistake. I shouldn't be here. I should be at home with dad, helping him with Danielle. This is the very last place I need to be. I don't even know why I came. Oliver's off with some bimbo he picked up after the fight, so I can't even use him as an excuse. All I know is, after my phone call with dad tonight, I didn't want to go home. I wanted, no *needed*, a break from the harsh realities of life. I'm an asshole and a coward because of it, but I wanted to get away from it all for a little while.

Rylee was the first person I thought of. Maybe it was because of the way she looked at me tonight, or whatever weird connection we shared. All I *do* know is I needed to see her. It was an impulse I had no way of curbing. And it's confusing as fuck, because I don't like the chick. She's still the same spoiled girl as before. Except, I'm beginning to wonder if there's more to her than the money she was born into.

Rylee looks at me like I'm some caged wild animal, unsure if and when I'll pounce. Her arms are crossed over her chest, like she's protecting herself. I feel close to the edge, but the last thing I want from her is wariness, so I try to relax my features and loosen my tense muscles.

"Do you… uh…." She gestures to the wicker furniture set on the porch. "Do you want to sit?"

I jerk my chin up and wait until she's seated at one end of the couch before sitting down on the opposite end. I probably should have taken the chair, but for some unexplainable reason I want to be closer to her.

"I can grab you something to drink if you like," she offers. "Tea, Coke, water?"

"I'm good."

"Okay."

She licks her lips nervously and tucks her hands between her knees. I lean back, resting an arm along the back of the couch, letting my knees fall open. She keeps her head forward, but her eyes dart toward me every few seconds.

"Do I make you nervous or something?" It's a dumb question. The answer is in the bounce of her knees and the stiff set of her shoulders. But I want to see if she'll answer truthfully.

"Or something," she mutters, barely loud enough for me to hear.

"What was that?"

"Nothing," she answers louder.

I smile, but keep my laughter in. We're silent for a few moments, both listening to the rustling of the leafless branches with the light breeze.

"Can you blame me?" I glance over at her sudden question. "One minute you're trying your best to make my life hell, the next you're warning me about dangers, and now, here you are wanting to talk. You hate me."

I blow out a long breath and run my hand over my face then the back of my head. "I don't hate you."

She lets out a bitter laugh. "Could've fooled me."

I turn so I'm facing her. "I don't hate you, Rylee," I state sternly. "I just don't particularly like you."

She lifts her head, her brows scrunched together.

"But why? I haven't done anything to you. And I get the feeling it's more than just Oliver hating me."

I shrug. "People like you, people with money, are always the same. Entitled, greedy, pompous, and undeserving."

Her lips press together into a scowl. "That's fucking stupid." I raise a brow at her outburst. "My mother may have money, but she's worked her butt off for it her entire life. It's not like it just fell into her lap, or mine for that matter. And I'm none of those things. For you to think you have the right to judge me when you know nothing about me makes you a judgmental bigoted asshole."

"That may be true, but from my experience most rich people are."

"What about Oliver? You're friends with him, and he has more money at his fingertips than I do. And from *my* experience, he *is* entitled and pompous. Not to mention he's also an asshole."

"Oliver's different. We were friends long before the greed of money could grip him. As far as the way he treats you, you'll have to take that up with him."

She's silent for a moment before she asks quietly, "Why are you here, Zayden?"

Leaning forward, I rest my elbows on my knees and rake both hands through my hair. That's the million-dollar question. Why the fuck *am* I here? I still don't know the answer.

"I have some shit going on at home and I needed to get away from it for a bit," I find myself admitting.

The couch creaks as she turns, her knee bent on the cushion as she leans back against the arm rest.

"Do you want to talk about it?"

I look at her. Although her thick brown hair is drawn up into a ponytail, the ends still fall over her shoulder and reach the top of her breasts. When it's down, it falls past the middle of her back. The porch light is behind her, so her face is partially hidden by shadows, but I can see the concern in her gaze.

Danielle's illness isn't a secret. I'm not ashamed of her or what she's forced to go through every day. Even so, it's not something I care to discuss. It's too painful. The only people I don't mind talking about it with is Dad, Oliver, and, Hart. But for some reason, I want to tell Rylee.

I glance away and stare off into the darkness.

"My sister has emphysema due to an Alpha-1 antitrypsin deficiency. It's classified in the severe stage. She had an episode today."

"I'm so sorry, Zayden."

I nod. "Most of the time she's okay as long as she's not active. But there are times, when even something as simple as taking a breath can be too much for her. She has to use an oxygen tank often because of it. I spoke with my dad after the fight and he said it hasn't been a good night. She's only nine years old and she can't do anything other girls her age are doing. She can't have sleepovers, ride a bike, or go to school."

"I can't imagine how hard that must be for her," Rylee remarks. "Or how difficult it must be on you and your dad."

I jerk my head to her. "I don't care about myself. What I feel is nothing compared to what she's going through."

She nods, and her throat bobs when she swallows. "Absolutely, but that doesn't mean your feelings aren't important. It's obvious you care deeply for her, and something tells me you're a good big brother."

My lip curls up into a sneer. "I'm such a good brother that I'm here with you, instead of at home with her."

She slides her ass across the cushion until her knee touches my thigh. Her hand is warm when she lays it on top of mine.

"That doesn't make you a bad brother. It makes you human. Everyone needs a break sometimes."

"Danielle doesn't get any breaks from the pain she endures just from breathing. What makes it okay for me to have one?"

"She was given a crappy lot in life. That doesn't mean you have to stop living your own life. It's okay to take time for yourself. It helps to keep you sane during the difficult times."

I clench my jaw and turn away from Rylee. I want to believe what she's saying, but it's hard to want something when my sister only lives half a life. There are so many things I want for Danielle, things she'll more than likely never have.

"Her doctors want to put her on the transplant list, but insurance won't pay for it because they claim her case isn't severe enough," I spit the last part. Rage fills me every time I think about those uppity insurance bastards.

"What are you and your father going to do?"

I look down at my hands and curl my fingers into fists. The damaged skin breaks apart. "Fight until I can pay for it myself and hope it's not too late."

Rylee grabs one of my clenched fists and uncurls my fingers. She runs the tip of her pointer finger lightly over one of the busted knuckles. "So that's why you fight," she murmurs.

"Yeah," I answer huskily.

Having her hold my hand in her much smaller one, along with the way she daintily examines the damage on my knuckles feels good. Way more than it probably should.

Sitting this close, I smell roses. I wonder if it's her natural scent or if it's the shampoo she uses. Whatever it is, it's intoxicating.

She lifts her head and her gaze meets mine. There's something in her eyes that has my blood heating and traveling south, filling my cock to an uncomfortable level in my shorts.

I don't realize what I'm doing until my hand is tangled in her hair. I lean closer at the same time tugging her toward me. I have no idea what's come over me, but the need to feel her mouth against mine is something I'm unable to resist.

At the first taste of her lips, a low groan rumbles from the back of my throat. She tastes fucking incredible. Sweet. So goddamn sweet.

A little mewl vibrates from her lips and her fingers grip my thigh, sending shockwaves of pleasure racing through me.

This is wrong. She's Oliver's fucking stepsister, and he'd skin me alive and call me a traitor if he knew I was kissing his enemy. But right now, I don't give two shits what Oliver would say or do. This feels too good to ignore.

Using the grip I still have on her hair; I tilt Rylee's head at a better angle. Then I wrap an arm around her waist and hoist her onto my lap. Her knees go to either side of my hips as our kissing continues. She's not even pressing down on me and I still feel the heat of her.

I nip her bottom lip causing her to suck in a breath. A shudder ripples down my spine when she laces her fingers in my hair. Gripping her waist, I pull her hot center down until it meets my cock, groaning at the contact. Any control I have left is slipping away by the minute.

I trail my lips down the slender column of her throat, marveling in her delicious taste.

"Wait," she pants and tightens her fingers in my hair. I want to growl my disapproval, but the shakiness in her tone stops me. "I can't—" She shakes her head. "We can't do this."

I rest my head against the back of the couch and try to catch my breath. "Why not?"

She dips her gaze away from me and stares at the strings of my hoodie.

"We just can't."

My fingers flex against her waist. "Look at me, Rylee."

When she lifts her head, the beam from the porch light illuminates her face, revealing the redness tinting her cheeks.

"What's wrong?" I ask gently.

"Nothing's wrong," she mutters. "That's just it. It felt good. Really good. But I've never—"

She stops abruptly and bites her lip, uncertainty dimming her eyes. The look doesn't match the confident and self-assured woman I know.

Realization dawns, and my cock jerks in my shorts. Her eyes widen at the movement.

I lift my head and look straight into her eyes. "Are you a virgin, Rylee?" I keep my tone even, although my mind is racing a mile a minute. How in the fuck could a girl as hot as her still be untouched?

"Yes."

I close my eyes and release a shuddering breath. I don't know why the thought of no one having touched Rylee before makes me so happy, but it damn sure does.

Deliriously so.

"There's no need to be embarrassed."

She scrunches up her pert little nose. "I wouldn't say I'm embarrassed. Just… uncertain. I mean, you've got all this experience, and well… I don't. I'm not like the girls you're used to."

I tuck a loose piece of hair behind her ear. "You've been listening to rumors." I smirk.

Her hands settle against my pecks, her fingers slightly digging into the muscles. "Maybe."

"You shouldn't believe everything you hear."

She cocks a brow. "So, you're saying you don't like girls with experience?"

"I'm saying I don't *only* like girls with experience. I have no preference, so long as she's into me and I'm into her."

"Oh."

I lift her off my lap and set her beside me before getting to my feet. "It's all irrelevant anyway. You're right. We shouldn't be doing this."

Even as I say the words, I want to take them back. Being with Rylee the last few minutes has been relaxing and comfortable, something I don't normally feel with girls. But I know Oliver would flip his shit if he found out. No girl is worth fucking up a ten-year friendship for.

"Yeah."

I look back at Rylee when I reach the bottom of the porch steps. She has her hands stuffed between her knees again, staring off into space, with a frown marring her pretty face. I want to wipe it away, but I force myself to move toward the driveway instead.

Without another look backward, I quickly climb into my truck and leave temptation behind.

chapter eleven

RYLEE

"tell me you want me." Zayden hovers above me, his breath dancing across my face.

"I want you." My voice is muffled and distorted, causing the words to come out jumbled.

"Say it." He rocks into me, sending a wave of pleasure through my lower extremities.

Every inch of my body aches for him.

Every cell ignites for him.

Heat spreads through my limbs- an inferno that's threatening to swallow me from the inside out.

"I want you," I repeat, but again the words don't come out right.

"Tell me, Rylee."

"I want you."

"Tell me." He's growing impatient, his words sharp.

I try again, but this time not even the slightest sound comes out. It's like being in a dream—one where you're trying so hard to run but your feet feel weighted to the ground and you can't seem to move.

"Rylee." His voice grows louder, his weight pressing down on me. "Rylee."

My eyes shoot open, and I blink rapidly into the light of the room. My chest rises and falls in quick succession.

It was just a dream—I tell myself, unsure if it's relief or disappointment that settles in my gut.

"Rylee." I glance up to find my mom standing in my doorway, realizing it must have been her that woke me so abruptly.

"What?" I question, my voice heavy with sleep.

"You're going to be late for school. You were supposed to be up thirty minutes ago."

"What?" I turn, looking at the clock on my nightstand, seeing that she's right. I overslept. "Crap!" I shoot upright. "I'm up," I tell her, throwing back the covers before quickly climbing out of bed.

"I'm heading to the office. Make sure you eat something before you leave."

"Okay." I shoo her out of my doorway. "I love you. Have a good day." I practically shut the door in her face, knowing I need to get dressed like right now.

"I love you, too," I hear her call from the hallway, but I'm already completely submerged in my closet, frantically trying to find something to wear.

I had meant to do laundry yesterday, but instead ended up lying in bed all day, mindlessly watching reruns of *I Love Lucy* while trying to cyber stalk Zayden. Not that it did me any good. The man is like a ghost. Who doesn't have Facebook or Instagram these days? Even my mom has a Facebook account.

My mind once again floats back to Saturday night. The way he showed up unannounced. How he looked when he talked about his sister. The way it felt when he kissed me. The thrill that ran through me when I felt his erection pressing into me.

I flatten a palm to my chest, feeling like I might hyperventilate just thinking about it again. Everything that happened on the porch had been unexpected, that's for sure. But it was also really… amazing. Though I doubt it was nearly as big of a deal for him as it was for me. I'm sure he goes around kissing girls all the time. The thought twists my stomach into an unsettling knot.

I'd be lying if I said the thought of Zayden with another girl doesn't drive me insane with jealousy—it absolutely does. Even if I have no claim to him. Even if Saturday night was nothing more than a low moment for him, and I was the closest available female to distract him. Even if he has no real interest in me—it doesn't change how I feel.

Asshole or not, that kiss did something to me. Something surprising and unexpected. I've been physically attracted to Zayden since the first time I saw him—who wouldn't be? And while I've also been intrigued by him, I didn't expect to actually *feel* something. And not just the thrill and excitement of kissing him—but something real. Something deep in my chest that's been humming ever since—despite the way he bolted afterward.

I've tried to reason with myself several times since then—reminding myself who Zayden Michaels really is. A man who is rumored to only be interested in one thing. A man who is in cahoots with my asshat of a stepbrother. A man who helped make my first week at a new school absolutely miserable. I can't have feelings for him.

And then the thought dawns on me—something I hadn't considered before now. What if that kiss—what if him showing up the way he did—what if that was all part of some scheme he and Oliver cooked up? It's totally plausible, right?

A man who's made it clear he doesn't like me shows up on my porch and tells me some sob story about his sister, who probably doesn't even exist, in an attempt to lower my guard so I don't see what's coming next.

My anger flares.

He wouldn't—would he?

If I'm being totally honest with myself, I can absolutely see him doing something like that. Maybe he came here hoping to trick me into having sex with him so he and Oliver could video tape it or something. Maybe it was all part of some sick, cruel joke, but when he learned I was a virgin he changed his mind. And the way he left right after finding out—I don't know, something doesn't quite add up. Either he's a complete fraud and the mask he wears around everyone else is just that—a mask, and the Zayden I saw last night is the real Zayden. Or he's toying with me on purpose. As much as I hate to admit it, my gut instinct is telling me it's the latter.

"hey." pierce slides up next to me, leaning his shoulder against the locker next to mine. "I tried calling you yesterday to find out how Saturday night went. When you didn't answer I started to worry that maybe they did suffocate you with a pillow." He grins.

"Nope. I'm still breathing." I grab a couple of books from my locker.

"I see you got your new lock." He gestures to my locker.

"Yeah, I stopped by the office and picked it up this morning. The janitor cut the other one off over the weekend. I'm taking bets on how long it will be before this one mysteriously stops working." I shove the books under my arm before closing the door and sliding the lock in place.

"Who knows? Maybe they'll start playing nice."

"Not likely." I roll my eyes, following Pierce when he turns and heads in the direction of my first period class. It's kind of become our thing. He meets me at my locker and we play catch up as he walks me to class.

"So…." He gives me a sideways glance, clearly waiting for me to say something.

"So, what?" I shift my books from one arm to the other.

"So, are you going to tell me what happened Saturday after I left?"

"Nothing happened," I answer too quickly.

"Don't think I can't read you. Spill." He knocks his shoulder into mine.

"There's nothing to spill." I shake my head, not sure how much, if anything, I want to tell him. It's kind of impossible to talk about something you don't understand yourself.

"Now why don't I believe that?" He turns and pulls me to the side as we reach my class.

"Can we talk about it later?" I shift nervously from one foot to the other, my gaze sweeping down the hallway in search of the one person I'm both terrified and excited to see.

"Is it that bad?" he questions, misreading my expression. Then again, maybe he's not misreading it, especially if the epiphany I had this morning actually ends up being true.

"I guess it depends on what you define as bad." I knead my bottom lip between my teeth.

"Now you've really piqued my interest."

"I'll fill you in at lunch," I promise, the second warning bell sounding through the halls.

"Fine," he groans. "I can't be late to first, anyway. One more tardy and Ms. Mullins will likely have me sitting in detention for a week."

"Well we wouldn't want that." I smile when he wraps an arm around me and pulls me in for a half hug.

"Try not to get yourself into trouble between now and lunch." He pulls back, tipping my chin upward with his hand.

"I'll do my best," I tell him, freezing when I catch sight of Zayden heading toward us. I groan at the sight of him but not for the reason I'm sure others would think.

When he wasn't at his locker this morning, I wondered if he was even here. Turns out he was probably just avoiding me.

His expression is hard, his shoulders tense—straining against the fabric of his gray t-shirt as he stalks in our direction. Our eyes meet for the briefest of moments before he snags my arm.

"We need to talk," he growls as he hooks an arm through mine and hauls me backward, away from Pierce.

"Zayden." I shake loose of his hold.

"You can go now," Zayden tells my friend, who seems to be frozen in place.

"It's okay," I mouth, meeting Pierce's confused expression. I have no idea what Zayden wants, but based on the curtness of his voice and the look in his eyes, I'd venture to say it's not something I want Pierce to witness.

I can tell he's not sure if he should leave me alone with Zayden, but after a long moment he nods and turns, heading in the opposite direction.

"What the fuck did you tell him?" Zayden clips the moment Pierce is out of earshot.

"What?" I draw back, taken aback by the harshness of his tone.

"You heard me. What did you tell him?"

"What are you talking about?" I square my shoulders, refusing to shrink under his intimidating glare.

"Don't play stupid with me, Rylee. We both know what I'm talking about." His tone eases, but his expression doesn't.

"I don't have time for this," I tell him. "I have to get to class." I try to move as the final bell sounds, but Zayden blocks my path.

I look to my left and then to my right, ensuring that we're alone and Oliver isn't lurking somewhere close by, ready to deliver his next round of humiliation.

"If you're referring to what happened Saturday, I didn't tell him anything," I answer after a long pause. "As far as I'm concerned, there's nothing to tell." This seems to get his attention and he steps closer, backing me into the lockers behind me.

"Nothing to tell, huh?" he grunts, leaning in until his face is so close to mine I can feel his warm breath on my face. "That's not the impression I got when my mouth was on you, tasting your sweet skin." I jump when the back of his hand grazes my collarbone.

"What do you want, Zayden?" I try to keep my voice even, despite the fact that my insides are trembling.

"I just wanted to make sure we understood each other, which it seems we do." He takes a full step back, and I swear I nearly protest the loss.

What the hell is wrong with me?

"Now that you've cleared that up—is there anything else you need? Or do you want to play on my emotions with another sob story and see how far you can take this little game of yours?"

"Come again?" His gaze narrows, and I can tell I've struck a nerve.

"I'm just saying, if you want to fuck with me, there are more creative ways you can do it."

"Is that what you think I'm doing?" His expression softens slightly.

"I don't think—I know. So whatever it is you're playing at, whatever you and Oliver have cooked up, I'm not falling for it. Guess you two will have to go back to the drawing board."

"You think Oliver had something to do with me kissing you?" He closes in on me again, dipping down to meet my eyes. I swallow, not able to push any words out past the sudden lump in my throat. "Let me make one thing clear, me kissing you had *nothing* to do with Oliver. Maybe I kissed you because I wanted to."

"Yeah, because you like me so much." Sarcasm drips from my voice.

"I *don't* like you, Rylee." If words could slice flesh, I'd be bleeding out all over the floor right now. It's not like I didn't already know he hated me but hearing him say as much stings a hell of a lot more than it should.

"Well I don't like you either." It's a lame rebuttal, but the only thing I can come up with on the spot.

Before I even know what's happening, Zayden's lips crash down onto mine. I can't think, can't breathe, or even move. I'm lost to the sensation—to the way his mouth moves skillfully against mine.

He grabs both of my hands and pins them to the locker behind me—my books crashing to the floor as his tongue slides past the seam of my lips and dips into my mouth. A full body tremor runs through me. My body arches into him, aching for his touch.

I can't explain my reaction to him—hell, I don't even understand it myself. But it's like my body is acting on its own accord—betraying the voice in my head screaming for it to stop.

Zayden kisses me hard, unforgiving, almost punishing, and I drink every ounce of it in—not able to get enough. I hate myself for how badly I want this—for how badly I want *him*.

The kiss ends as abruptly as it began, and my eyes flutter open to find very heated ocean blue eyes staring back at me.

I open my mouth to say something, but nothing comes out. I'm not even sure what I would say if I could find words. My body feels like I just touched a live wire—the aftereffects of the shock are still coursing through me.

"Seems like you like me just fine," Zayden scoffs, his hard mask slipping back into place.

As if this were the reaction I needed from him to snap out of it, I take a deep breath and step toward him.

"Do not ever fucking kiss me again." I stab at his chest with my pointer finger.

"And what are you going to do if I do?" He seems amused by my reaction, which only pisses me off more. If I had any doubt he was playing some kind of game, I don't anymore.

"Trust me when I say, you don't want to find out." With that, I snag my books off the floor and spin around, stomping into class without so much as a backward glance.

I nod an apology to the teacher, who pauses for a brief second when I enter before diving back into the day's lesson. My hands tremble as I slide into my seat, and tears sting the backs of my eyes, threatening to spill over at any moment.

I don't know what bothers me more—learning that this really is just a game to Zayden or the fact that I let myself hope that it was something more.

When Zayden enters the classroom a couple of minutes later, I don't make any attempt to look at him. His scent invades my nostrils as he glides past me, and even though I'm so mad at him and myself for what just transpired in the hallway, it doesn't stop me from breathing him in as deeply as my lungs will allow.

I guess I really am a glutton for punishment….

chapter twelve

ZAYDEN

i throw my booted feet up on the chair in front of me and watch as students come in droves into the cafeteria. Some head for the lunch line, while others join their cliquey groups at their usual tables. I roll my eyes when a couple of cheerleaders prance by in their uniforms and a group of guys whistle and jeer at them. Of course, the girls eat up the attention; flipping their blonde hair over their shoulders, pushing out their tits, and casting the guys a come-fuck-me look.

Behind them, Tiffany walks in. I bite back a curse when she immediately sets her eyes on me. I really need to start spending my lunches outside with the potheads; thirty-degree weather be damned. I'm in no fucking mood to deal with her today.

Being the cheer captain, she's also decked out in her cheer uniform. Tonight is a rival basketball game between Parkview and Westerland, so there's a prep rally at the end of the school day to pump up the team. Parkview High has always been very competitive when it comes to sports.

"Hey, Z," Tiffany croons, plopping her ass down on my lap, as if it's her place to do so, when it sure as fuck isn't. The bitch knows this too, because I've told her multiple times.

I grab her waist, about to shove her ass to the floor, when I feel an intense stare on me. I glance toward the doorway and find a pair of angry brown eyes drilling holes in my skull. I don't know if her ire is left over from what happened in the hallway yesterday or from the girl currently occupying my lap. I decide to find out. Grabbing Tiffany's waist, I pull her closer to me instead of pushing her away. My lips quirk up into a smirk when her glare intensifies.

Yep, Rylee doesn't like Tiffany snuggled up to me. Jealousy is a bitch, but I find I like it on Rylee.

"God!" Tiffany draws out the word. "I can't believe Mr. Bernard gave us homework on a game night."

Her whining grates on my nerves, and my fingers twitch to get her the fuck off me, but there's something I want more. If I can't have Rylee sitting on my dick, then the next best thing is seeing her green with envy, wishing it were her in my lap. She can deny it all she wants. The look in her eyes says she's visualizing scratching Tiffany's eyes out and sliding into her place.

"Are you even listening to me, Z?"

I peel my eyes off Rylee and look at Tiffany's made-up face.

"It's five fucking questions, Tiffany. I think you can manage," I tell her with as much patience as I can muster.

Her bottom lip sticks out into a pout. “Yeah, but it’s the point. He knows our focus needs to be on the game and not some dumb questions about what the government did a hundred years ago.”

Yeah, because it’s the cheer team who works their asses off to win each game. Give me a fucking break.

Her eyes light up and a smile creeps across her face. “I’ll get Neville to do it for me.”

I grunt. Neville, the smartest guy in the school, is a pathetic fool who follows Tiffany around like a lovesick puppy, no matter how shitty she treats him.

Oliver slides into the seat beside me, a sated look in his eyes. His hair is mussed up and there’s a huge red mark on the side of his neck. He slouches in his chair, his knees falling open.

“I see Karla finally found you,” Tiffany snarks with a giggle.

He offers her a lazy grin. “She sure as fuck did. Cornered me in the bathroom.”

“Eww….” She wrinkles her nose. “You fucked her in the bathroom?”

“Nope.” He tosses a handful of Red Hots into his mouth. “But she did blow me,” he finishes with a wink.

“Gross. That’s even worse.”

“Whatever, Tiff. It’s not like you haven’t been on your knees in the boy’s bathroom before.”

I know for a fact she’s been on her knees in the boy’s bathroom. The first disastrous blowjob she gave me was in the boy’s bathroom.

She nibbles on the tip of one of her manicured nails for a moment. Her eyes slide to me before she shrugs.

A peel of laughter has the three of us looking over at Rylee’s table. She has her hand over her mouth, her face red from whatever she found funny. Her eyes dart around the room, noticing she's drawn attention to herself, and her face becomes an even darker shade of red. Her eyes briefly dart to mine, but just as quickly she looks away.

"I can't stand that bitch," Tiffany grumbles, curling her lip up into a sneer. "She needs to go back to wherever she came from."

"What'd she do to you?" I ask, suddenly annoyed.

"I just don't like her. You'd think after the party last weekend, she'd be too scared to show her face. She actually had the nerve to show up at the fight on Saturday."

"She was at the fight?" Oliver asks, his brows lifting in surprise. "I didn't see her there."

She lifts a hand and inspects the tips of her nails. "Probably because she had that weirdo Pierce shielding her all night."

Oliver grunts, but doesn't say anything else, which surprises me. Rylee is always a sore subject for him, and he never gives up an opportunity to talk shit about her. His incensed stare is pinned on her. His jaw tics, but he keeps his thoughts to himself.

I steer my eyes back to Rylee, biting the inside of my cheek to keep the growl from rumbling from my chest when I see Charles sitting too fucking close to her. I want to break each of his fingers when he sets his hand on her shoulder to whisper something in her ear. Rylee is a beautiful, if somewhat frustrating, girl, and Charles bats for both teams. It wouldn't surprise me if he's tried hooking up with her.

I may enjoy the look of jealousy on Rylee's face, but I sure as fuck don't want to feel it myself.

She lifts her head, and her eyes slide from me to Tiffany, then back to me. I hold her stare and lick my bottom lip, satisfied when her eyes flare with heat.

A vision of the night on her porch comes to mind. The remembered taste of her on my tongue and the way her body felt against me. It took iron will to walk away from her that night. Then yesterday in the hallway wasn't any easier. I wanted to yank her into the nearest room and devour her whole. When I saw her talking to Charles at her locker, I nearly lost my shit. My mind screamed at me to claim her, to make her see that she was mine. When she sprouted that shit about Oliver, it pissed me off. How the fuck could she think I would let Oliver dictate who I saw or touched?

The kiss I gave her against the lockers was not only to satisfy my need to see if she tasted as good as I remembered—she tasted better, but to also show her I make my own decisions, and *I* fucking chose to kiss her.

My dick hardens in my jeans at the thought of tasting her again. I'm just about to push Tiffany from my lap when she starts wiggling around.

"Oh, baby. Is that a cucumber in your pocket, or are you happy to see me?" She flashes me a wicked grin and presses herself harder against me.

"It's definitely not you," I bite out. "Now get off."

Grabbing her waist, I hoist her none to gently from my lap. She stumbles back a step and has to catch herself on the table so she doesn't fall.

"What the hell, Zayden?" she complains, smoothing down her skirt. "You don't have to be an asshole. What did you do that for?"

"You know my lap isn't a place for you to park your ass, Tiffany. How many times have I told you before?"

"You seemed fine with it a minute ago."

"Well, I'm not fine with it now. Be lucky I didn't dump you on the floor."

She rolls her eyes, flips her hair, and stomps off.

Good riddance.

Oliver chuckles beside me. "I don't know why you just don't tap her and get it over with. Maybe she'll leave you alone afterward."

"Doubt it. Girls think they have some misguided claim after you put your dick in them, no matter how much you tell them otherwise. Speaking of… bet you fifty bucks by the end of the day, Karla tells everyone you're dating."

"If the bitch knows what's good for her, she won't."

"Apparently, she doesn't." I tip my chin in the direction of Karla, who's snickering with a couple of other girls. All three are looking at Oliver. Karla waves her fingertips at him.

I laugh. "Good luck with that."

His jaw clenches as he gets up and stalks over to Karla's table. Uninterested in his shit, I turn my eyes back to Rylee. She has her head turned away from me, but as if sensing my stare, she looks over and our eyes clash. My body instantly heats and blood rushes south. I want nothing more than to go to her and do what I just told Oliver girls are known for. Claim the fuck out of her in front of the entire school. The girl drives my libido and mind crazy, and I can't for the life of me figure out why.

Out of the corner of my eye, I catch Tiffany approach Oliver and pull him away from Karla's table. They huddle together, talking quietly. Anger spikes when Tiffany snickers and slides her eyes to Rylee.

What the hell are they planning?

Shit has shifted between Rylee and me. While I may not be opposed to Oliver pulling harmless stunts against Rylee, I refuse to let anyone else fuck with her. That includes Tiffany and her gaggle of girls.

I stand, ready to demand some answers, when Tiffany spins around and flounces out of the cafeteria. I stalk over to Oliver.

"What the hell was that about? What are you two up to?"

There's something in his eyes that I don't like. Something calculating and sinister.

"Not a clue. She just told me to keep an eye out for something big."

I'm not sure if I believe him or not, but unless I'm prepared to beat the truth out of him, Oliver won't say shit. He's a stubborn bastard when he wants to be, and from the hard set of his jaw, I know this is one of those times.

He smiles and winks at Rylee, before turning and walking away, whistling a happy tune.

I have no clue what he and Tiffany are up to, but whatever it is, it can't be good.

Not for Rylee anyway.

chapter thirteen

RYLEE

"Um, what the hell was that?" Pierce looks about as confused as I feel when Oliver smiles and winks at me.

"Oh, so you saw it, too. Here I thought maybe I was seeing things," I admit, shaking my head slightly as I watch Oliver speed out of the cafeteria, Zayden following directly behind him.

"He's up to something," Pierce voices the very thing I was thinking.

"I agree. Unless…." I trail off.

I think about the conversation I had with my mom yesterday. I might have expressed some concerns over Oliver's behavior toward me—though I left out the part where he's harassing me every chance he gets. She didn't seem too concerned. Probably because she doesn't know how badly he's actually treating me. But I still have no doubt that she talked to Paul about it. Maybe Paul said something to Oliver. Maybe this is his way of being a sarcastic asshole about the whole thing. I can't very well complain that he's smiling and winking at me now, can I?

"Unless?" Pierce presses when I haven't finished my thought.

"Maybe his dad said something to him." I shrug. "I talked to my mom yesterday. I kept it pretty vague, but I got my point across that I was having a hard time. If his dad said something to him, maybe that explains his overdramatized smile. He can't be genuinely nice to me, so he's going for asshole nice instead."

"What's his problem with you anyway?" Brielle chimes in. She's a friend of Pierce's, and though I've only just met her this week, I really like her.

"That's the million-dollar question, isn't it?" I shrug. "He hates that my mom married his dad."

"So he messes with you because he's mad at his dad?" Brielle doesn't know the full extent of Oliver's shenanigans, but like everyone else who goes to this school, she's heard about a lot—especially the party fiasco. That seems to be what most people are still talking about. I can't walk down a hallway without someone snickering or offering up their detachable shower head for me to use. "Seems pretty childish if you ask me," she tacks on.

"I'm not going to argue with you there."

"Come on." Pierce stands, grabbing his half-eaten tray of food. "We should probably get going."

"Is anyone else dreading this pep rally?" Brielle asks as we drop our trays off on our way out of the cafeteria.

"That would be me," Pierce agrees.

"I don't know. It might be fun." I shrug.

I used to live for things like football and basketball games and pep rallies. Of course, that was back when

I had a lot of friends and school was less of a prison and more like social hour. At Bristol I was involved in everything. Student council, dance committee, volleyball, and I ran track, among other things.

I miss it. I miss walking through the halls, laughing with my friends without the worry of someone doing something to embarrass or hurt me. You don't realize how incredible it is not to have to look over your shoulder until you're forced to do so with every corner you turn and every hallway you walk down. It also doesn't help that I seem to be the laughingstock of the entire school.

I'm trying so hard not to let it get me down, but some days it's really quite exhausting. The constant laughing and finger pointing. The whispered comments. The looks. A smarter person would probably try to be less visible—maybe hoping to melt into the background. But that just isn't me. My mom didn't raise me to cower.

So I take it all—everything everyone throws at me. I absorb every ounce of it, and I do so with a smile on my face. If they think it doesn't bother me, maybe they'll stop… eventually. Or at least, that's my hope. To this point it hasn't done me much good. But as I said, I'm not a tuck my tail between my legs kind of girl.

"Did I hear you right?" Pierce finally comments. "A pep rally… fun?"

"What? At least we get to skip seventh period."

"I'm this way, guys. I'll see you later." Brielle throws up a wave as she veers right, heading toward her locker, which is on the opposite side of the school from mine and Pierce's.

"Bye," I call after her before turning my attention forward. "I really like her."

"Yeah, Brielle is good people. Not the best girlfriend, though." He smiles when my shocked gaze swings his way.

"You guys dated?"

"For six months, sophomore year. It was a disaster. She's kind of a jealous person, and that's when I was trying to figure out who I was. Needless to say, I gave her a lot of reasons to be jealous."

"Sounds to me like maybe you weren't the best boyfriend." I shake my head at him.

"Yeah, I guess you got me there." He slows, stopping next to my locker. "So, have you spoken with Zayden at all?" He crosses his arms in front of his chest and leans against the locker to the right of mine.

"No, and I don't plan to either," I tell him, working the combination to my lock—which thankfully clicks open on the first try.

"I still can't believe what you told me yesterday."

"Which part?" I give him an annoyed look. "The part where he told me he didn't like me, or the part after that when he kissed me?"

"The kissing part. Definitely the kissing part." He smiles.

"We've been through this already. He did it to mess with me." I grab a book from my locker before pushing it closed.

"The first time, maybe. But then again in the hallway where anyone could see? I don't know. I'm not convinced."

I turn, weaving through other students to follow Pierce a few feet to where his locker sits on the opposite side of the hallway.

"Did you not see what just happened in the cafeteria?"

"What do you mean?" He pretends to not know what I'm talking about.

"Um, Tiffany practically riding his lap."

"That's Tiffany. That girl wouldn't know what to do if she wasn't throwing herself at Zayden every chance she got. Trust me, he doesn't want her. If he did, he wouldn't be such a dick to her."

"As opposed to the way he treats me." I give him a funny look. "Your logic doesn't make much sense." I watch him grab a few things out of his locker before closing it and turning toward me.

"It's not so much about how he treats you. It's more about how he *looks* at you."

"And how does he look at me?"

"Like that." He gestures behind me with a slight nod of his head.

I turn and see Zayden closing in on us, his gaze locked directly on me. My heart instantly picks up speed as a wave of nervous energy runs through me.

"We need to talk." Zayden stops directly in front of me. "*Alone*." The word is clearly aimed at Pierce.

"Yeah, uh, I… I'll see you later," Pierce mutters before quickly sliding past me.

"What do you want, Zayden?" I try to act as uninterested as possible as I turn and start heading in the direction of my next class.

"Oliver's up to something." He easily keeps up with my quick pace.

"And…? That's different from every other day how?"

"I'm not talking about spouting off at a party for a few dozen people or dumping a milkshake on your head." His nostrils flare. "I know him, and I'm telling you, he's up to something."

"And why would I believe you?" I ask, stopping so abruptly that Zayden walks past me and has to turn back around. "You've been in cahoots with Oliver this entire time—making my life miserable right alongside him—and now what? I'm supposed to believe that suddenly you've had a change of heart and you're on my side?"

"I'm not on your side. But I am trying to fucking warn you."

"Oh, is that what you're doing?" I give him a look that says I don't buy it. "Well, here's a newsflash for ya, I'm a big girl. I can take care of myself."

"You know what? Fine," he grinds out, a slight tic in his jaw. "You don't want to listen to me, don't fucking listen. But don't say I didn't warn you."

"Okay, I won't."

"Fuck." Zayden pinches the bridge of his nose and blows out a heavy breath. "You're really fucking frustrating, you know that?"

"Me?"

"Yes, you. I'm trying to do the right thing here and you're making it really hard to do."

"The right thing. Yeah, I bet. Zayden Michaels—Parkview's resident badass and… closet nice guy? I don't think so."

"You know what…." Zayden steps toward me, and even though my instinct is to step back, I stand my ground. He lowers his face so that we're eye level and my breath immediately catches in my throat. "You deserve whatever is coming your way," he growls, his gaze dropping to my lips for a brief moment before he straightens his posture.

"And so do you," I spit. "Based on the girls you have on rotation; I'd say an STD might be among them."

I have no idea where that came from, but I can't deny that it felt good to say. Even if it was childish.

"Careful," he warns, a smile playing on his lips. "You don't want people thinking that you're jealous."

"Jealous?" I draw back like it's the most ludicrous thing I've ever heard. "I am not jealous of your trashy girlfriend or any of the other floozies you surround yourself with."

"Tiffany is *not* my girlfriend."

"No?" I cock my head. "Perhaps you should tell her that, because I'm not sure she got the memo."

"Are you about done?" He looks like he can't decide if he should be laughing or lashing out.

"Are you?" I throw back at him.

He stands there for a few seconds, his glare locked firmly on my face before he finally breaks the standoff.

"Shows over," he announces and it isn't until then that I realize we've drawn quite the audience. I watch as several students avert their gaze and scatter in different directions. Zayden gives me one more hard look, shaking his head slowly as he slides past me without another word.

"So, what did lover boy want?" Pierce slides up next to me right as I reach the entrance to the gymnasium where the pep rally is being held.

"I'm not sure," I answer truthfully, still not sure what his motives were for *warning* me about Oliver.

"What do you mean you're not sure?" He throws me a sideways glance as he follows me to the front row of the bleachers—plopping down next to me seconds later.

"That's exactly what I mean. I don't know." I blow out a breath. "Anyway, I don't want to talk about him. How's your afternoon been?"

"Same old shit, different day." He grimaces when Principal Harris taps the microphone in the center of the shiny gymnasium floor.

The room quiets.

"This shit is so stupid," Pierce grumbles under his breath as the cheerleaders storm the room, waving their pom poms over their heads.

"Stop it," I whisper, nudging him with my elbow.

I roll my eyes at least ten times as I watch the cheerleaders dance routine. Not because it's bad, but because the cheerleader in the middle dances like she's at a strip club rather than a high school. Tiffany may be the head cheerleader, but it's clear she got that title based on popularity and not talent.

After their dance, the basketball team rushes in, taking seats in the middle of the front row as a projection screen is lowered. The lights dim as Principal Harris announces that the cheerleaders have put together a video for the players.

It starts off with clips of each player. Some pictures, some short videos, followed by a skit the cheerleaders put on impersonating the basketball players. Even though I don't want to admit it, it's actually pretty creative. And while I may dislike half of the cheer squad, I still find myself laughing at their antics right alongside everyone else.

But then the feed cuts and suddenly it's me on screen. My stomach doubles over, and even though every instinct I have is screaming for me to run, I sit frozen on the bleachers, not able to look away.

I'm standing in my room, in a white tank and black underwear, a hairbrush held up to my mouth as I belt out Taylor Swift in the mirror. I hear people snicker and laughter filters around me, but still I don't move.

The video skips and now I'm sitting on the edge of my bed, my phone pressed to my ear.

"I know. I want to hate him. But oh my God, Savannah, if you could see this guy. Zayden is seriously the hottest person I've ever seen. And don't get me started on those arms," I practically moan into the phone. "Sleep with him? Hell yes, I would. I'm pretty certain I'm going to wear my fingers out just thinking about him." And then, because I just couldn't help myself, my hand slides between my legs.

The video cuts off at the worst possible moment, because even though I know I pulled my hand away following that brief touch, everyone no doubt will think I probably masturbated while talking to someone on the phone about Zayden.

Heat piles in my chest before sliding up my neck and across my face. The laughter is deafening, and yet I still haven't moved.

I hear Pierce. I'm not sure what he says. I can't make out his voice through the sudden ringing in my ears. I blink. Once. Twice. And when I look up again, Pierce is standing in front of me.

Seconds later, he pulls me to my feet and guides me out of the gymnasium, but not before I hear several people yell obscenities at me when we pass in front of them.

How could anyone do that to another person? To record someone in private and air it to the entire school? It's unthinkable. It's inconceivable. And yet, it's exactly what Oliver did.

Tears prick my eyes as Pierce navigates me through the empty hallway, but it isn't until we reach the parking lot and the cold wind hits me in the face that everything seems to catch up with me.

The video.

The laughter.

The taunting.

I want to be strong. I want to pretend like this isn't that big of a deal. But the grasp on my control has slipped and there's no hiding it. This stunt far surpasses anything Oliver's done up to this point and anything I ever thought he was capable of. Saying I did something is one thing, because I have deniability—but airing a video to the whole school—even if it didn't end the way I'm sure they all assume it did, can't be undone.

chapter fourteen

ZAYDEN

"*son of a bitch*," I mutter, my jaw clenched so hard my teeth hurt. I get up from my spot at the top of the bleachers and stomp my way down. "Move," I growl. "Get the fuck out of my way."

People part like the red sea, scrambling over themselves before they get trampled by my boots. Raucous laughter fills the room. Principal Harris yells into the microphone, demanding everyone to quiet down, but it doesn't do shit to calm them. They're all too hyped up over what they just saw on the projector screen to care that the principal looks like he's going to have a coronary.

I'd like to bash every single one of their heads in. I'm going to fucking strangle Oliver and Tiffany. This shit is over. No one deserves what they just pulled.

I jump from the last bleacher to the floor and head toward the end where the door is. Oliver's against the wall, his face a blank mask. Instead of going for the door, I stalk over to him.

He doesn't see me coming, so he's surprised when I shove him against the wall, my hand on his chest.

"What the fuck, Z?" He frowns, glancing from my hand to my face.

"I could ask you the same thing. You hate her so much you'd pull that shit?" I point to the blank projector screen over my shoulder.

His jaw twitches. "I didn't do shit. That was all Tiffany."

"That's bullshit, and you know it, Oliver. The only way she could have gotten that video is if you recorded it and gave it to her."

"I don't know how she got that video." I bare my teeth at his lying face. "I mean, yeah, I took it last week, but I sure as hell didn't give it to Tiff." His brows drop, and after a moment he lets loose a low curse. "Fuck." His eyes snap to mine. "Tiffany borrowed my phone a couple days ago because hers was dead. Said she needed to call her parents. She must have seen the video and sent it to herself."

I bunch up his shirt into my fist, barely restraining myself from clocking him in the jaw for being so stupid.

"Why the fuck were you videoing her in the first place?"

"I wasn't planning on doing anything with it, except to show her I had it."

He grabs my wrist and tries to pry it away from his shirt. But I tighten my grip, and he narrows his eyes.

"This shit stops now. You got me, Oliver? It's over."

"Fuck you, Zayden," he growls. "You've got no business in what happens between me and Rylee."

I get in his face. "I'm making it my business."

"You're going to let some girl, especially *her*, fuck up our friendship?"

I let go of his shirt and take a step back. "I was fine with the petty shit. Hell, I helped with some of it. I even let the stunt you pulled at the party slide, although I felt that was taking it too far. But this," I gesture to the still laughing crowd behind me, "this shit is not funny. It's over."

Before he has a chance to say anything else that might have my fist landing against his face, I turn around and leave the gym. There are a few people in the hallway, but from the savage expression on my face, they stay out of my way and keep their mouths shut. The school doors slam against the building when I sling them open.

I expect Charles to have already gotten Rylee out of here, so I'm surprised to find them beside her car. She has her back pressed against the trunk, her arms crossed protectively over her chest, and her head lowered, looking at the ground. Her hair has fallen forward, so I can't see her face. Charles is standing in front of her, saying something quietly, and she nods.

I have no fucking clue what I'm going to say, but I still go over to them. Charles notices me first and stiffens, then steps protectively in front of Rylee to shield her.

"I'm getting her out of here," I tell him, pulling my keys from my pocket.

"Like hell you are," Charles states angrily, fisting his hands at his sides. "You really think I'm going to let you take her anywhere when you—"

I cut him off and bump my chest into his, forcing him back a step. "If you were smart, you wouldn't finish that statement," I warn with a deadly calm voice.

"I had nothing to do with that shit, and had I known, I would have stopped it."

"And we're supposed to just believe you?" he scoffs.

"I don't give a fuck if you believe me or not. All I care about at this moment is getting Rylee the hell out of here before the parking lot fills with nosy people. School's out in ten minutes. I suggest you get the fuck out of my way so I can get her home."

He crosses his arms over his chest, staying in place. I have to hand it to the guy. I could lay him out with one swing, and he knows this, but he still places himself in harm's way, all in a misguided attempt to protect Rylee from me.

I unlock my fists, ready to forcefully move him out of the way, when Rylee steps up beside him with her back facing me. She lays her hand on his arm.

"It's fine, Pierce. I'll be okay," she says quietly. I fucking hate the cracks in her voice.

"You sure? I can take you somewhere myself."

"You can't. You have your appointment with Mrs. Miller, remember?"

He scowls. "Fuck Mrs. Miller. You're more important."

She shakes her head, her silky brown hair swishing against her back. "I am not more important than your future. You need to go and rock the hell out of your presentation."

They have a stare down, but after a moment, Charles nods. Leaning down, he presses a kiss to her forehead. "They're all assholes. You hear me?" She nods. "Call me later."

After a promise from Rylee that she'll call, he lifts his eyes to me. His gaze loses some of its warmth. "Take care of her."

I jerk up my chin.

It's not until he walks away that Rylee turns toward me, and the look on her face brings my anger back tenfold. She's deathly pale and her eyes are red and glossy. She hasn't shed a tear, but I know she's barely holding it in. Most girls would have been in hysterics, but Rylee has shown her resilience over and over again. Despite all the shit she's been through, she's never looked so close to breaking down as she does at this moment.

Some of my anger is pointed at myself. I'm no fucking better than the other assholes at this school. I'm just as responsible, because I played my part. Guilt and shame hit me square in the chest.

She doesn't look at me, instead keeping her eyes pointed ahead at my truck several spots over. Her arms are tightly crossed over her chest still. I gently unclasp one of her hands from around her bicep, interlocking our fingers together. Her hands are cold and clammy, and even though I'm touching her, she still keeps her eyes forward. I fucking hate it. I wish she'd look at me; give me something. I'd even take the venom-filled look she's given me several times in the past. Lord knows I fucking deserve it as much as everyone else does. Anything to make that horrific look leave her eyes.

Neither of us say anything as we walk to my truck. I open the door for her, and she quickly climbs into the seat, not once making eye contact with me. I rake my hand through my hair as I walk around and climb behind the wheel. As I start my truck, I glance at her. Her arms are back across her chest, attempting to protect herself.

"Where do you want to go?" I ask her quietly.

Her shrug is stiff. "I don't care. Just not home."

I lock my jaw and put my truck in gear, pulling out of the parking lot and turning left. I drive for about twenty minutes before I turn down an overgrown gravel road. I haven't been here since I was a kid, but I chose this spot because I know no one ever comes out here.

The road is bumpy and the brush is so thick that it scrapes against the side of my truck, no doubt leaving scratches in the already rusted paint. The clearing opens up, and I drive over the small mounds of dirt until we're directly in front of the big screen. One corner is broken off and graffiti covers most of the rest.

I put my truck in park, but keep the engine running for warmth.

"This used to be the hot spot when my parents were younger," I say to fill the silence. "It shut down when I was eight. The last movie I saw here was *Iron Man*. I sat in the front seat between my parents."

Rylee doesn't move; not even a twitch of her fingers.

"I should have listened to you," she says after a few painful minutes of silence have filled the cab of the truck between us. "You tried to warn me, but I ignored you." Her voice breaks and a lone tear slides down her cheek. "Why does he hate me so much?"

"I don't know."

My stomach plummets to my goddamn toes when she finally looks at me. Devastation fills the pretty brown orbs. Never has a simple look bothered me so much as seeing the desolation on Rylee's face.

Before I realize what I'm doing, I've unbuckled us both, scooped her in my arms, and set her sideways on my lap, her back against the door. Her eyes widen for a brief moment at the sudden movement.

Her bottom lip wobbles, and it's only a split second later that she finally breaks. Her eyes fill with tears and her face crumples. I pull her to my chest and she buries her face in the crook of my neck, clutching my shirt in her small fists- like there's even a chance in hell I would let her go. Her sobs crack something inside my chest, and I can barely catch my breath along with her. I rub her back and brush her hair from her face, trying my damnedest to offer her comfort. It doesn't feel like it's enough, but other than going back to school and beating the shit out of Oliver and Tiffany, this is the only thing I can give her at the moment.

My shirt is soaked by the time Rylee begins to calm down. Her breaths come in shuddering pants, but at least it's not the hiccupping sobs of a moment ago. She keeps her face in my neck, and I'm not ashamed to admit I like having her there. I just wish the circumstances were different.

After a few moments, she sucks in a shaky breath and lifts her head. With the steering wheel in the way, she can't go very far. She tries to move from my lap, but I don't want to let her go yet, so I hold her in place by her hips.

"Stay for a couple more minutes," I request gruffly. Seeing her so broken has really fucked with my emotions. "Please."

She nods and her eyes slide to my neck. "I'm sorry about your shirt."

"I don't give a fuck about my shirt, Rylee."

She nods again. Lifting her hands, she scrubs them across her face, wiping away the evidence of her break down. Even with her eyes puffy, her complexion red and splotchy, and her hair a tangled mess, she's still so damn beautiful.

"This is so embarrassing," she mumbles, fisting her hands in her lap and darting her eyes away from me.

"What is?"

She gives a humorless laugh. "You know what, Zayden. This. All of this." She gestures around the truck. "And that video…." She trails off, closing her eyes.

I gently grip her chin and turn her face back toward me. It takes her several seconds to open her eyes, and even then she has a hard time meeting mine.

"There's nothing to be embarrassed about."

"Says the guy who wasn't just humiliated by a video showing very personal things in a very public way."

"First off, you did that in the privacy of your room, and it should have stayed that way."

"Yeah, but it—"

"Secondly," I say, cutting her off, "who the fuck cares if you touch yourself? People do it all the time. It's normal, I bet every single one of those fuckers in that gym do it, too."

She bites her lip and her brows form a deep V as she frowns. I remove my hand from her chin and tuck a piece of hair behind her ear.

"Lastly," I add, dropping my voice, "and I'm sorry if this embarrasses you further, but do you have any fucking clue how much of a compliment it is to know you've touched yourself while thinking of me?"

Her face flushes red for an entirely different reason now. She releases her lip from her teeth, and I'm tempted to take it between mine. Only the seriousness of the current situation prevents me from doing so.

She shakes her head, dislodging the hair I'd slid behind her ear. "I didn't…." She licks her lips. "That video cut off right before I moved my hand away."

"Well, that's really fucking disappointing." My voice is husky.

She purses her lips together, a slight scowl forming on her face. "Are you joking right now? Really?"

I settle one hand on her thigh, keeping it close to her knee.

"Fuck no, I'm not joking. Do you know how many times I've jacked off to the thought of you?" Her mouth drops open and her breath hitches. "Too many to count. I expect calluses to start popping up on my palms any minute."

"You're lying," she accuses, narrowing her eyes.

"Actually, I'm not. It wouldn't surprise me if my dad starts charging me for water. I've taken so many showers lately."

Her lips twitch, but she doesn't smile, which is a pity, because I'd give damn near anything to have her smile right now.

Suddenly, her eyes glaze over with that despondent look again and she glances down at her hand. "I'm never going to be able to show my face again. Oliver has officially ruined my last year of high school."

"Fuck Oliver, fuck Tiffany, and fuck everyone else. Don't let them win by admitting defeat." I take one of her hands and lace our fingers together. She uses her other hand to trace the veins in the back of mine. "You're one of the strongest and most resilient people I know, Rylee. Don't let them take that strength from you."

"I just don't understand how he could hate me so much to do something like that."

"I don't think his part was intentional." Her head jerks up at that, anger making the brown in her eyes darker. "I spoke with him before I came out to the parking lot. He said he took the video only with the intention to show you- something he could hold over your head. Tiffany found the video on his phone and must've sent it to herself."

"And you believe him?" she asks incredulously.

It's my turn to frown.

"Yes. Oliver *is* an asshole, and we've done some pretty shitty things to you." I swallow thickly, thinking about my part in her torment. "But I don't think he'd go that far."

"Maybe you don't know him as well as you think."

"Maybe," I concede with a nod. "But one thing I do know is he won't be fucking with you again."

She tilts her head to the side, studying me. "And how do you know that?"

"Because I'll beat his fucking ass if he even tries."

Her brows jump up so high her forehead wrinkles. "But he's your best friend."

"Best friend or not, you're now off limits."

"Why? You don't even like me. You said so yourself."

I lean forward until only a couple of inches separate our mouths. "Maybe I've changed my mind."

"Oh." Confusion clouds her eyes. "You have?"

"Yes, Rylee. I have."

I close the gap between us. The second my lips touch hers she releases a little sigh and her body relaxes against mine. I know I need to keep this kiss simple, because now isn't the time for anything more, but it doesn't stop my body from reacting. My cock grows stiff underneath the plumpness of her ass, tempting me to press my hips upward at the same time I pull her down. I wasn't lying when I told her I've jacked off multiple times with her in mind. And it looks like tonight will be no different.

With a groan, I lift my head. Rylee's eyes flutter open, a glazed look on her face. I drop my forehead to her temple and pull in several deep breaths to rein in my desire. I think about Danielle and her illness, my grandmother and her chocolate cookies, and the assignment I still need to do in my economics class. Anything to take my mind off the girl in my arms and what she does to my body.

Soon, my erection begins to wilt, and I've managed to get myself under control enough to lift my head. Rylee watches me with wary eyes.

"What's going on here, Zayden?" Her voice comes out small and unsure.

"I don't know," I answer truthfully. "I just know I'd like to find out."

"Swear to me right now," she states, strengthening her voice, "that whatever this is, it isn't something you and Oliver have cooked up to screw with me even more. I honestly don't think I can take another thing. Especially not that."

My jaw clenches and anger makes the vein in my temple pound. She has every right to be suspicious of my motives. Fuck knows I would be too if I were in her situation.

"That's the second time you've brought that up. I've given you no reason to trust me, but I'm asking you to do so now anyway. Oliver has not one damn thing to do with whatever is going on between us. In fact, I think it's safe to say this is not something he would be okay with."

After several tense seconds, she nods. "Okay."

That one word has my shoulders relaxing.

She leans back against the door, resting one hand on the steering wheel and laying her other arm around my shoulders. She looks out the windshield to the big screen in front of us.

"My parents brought me here once. Funnily enough, the movie we saw was *Iron Man*." She looks at me, her lips curling wryly.

"No shit?" Small world.

She smiles, and the weight on my chest doesn't feel quite so heavy. "Yep. It was my first and only time going to a drive-in theater."

I recline my seat back a couple of inches and pull her closer to me. She lets go of the steering wheel and places her hand on my chest.

"The night my parents brought me here was the last night we ever went to the theater. Mom had just found out she was pregnant with Danielle. She started her affair not long after Danielle was born."

"I'm sorry," Rylee says quietly.

I shrug. "I got over it a long time ago. Mom and Dad divorced four years ago." I twist my neck to dislodge one of her hairs stuck on the bristles on my chin. "The guy she cheated on my dad with is some big business mogul. She was his secretary. Her affair came to light when Dad and I went to visit her at the office. We saw them kissing outside her car in the parking garage. Mom left; didn't even try to work it out with Dad. When she left, she left for good. I've only seen her a handful of times since then. And she's seen Danielle even less."

"What a bitch," Rylee mumbles. Her eyes go wide and she slaps a hand over her mouth. "Sorry," she mutters, the word muffled.

I kiss the back of her hand. "Don't be. It's the truth. She stopped being a mother to Danielle and me long before she left, so it wasn't that much of a shock."

She slowly drops her hand back to my chest. "That's why you don't like people with money, isn't it?"

"It wasn't until I heard them arguing one night that I found out Mom resented Dad because he wouldn't let her have an abortion when she found out she was pregnant with me in college. She was pre-law and was forced to quit during her sophomore year when she almost miscarried. The doctors ordered bedrest. She never forgave him."

Her hand bunches my shirt into her fist. "It takes two people to get pregnant. She took that risk just as much as your father did when they slept together. She's just as much to blame as he is."

"She doesn't see it that way."

"Well, I'm sorry, but your mom is blind. And selfish," she adds vehemently.

"You'll get no arguments from me."

"Is she still with the mogul?"

"Yes. They married six months after the divorce went through."

"Please tell me she didn't have any more kids."

I rub circles over her jean clad thigh. "No. She can't. After she had Danielle, she had her tubes snipped and tied. Didn't even bother to tell Dad she had it done."

"Your mother sounds like a real piece of work. I hope you know that."

I grunt. "I've known for a while now."

"What about your dad? Did he ever remarry?"

"He's dated a couple of women, but nothing serious. I think the shit that went down really fucked his head up."

Rylee's lips pull down into a frown. "He really loved her." She observes.

"He worshipped the ground she walked on. That's what's so fucked up about the situation. He loved my mom so much, and for a while I thought she felt the same way. Or the innocence of my youth made me see it that way. Love can be a fickle bitch sometimes."

It turns quiet for several beats, only the hum of the heater filling the silence.

"What about your dad?" I ask, wanting to know more about the girl invading my thoughts lately. "Did he remarry?"

Rylee lets out a dull laugh. "Oh yeah. Remarried, started a new family, and all but forgot about his old one."

"Sounds like we're cut from the same cloth. One parent who cares and another who doesn't."

"Yeah."

Taylor Swift's "Blank Space" cuts through the cab, and I glance at Rylee with a lifted brow. Danielle likes Taylor Swift as well, so I've heard all of her songs what feels like hundreds of times.

With an eye roll, she slides from my lap to the middle seat and reaches for her purse on the floorboard. She blows out a breath, and instead of accepting the call, she chooses to ignore it.

"It's my mom," she murmurs, dropping her phone back in her purse. "I'm not ready to deal with her yet. I'm sure Principal Harris called her to give her a heads up about what happened."

"Which also means he probably called Oliver and his dad in for questioning."

"And that'll just make my life even better," she says bitterly. "Oliver's going to love getting reamed by his dad. One guess who'll be taking the brunt of his anger."

"Oliver will take whatever his father dishes out like a man. I'll be damned if he blames that shit on you. I was serious when I said he's done tormenting you. He'll learn to deal with his shit a different way."

Her smile is sad. "Thanks, but I live with the guy. I'm sure he'll find ways at home to make my life miserable."

"The fuck he will. Oliver isn't dumb. I've set down the new rules that include you being off limits. He won't do anything stupid."

Her eyes hold doubt, but she nods anyway. She may not believe it, but Rylee's under my protection now. I don't know how or when it happened, but she's wormed her way inside me. My initial feeling of dislike has not only changed but has grown into caring. And the fucked-up thing is, I never even saw it coming.

chapter fifteen

RYLEE

"*you sure you're* going to be okay?" Zayden asks as he pulls into the driveway and shifts his truck into park.

Today has taken one crazy turn after the other, none of which I saw coming. But not all the twists have been bad.

"Yeah, I'll be fine." I blow out a breath, not sure what to do next. Do I just say goodbye and leave the truck? Do I lean over and hug him? Maybe kiss him? I feel a bit uncertain about what's happening between us and as such, I'm not really sure how to act.

Before it was easy—I hated him, or at least I pretended I did, and he hated me. But now? Now I'm not so sure how I feel. Or how he feels for that matter. The only thing I know for certain is that Zayden made this day a hell of a lot easier to stomach. Even if I'm still convinced I'll never be able to show my face in school again, him being there for me has meant more than I could ever say—and more than I expected it to mean.

"If you're worried about Oliver, don't be. He's not going to mess with you," he reassures, his dark gaze swinging to the front porch before coming back to me.

"At this point, I don't think he could do anything worse than what he pulled today." I let out a broken laugh.

"Look at me." His fingers graze my chin before he's turning my face toward him. "Don't let him see what he's done. He doesn't deserve the satisfaction. If I know Oliver, and I do, you walking in there like nothing happened will be the last thing he wants or expects. If he's trying to break you, don't let him believe he has."

"Well, considering there's no way I'm showing my face in school for the rest of the year, I think he's going to know he won."

"No one at school is going to say one word to or about you, believe me on that."

"You can't control what people say to each other, Zayden." I wrap my fingers around his and pull his hand away from my face. "And even if you could, it won't stop them from thinking it."

"So then let's change the way they think about it."

"And how do we do that?"

"Ride to school with me tomorrow."

"That's going to help me how?"

"Just trust me on this, yeah?"

I give him a questioning look; not sure I have the ability to trust anyone at the current moment.

"I don't know. I think maybe I'm going to stay home tomorrow. That will give people three days to get it out of their systems before Monday morning. Or maybe I'll see if my mom will let me do home schooling for the rest of the year. Anything would be easier than having to go back there after what happened today."

"Fuck that." His nostrils flare. "You're going to school tomorrow and you're going there with me. I'm not taking no for an answer."

"Zayden," I start to object.

"I know I don't deserve it, Rylee, but I'm asking you to trust me here. I can make this go away."

"And how do you plan on doing that?"

"By giving them something else to talk about." He grins and the action causes a nervous flutter to run through my stomach.

"I don't know." I mull over his proposal. I know that going on like nothing happened is my best course of action. But knowing what I should do and actually seeing it through are two very different things.

"You're going to have to go to school at some point and get your car anyway," he tacks on, as if this will somehow sway me to his side.

"Yeah, on Saturday when no one is there."

"Listen, what happened today was beyond fucked up. I can't imagine how hard the thought of going back there probably is. But if I can make it easier for you, then you have to let me. I feel fucking awful for how I've treated you. Consider this me making it up to you."

"I can't figure you out," I tell him honestly, getting a little lost in the incredible depths of his blue eyes.

To say Zayden has been back and forth since we first met would be the understatement of the year. I've never been growled at so many times in my life. But I've also never felt safer than he made me feel today.

I had no reason to get into his truck earlier. No reason to believe that he wasn't in on this right along with Oliver and Tiffany. And yet, without even saying it, I knew he wasn't. Zayden Michaels might be the resident bad ass, but he also has a softer side. One that I'm willing to bet most people have never seen.

After spending two hours talking in his truck, I already feel like I know more about him than most people who have known him for years do. He talked to me about his parents, his sister, fighting, his friendship with Oliver. I saw a different side to him today, and I really, really liked what I saw.

I didn't think it was possible to find him more attractive, and yet every time I think that, he has a way of proving me wrong.

I don't know what's going to happen next or what, if anything, will transpire between Zayden and me, but for the first time since moving here, I actually feel excited about something… even after everything that happened today.

"So, tomorrow morning? I'll pick you up?" he asks again, clearly sensing the weakening of my resolve.

"Tomorrow morning." I nod, reaching for the door handle before I change my mind.

"Rylee." I turn back toward him, my heart skipping inside my chest at his sudden close proximity.

Before I can say anything, Zayden's mouth is on mine. It's not rough or forced the way he kissed me the first two times, but tender and sweet—which is a total contradiction to the persona he embodies.

"I'll see you in the morning," he murmurs against my lips before pulling back.

"Okay," I croak, not able to think of a single other thing to say.

Pulling the handle, I shove the door open and step out into the frigid evening air.

"*I'm sorry, he did what?*" Savannah practically screams in my ear after I've given her a brief run through of the events that took place earlier today.

"You heard me," I groan, flopping back onto my bed to stare up to the ceiling.

"Please tell me his ass got expelled and his dad is kicking him the hell out. What the actual fuck? Who the hell would do something like that?"

"Those were my thoughts exactly. But no, he didn't get expelled. In fact, he didn't get so much as a slap on the wrist. Apparently, everyone involved covered for each other and since no one is talking, they had no way to prove that it was Oliver and Tiffany who aired the video."

"Are you kidding me?" Her voice vibrates against my ear.

"I wish I were."

"What about his dad? Certainly he's not that stupid."

"No, I think Paul knows it was him—even though Oliver swore to him and my mom that he had nothing to do with it. I've never seen Paul so angry. When I got home I could hear him yelling all the way from his study at the back of the house. And my poor mom. I'm not sure if she was more embarrassed of me or for me."

"Why would she be embarrassed of you?"

"Did you miss the part where I touched myself in the video?" I say flatly.

"Yeah, but hello, what teenage girl hasn't touched herself? Besides, it's not like you were full on masturbating, right?"

"God no. My hand barely grazed the outside of my underwear," I say for a second time. "But the video cuts off in a way that makes you think more is about to happen. It's so bad, Savannah. I honestly don't know how I'm going to show my face at school tomorrow."

"Wait. You're going to school tomorrow? After what happened today?" She seems as surprised as me by this news.

I don't know why I agreed to show my face back in that building so soon after the video. Maybe because Zayden asked, and for whatever reason I couldn't tell him no. Or maybe it's because I know he's right. Hiding is letting them win, and anyone who knows me knows that I'm way too damn stubborn to roll over and hand them a victory that easily.

Maybe that makes me stupid. Maybe that's me asking for more trouble. But it's the only way I know how to defend myself at this point.

"I have to," I tell her after a long moment has passed. "It'll only be worse if I stop showing up for a while. I can't let them think that they've won."

"You are a bigger person than I, Rylee Harper. I think I'd drop out of school and leave the state if something like that happened to me." She pauses. "I still can't believe Oliver would do that to you. Don't get me wrong, I believe it, given everything else you've told me, but I don't get it. You would think he'd want to get to know you before he tries destroying you."

"It has something to do with his dad and my mom. It has to. There's no other explanation."

"But what does he hope to accomplish if that's the case?"

"Maybe he thinks if he does something drastic enough my mom will leave his dad…. I don't know," I admit.

"You think he hates you guys being there that much?" she questions.

"He must. Otherwise he wouldn't be going through so much trouble. I just wish he would talk to me, ya know? Maybe if he would he would know that I'm no happier about being here than he is about having me here. He's so convinced that we're money hungry, free loaders out for his dad's money."

"Your mom is a freaking brain surgeon, for goodness sake. She makes plenty of money for herself," she objects.

"Exactly," I agree. "Honestly, I don't have the mental capacity to try to break down why he does the things he does, and what he hopes to accomplish by doing them. Clearly his issue isn't with me, but for whatever reason I'm getting the brunt of his anger."

"Not only his anger, but all his little minions' anger, too. Zayden was in on it as well, I assume?" she asks, already knowing I've had my fair share of issues with him.

"I don't think so," I tell her truthfully. "In fact, he's the one who kind of rescued me after everything went down."

"What do you mean he rescued you?" she asks, and I can hear the smile in her voice.

Savannah knows I've had a serious crush on Zayden since the first time I saw him. Now granted, I also hated him because of how he's treated me—or at least I claimed to—but that hasn't stopped me from mentioning his name every time Savannah and I have spoken over the last couple of weeks.

I spend the next several minutes filling her in on everything that transpired after I left school with Zayden. She hangs onto my every word like she can't get enough—meanwhile, I'm having trouble grasping any of it as I recount the events that took place this afternoon. I know it happened because I was there, but it feels more like a dream than reality. In what world would a guy like Zayden Michaels be interested in me? Especially when up until today he's treated me more like a nuisance than anything else.

"I knew it," she announces after I've finished.

"Knew what?" I don't try to hide my confusion.

"That you two were gonna end up together." She giggles. "I could tell just by the way you talked about him. No man kisses someone the way he kissed you in that hallway if he's not interested."

"Um, no," I cut her off before she can go any further. "One, we are *not* together. And two, have you not been listening to anything I've told you over the last few weeks?"

"Actually, I have. You told me he got mad at you because he was worried someone would slip something in your drink at a party. Then, he got all bent out of shape that you showed up at his illegal fight because he claimed it wasn't safe for you. Swoon." She sighs dramatically. "And *then* he showed up at your house when he knew Oliver wasn't there and he kissed you. *Then*, he picked a fight with you in the hallway the next day and kissed you again—because let's be real, it's probably all he could think about after kissing you the first time. Then, he tries to warn you that Oliver is up to something, and when you didn't listen, he swooped in and saved the day—taking you away. Do you want me to keep going, because what happened next is even juicier?"

"No, I think I got your point." I shake my head even though she can't see me.

"He's into you, Rylee. He knows it. I know it. So do us all a favor and stop pretending like you don't know it."

"I don't know, V. I mean, sometimes when he looks at me, like today, I feel like maybe he feels it, too—this overwhelming chemistry we seem to share. But he's so all over the place that I don't feel like I can get a good read on him. I can't help but feel like maybe he's just messing with me."

"Why would he be messing with you?"

"The same reason he's been messing with me from the beginning," I say like it should be obvious. "Oliver."

"If what you told me about today is true, I don't think he's messing with you, Ry. Don't get me wrong, I get your hesitation, I really do, but don't let that hold you back from exploring things with him. I haven't heard you this excited about a guy since Jackson Bradley in fifth grade."

"That's not true. Or are you completely forgetting about Parker?"

"That's my point. You dated Parker for how long? And even then you never talked about him the way you talk about Zayden. And it's not about what you're saying, it's about how you're saying it."

"You act like you know me so well." I don't try to hide my annoyance, even though I know she's right.

She really does know me that well. And she's not wrong about Zayden. There's something there. Something I can't put my finger on. Something beyond his obvious good looks and popularity status.

Something raw and real. Something that I cannot shake. And truthfully, I don't know if I want to shake it.

"I think sometimes I know you better than I know myself." She laughs.

"And that is why I miss you so damn much," I whine. "If you were here, things would be so much easier."

"I may not be at school with you, but I'm still here. Always. You know that."

"I do." I let out a puff of air, rolling to my side on the bed. "But it's not the same. I hate always looking over my shoulder, never knowing who I can trust."

"I get that. But you have Pierce. And you mentioned another friend you made—what's her name, Brielle?"

"Yeah."

"See, you have friends. Maybe you haven't known them as long as you've known me, but that doesn't mean they don't have your back. Pierce seems like a pretty awesome friend. I'm actually looking forward to meeting him."

"Speaking of meeting people—are you still planning on coming over Saturday? I feel like it's been forever since we've hung out."

"Yes, and I cannot wait. I think this is the longest we've ever gone without seeing each other."

"It *is* the longest we've ever gone," I confirm.

"I've already got a list of everything I need to bring for the night's festivities. Facials. Manis and pedis. All the junk food your little heart desires. I'm bringing out the big guns. After the week you've had, I think you need it."

"God, that sounds perfect. I just want to forget about everything that happened today and spend some much-needed time with my best friend."

"*Everything* that happened today?" she questions knowingly, bringing Zayden back to the forefront of my mind.

I close my eyes, and I can see his face perfectly. The dip in his chin, his unruly hair, his stark blue gaze. Just the thought of him causes my heart to do a little flip in my chest. As much as I hate to admit it, he's all I think about most days. I can't help it. And after today, I feel utterly consumed by him.

"Okay, almost everything," I admit, a smile gracing my lips.

I didn't think it was possible to feel this good after what happened at school today, but Zayden seemed to know exactly what I needed and how to push me past it. Hell, he even got me to agree to go to school tomorrow when hours ago I was swearing I'd never step foot in those hallways again.

Something tells me there's very little Zayden couldn't talk me into. I'm just not sure if that's a good thing or not.

And while I'm still mortified by what Oliver did today, facing it seems a lot less scary with Zayden by my side. Which makes no sense at all considering he's been on the opposing team up to this point, playing against me. But it's still true. He makes me feel... better. Stronger. Braver. And I don't know if he even realizes it.

"That's what I thought." Savannah pulls me from my thoughts. "I gotta say, I think I'm looking forward to meeting him the most."

"Who says you're going to meet him? I thought we were having a quiet girls' night in," I remind her.

"Oh we are. I'm just hoping he happens to stop by when I'm there. Either way, I'm sure I'll meet him eventually."

"I'm sure you will."

"It's just yet to be seen whether or not I'm going to hug him or offer him a swift knee to the balls."

"V." I snort.

"What? He's walking a fine line right now. As for Oliver, let's just hope he doesn't try to pull something while I'm there. I'm not above putting hair remover in someone's shampoo."

I cough out a laugh, knowing full well if anyone would have the balls to do something like that it would be Savannah.

"Well, let's hope it doesn't come to that. I'm hoping after Paul gets done with him he won't be leaving his room for a few days. Lord knows he's the last person I want to see."

"Can't say I blame you there." I hear papers shuffle in the background. "Though if it were me, I'd already be planning my revenge."

"Don't think I haven't been tempted. But what does it say about me if I stoop to his level?"

"It says you're a badass who doesn't take shit from anyone."

"Or it says I'm just as heartless as he is and I'll end up feeling even worse about myself because of it. You know me, I can run my mouth with the best of them, but when it comes to actually doing something about it, I'm just not that type of person- no matter how much I wish I were."

"I know. It's one of the reasons I love you so much." She pauses. "Now, if I'm going to come over this weekend, I really need to get off here. I have an

English paper due Monday that I have to finish tonight to free up my weekend."

"Okay, well, I won't keep you."

"You'll call me if you need anything?"

"Always."

"I'll text you Saturday when I'm headed over. I still need you to send me the address."

"Okay, sounds good."

"Love you, Ry."

"Love you, too."

The phone disconnects moments before there's a knock against my bedroom door.

"Come in," I holler as I sit up in bed, assuming it's my mom.

When the door swings open and Oliver appears in the doorway, I'm not sure if I'm more surprised or pissed. It's the first time I've seen him since what happened at school today, and while I knew I was mad, I don't think I realized just how mad until this very second.

"Hey." He shuffles from one foot to the other, looking extremely uncomfortable. "I, uh, I just wanted to say sorry for the role I played in what went down today." He doesn't meet my gaze, instead choosing to stare at the wall behind me.

"Little late for apologies, don't you think?" I clip, knowing the only reason he's here is because Paul likely made him come up to apologize.

"Yeah, well, for what it's worth, I didn't record that video with the intent of showing it to anyone. I was just planning on threatening to use it."

"Like that makes it any better?" I draw back.

"Anyway," he continues like I didn't say anything. "I know you left your car at school today, so I was thinking maybe I could give you a ride tomorrow."

"You're joking, right?" I let out an angry laugh. "You humiliate me in front of the entire student body and you think offering me a ride to school is somehow going to make up for that?"

"No, I just… I don't know. I thought it was a start."

"You mean your dad told you that you had to," I cut him off. "Well thanks, but no thanks. Zayden has already offered to pick me up in the morning, and I said yes." This seems to get his attention and his gaze finally lands on me.

"Zayden's giving you a ride tomorrow?" he repeats slowly like he's trying to process it.

"He is. That's where I was this afternoon after your little stunt. I was with Zayden."

"So, that's your play." An angry snarl pulls at his lips. "Trying to get between me and my best friend."

"There is no play, Oliver. In case you haven't noticed, I'm not like you. I don't play games and I don't purposely mess with people because I'm too chicken to say what it is that's bothering me. Now if you don't mind, I have things to do." I stand and stomp toward him. "You know, the sad thing is, had you actually given me the time of day, I think you might have found that I'm a pretty good person to have in your life. But instead, you chose to make me the enemy. Well I'm done being your punching bag. The next time you swing, I'll swing back. And that is a promise." With that, I shove the door closed, forcing him into the hallway without another word.

chapter sixteen

ZAYDEN

i pull to a stop in front of Oliver's house right as Rylee exits the front door. I can tell by the way she drags her feet that she's still nervous about showing up at school today. I wish she'd look inside herself and see the strong person I see. Yes, anyone would be reluctant to show their face after what happened yesterday, but I'll be damned if I let anyone fuck with her either. She's been through enough already. Oliver got to play his games; it's time he gets over his shit.

As soon as Rylee's ass hits the seat, I don't even give her a chance to say hello before my hand is behind her head, and I'm tugging her lips to mine. The move is more to distract her from the impending stress of walking into school, but a bigger part, a part I'm growing used to, is for me. I simply want to taste her.

I pull back just enough to see her eyes. They flutter open and the chocolatey brown depths stare back at me softly, giving me the look I was hoping for. It's me she's thinking about now, not the assholes at school or Oliver.

"Morning," she whispers, her voice slightly husky.

I run my nose along the side of hers before pecking her lips one more time. "Morning."

Her smile is lazy and relaxed.

"Nah uh." I stop her from buckling herself in and pat the seat next to mine. Thank Christ for bench seats. "I want you right here."

She bites her lip, indecision warring on her face. After a moment, she relents and scoots over until her thigh and hip press against mine.

Once she's pulled the middle strap over and has buckled herself in, I put the truck into gear. Before I pull away, I glance out the window and find Oliver at his car, staring at us. His expression is a mixture of anger and betrayal. I hate that we're at an impasse right now, but he's leaving me no choice. I may come across as an asshole and most people know to stay the fuck away from me, but I have my limits, and Oliver crossed them. Until he realizes this, he can go pout in a fucking corner.

I tip my chin at him. His jaw clenches, but he does the same seconds before I pull away from the curb.

Rylee sits quietly beside me for most of the ride. When her knees begin to bounce and she picks at a loose string on the bottom of her shirt to the point the hem comes loose, I reach over and grab her hand.

"Relax, Rylee, before you unravel your whole shirt."

She grumbles something too low for me to hear.

"How did it go last night when you got home?"

She lets out a long breath. “Well, I overheard Paul giving Oliver hell in his study.” She pauses. “Then Oliver came to my room later.”

I jerk my eyes off the road to look at her. “What did he say?”

“He actually had the nerve to apologize.” She snorts. “As if I’d believe him.”

As much as I want to believe Oliver does feel remorse for what happened, I’m not sure I believe him either, especially given the look he gave me a few moments ago. He may not have had a hand in releasing that video, but I’m sure he’s not broken up over it either.

“Just stay cautious, and if I’m not with you, try to stick with Charles.”

She huffs, her fingers tightening around mine. “This is ridiculous,” she growls. “I can’t believe I have to watch my back at school, all because my stepbrother has a stick up his ass.”

“It’s only until I take care of some shit and let it be known that you’re not to be fucked with.”

“It shouldn’t have come to this. If Oliver had just come to me and told me what his problem was, this all could have been avoided. Has he told you what his issue is with me?”

“No. All I know is it has something to do with your mom marrying his dad. I assume it’s because of how fast it happened.”

“That’s dumb. I understand him being angry at my mother and his father, but what the hell do I have to do with it? It’s not like I could have prevented them from getting married.”

“Because you’re more convenient. He can’t take his anger out on your mom and his dad.”

I pull into a parking space at school and shut my truck off. Rylee is back to bouncing her knees, so I grab her thigh until she stops. When she lifts her head to me, I lean forward and kiss her.

"It's going to be fine. Stop stressing," I murmur against her lips.

"Yeah, yeah," she grumbles.

I grin and nip her bottom lip before I open my door, pulling her out on my side by the hand. The parking lot is already full, and several pairs of eyes watch us as we walk across the lot. More follow as the whispers begin, alerting their friends. I keep Rylee's hand in mine, and I'm damn proud of her when she keeps her head held high.

The bustle of the hallway quiets down when we walk through the doors. A couple of people actually have the balls to snicker and point while several others whisper among themselves. I want to smash every single one of their heads in.

"Unless any of you fuckers have anything to say loud enough for us all to hear, I suggest you turn the fuck around and keep doing what you were doing before we walked in," I boom, meeting the gaze of several people.

Wide eyes dart away and everyone scurries on their way, peeking glances over their shoulders.

"I don't know if having you here with me is making things better or worse," Rylee says just loud enough for me to hear.

"Why's that?"

"Because now everyone will think you're my bodyguard or something."

"So?" I stop us at our lockers and turn to face her. "How is that a problem?"

"It makes me look weak. Like I need the hot, tough guy of school to protect me."

"Hot and tough, huh?" I smirk and lean against my locker.

She rolls her eyes and turns to enter the combination on her lock. "It's not like you don't know you're the hottest guy in this school."

"So, I'm not just a hot guy, I'm *the* hottest guy? I'm really liking where this conversation is going." My grin is big.

She laughs, pulling a couple of books from her locker before slamming the door shut. "Just so you know, flattery isn't attractive, so you just lost a 'hot guy' point."

"Well, since I'm the hottest guy here, I can probably manage to lose a few points and still be at the top."

"You're ridiculous," she states, shaking her head and smiling.

"And you're sexy as fuck." I step in so close that she's forced back into the lockers. I put my fist above her head. "And just so you know, *you're* the hottest girl in this school. It makes total sense that you and I should be together, since we're both the hottest and all."

I lean down and brush my lips against hers, no doubt adding more fuel to the gossip raging on behind us. I couldn't care less if people see me kissing Rylee. Hell, I'm glad they do. If everyone sees Rylee with me, then it's less likely they'll fuck with her to avoid my wrath. Not to mention, it'll keep any interested guys away.

I wrap my arm around her waist and press my chest against hers. Her generous tits smash against me, tempting me with their softness. I bet they'd feel fucking divine in my hands.

Her nails bite into my biceps and she releases a little whimper. I'd give my left nut to be alone with her right now. But we're not, so I reluctantly lift my head and put a couple inches of space between us.

"Are you fucking kidding me?" a snide voice comes from behind me.

I turn around slowly and narrow my eyes at Tiffany. Her hand is thrown up on her cocked hip and her face is scrunched up in disgust. Her posse is behind her.

"Walk away, Tiffany," I warn with a low tone, still enraged about her part in yesterday's events.

"When I heard you rode in together, I thought they must have saw wrong, or maybe you were playing nice because you felt sorry for the bitch." Her heated gaze flicks behind me to Rylee before settling back on me. "Holy shit, Zayden, are you fucking her?"

I take a threatening step toward her, and her eyes widen in fear. I've never hit a girl in my life, and I won't be starting now, but the more scared Tiffany is of me, the better.

"It isn't now, and it never will be, any of your business who I fuck, Tiffany. I don't hit women, but I'm sure I can find a girl here who you've done wrong who will gladly do it for me. I suggest you mind your own business, and while you're at it, leave Rylee the fuck alone."

She looks at Rylee again. "You don't honestly think he actually wants you, do you?" She laughs sinisterly. "He's only with you because of that video and he knows you'll be an easy lay."

I'm about to open my mouth and lay into her, when Rylee places her hand on my arm. She appears beside me, and I'm surprised at the serene smile tipping up her lips.

"I think someone might be jealous that I've got the guy and she doesn't. You worried I might be better than you?"

Tiffany's lips twist into a nasty sneer. "I've had him, bitch, and believe me, he'll come back for more after he's done with your ass."

I bark out a laugh. "You've had my dick in your mouth and your teeth scraped half of the skin off. *Twice*. I wouldn't count on a third time."

She scoffs, rolling her eyes. "You loved my mouth. You just don't want to admit it in front of her."

"Hate to break it to you, but most men aren't into pain when they're having their dick sucked. Might want to use a mouth guard for the next unfortunate soul."

A few people break out into laughter, and Tiffany's cheeks heat in embarrassment. If she wasn't such a bitch, I might feel remorse for being an asshole, but she's treated Rylee worse. All of my fucks have been spent when it comes to Tiffany.

With a huff and a glare tossed Rylee's way, she spins around on her heel and stomps off, her band of followers trailing behind her.

"Shit," Rylee mutters beside me. "She's going to be out for blood now."

I throw my arm over her shoulder and steer her toward our first class. "Fuck Tiffany."

"Yeah, I bet she'd just love that."

"Probably, but my dick isn't going anywhere near her again."

She brushes some hair off her face and looks up at me. "Did she…." She looks down in the vicinity of my dick and quickly looks back up. "Did you really let her suck you off?"

I stop her right outside the classroom door. "Yes, but she was just a convenience."

Her gaze moves to my neck and she clears her throat. "Is that what I am?"

I tip her head back up so I can see her eyes. "What do you think?"

"I don't know," she admits quietly, nibbling on her bottom lip. "I don't want to think so, but I don't know."

"I guess I'll have to prove to you you're more than that."

"Holy hell, Rylee," Charles says, coming to a stop beside us. His gaze moves to me. "Oh, hey, Zayden."

I tip my chin. "Charles. How's it going?"

"Better now that I heard what you said to Tiffany." His lips twitch, giving away his mirth.

"It was nothing more than she deserved," I respond truthfully. "I need a favor."

"What's up?"

"If Rylee isn't in class or with me, stay with her."

"Zayden, I don't—" Rylee tries to protest, but I talk over her.

"Tiffany's pride has been hurt. She might try to retaliate against Rylee."

He nods. "Got it."

I turn to Rylee and find her lips pressed into a firm line. "I'm not afraid of Tiffany."

"I know, but for my peace of mind, I'd prefer if Charles or I were with you until we know for sure if she's planning anything. Tiffany can be a crazy bitch if provoked."

She doesn't like it—I can see it in her eyes—but she appeases me anyway. "Fine."

"I'm heading in. Sit with me in the back?"

After she nods, I press a quick kiss to her lips, ignoring Charles' pleased grin as I walk through the door.

"So, it's like that, huh?" Oliver asks as I walk toward him, wiping the grease from my hands. I've been expecting this conversation; I'm just surprised he waited until I was at work and didn't try to confront me at school. Of course, that may have been because he hasn't had the opportunity since we've either been in class or I've been with Rylee.

I stuff the rag back in my pocket.

"I saw the two of you all cozied up at lunch," he continues. "Trading in your best friend for a girl?"

"That's entirely up to my best friend. Is he going to make me choose between the two?"

He shoves his hands into his pockets and works his jaw back and forth. "You had to pick the worst fucking girl in school, knowing how much I can't stand her. You even hated her yourself."

"I didn't know her."

"And now you do? After what? Spending only a few hours with her?"

I blow out a breath. "If you spent half the time getting to know her that you've spent trying to ruin her life, you'd know she's a good person, Oliver. Just because your dad married her mom so soon after divorcing your mom doesn't make *her* deceitful or *your* enemy."

"No, but it makes her a homewrecker," he snarls, anger making his face turn red.

"What the fuck are you talking about? Rylee had nothing to do with your parents divorcing."

He lets out a harsh laugh. "Her mother sure did. How am I supposed to get along with the daughter of the woman who had a hand in my parent's marriage ending?" He turns away and rips his hands through his hair before he spins back around. "You know what? Just forget it. It doesn't matter. You really want her, be my fucking guest, but don't expect her and me to become best friends. Unlike you, I refuse to let her ruin a ten-year friendship."

He turns away, walking toward his car.

"No more tricks, Oliver, and no more bullshit." I take a couple of steps after him. "I get that for whatever reason you don't like her. I love you like a brother, and I'd do damn near anything for you, but she's off limits. That includes anything that Tiffany may come up with." Oliver stops and turns back around, facing me.

"I told you before, I didn't give that video to Tiffany," he says heatedly.

"And I believe you. I'm just giving you fair warning."

His eyes narrow, but he delivers a tight nod before getting into his car. I stuff my hands into my pockets and watch as he speeds off.

From the first moment Oliver and I became friends, we've been tight. We've had the typical fights all boys go through over the years, but nothing that lasted more than a day or two. A couple of weeks ago, I would have never believed that a girl would come between us, but a couple of weeks ago Rylee wasn't a factor. I can't get the girl out of my fucking mind, and I'm not really sure I want to try. I hate that there's this now rift between us, but I'm sure he'll get over his beef, eventually. Once he sees her for the person she is and not the person he *thinks* she is.

Benny gives me a questioning look when I walk back into the garage, no doubt sensing the tension radiating off me. I give him a chin lift, silently letting him know everything's fine, and go back to the Mustang I'm working on.

chapter seventeen

RYLEE

"well, i see you survived," Savannah says the second I open the door to find her standing on my front porch.

"V!" I waste no time wrapping my arms around her neck and pulling her into a tight hug, despite the multiple bags she's currently weighed down with.

I knew I missed my best friend, but I don't think I realized just how much until now. Pulling back, I let my gaze settle on her—taking in her light blonde hair that's now streaked with dark blonde highlights and appears to have been cut since the last time I saw her. It used to hang halfway down her back but now barely brushes her shoulders. It looks good on her—then again, I think Savannah could pull off a buzz cut and still look beautiful.

She's one of those naturally stunning girls. With her piercing green eyes and bright white smile, V is the kind of girl every other girl wishes she looked like.

Unfortunately, she's never seen it this way. Body image is something she's struggled with since Junior High—despite the fact that she's off the charts on the hot scale.

"I see someone has missed me." She smiles, holding up the bags. "Mind helping me out here."

"Oh yeah, sorry." I laugh, immediately reaching for a couple of the bags before stepping to the side and gesturing for her to come in.

"Wow," she says, looking around the large foyer. "This place is massive."

"Not massive enough." I blow out a breath, kicking the door shut behind us. "It would take an entire country to put the kind of distance between me and Oliver that I need."

"Still no better on the brother front, huh?" she asks, following me to the kitchen.

"Stepbrother." I correct her. "And no, unless you count a forced apology as better."

"Well, have no fear, because now I'm here," she sings, laying the bags on the kitchen island.

"Did you just rhyme on purpose?" I give her a funny look.

"Shut up and help me." She laughs, pulling items out of the plastic grocery bags.

By the time we're done, the island is covered with enough snacks to feed twenty people.

"I think maybe you went a little overboard," I tell her, gesturing to all the food.

"I didn't know what you were in the mood for, so I bought all your favorites." She shrugs. "Plus, I have all the stuff for our facials and mani/pedis in my duffel. I raided my mom's bathroom and brought the good stuff."

"You seriously are the best, you know that?" I smile. "But really, you didn't have to do all this. We do have food here, ya know."

"Yeah, but if I know your mom, you don't have any of *this* stuff."

She's not wrong there. What is it with doctors and healthy food? I guess they see firsthand the effects of a bad diet. My entire life my mom has preached about how important it is to put the *right* foods into your body.

"Okay, you got me there."

"Let's stick the ice cream and stuff in the freezer and take the rest up to your room. I'm dying to see the rest of this place."

"Okay," I agree, gathering up some of the cold items to put away.

Once we finish in the kitchen, I give Savannah a brief tour that ends at my bedroom. I know Oliver is home, because his car is outside, and music is coming from his room, but other than pointing to his door to say that's his room, I make no attempt to introduce the two. Why would I? He'll probably be mean to her just because she's *my* friend—and I'm not having any of that. He can mess with me but messing with V is a line I'm not willing to let him cross.

"So let me make sure I've got all this straight. Zayden was in on the bullying in the beginning. And despite your better judgement, you were still crushing on him pretty hard. And now he's acting as your protector, and you're crushing on him even harder." Savannah blows on her fingernails to speed up the drying process, recapping my relationship with Zayden in a nutshell.

We started with facials and are now finishing up our nails. While we kept the conversation light at first—with V filling me in on everything happening at Bristol, it didn't take long for the conversation to turn back to me and the shit show that is now my life.

"I don't know if he was so much bullying me as he was just playing along with Oliver, but yes, I guess you could say he's protecting me now. Though in a weird way he kind of always has."

"Ry, I love you, but from what you've told me, bullying you was exactly what he was doing—regardless of why he was doing it."

"I guess. I just… I don't know. He's not who I thought he was. He's surprisingly really gentle. For a guy the whole school is afraid of, and rightfully so, he's got this really soft side to him. You should have seen the way he shielded me yesterday at school. He's protective but in a very Zayden, bad ass, type of way. I don't know, he's just really… sweet."

"Sweet?" Savannah smiles—not fully convinced. "A guy who does illegal underground fighting and helps your stepbrother make your life miserable?"

"I know how it probably sounds, but I'm telling you, V, there's something about him. A side to him I don't think many people know is there. Sure, he's a little rough around the edges and he's pretty damn intimidating, too. But when it's just me and him—I don't know? He's different. He's not the asshole he portrays to everyone else. He's caring and attentive. He even helps his dad take care of his sick little sister. How many teenage guys can say they do that? And he's smart. Like super smart. And my, can that boy kiss." I can't stop the smile that spreads across my face.

"He sounds awesome, Ry, but…." She nibbles on her bottom lip.

"But what?"

"I just want you to be careful, okay? I know you, and I can see you're already so smitten with him that you can't see past your own nose. And I don't want to see you get hurt because you let your guard down too quickly."

"Oh, trust me, my guard is way up." I shake my head. "But that doesn't mean I'm not enjoying what's happening between us. I just want to see where this goes, ya know? Good or bad."

"I get that. And I hope it turns out the way you want. But sweetie, he *is* Oliver's best friend."

"I know that. But I'm confused, I thought you were Team Zayden. Weren't you the one saying just the other day on the phone that you've known this whole time he was into me?"

"I did say that. And I meant it. But after we got off the phone I got to thinking."

"About?" I prompt when she doesn't continue.

"Think about us. If I had a problem with someone, is there anything you wouldn't do to help me settle the score if I asked you to?"

"I think I'd draw the line at physically harming someone, but no, I guess not."

"Exactly my point. I'm just asking that you don't forget that he and Oliver have been friends for a long time. Based on what you've told me, the only conclusion I can come up with is that he actually cares about you. But, that doesn't mean his intentions are completely honorable. Just be careful."

An uneasy feeling settles in my stomach, but I do my best to push past it. It's not like Savannah isn't saying exactly what I've been thinking since the first time Zayden kissed me—but somehow hearing it from her makes it harder to swallow.

I don't know what I'd do if this all turned out to be a ruse. But what if it isn't? Am I really willing to pass something up that could be incredible because I'm scared that it's not real?

I already know the answer to that question.

I'm not ready to give up Zayden just yet. Even if it means that it could all blow up in my face—I have to see this through. I owe it to myself to find out if there's really something there.

I'm not one of those girls who goes gaga over a guy, so when feelings this strong come on, I have to explore them.

"I will be," I promise.

Savannah claps her hands together. "Now that that's out of the way, what do you say we crack open the ice cream and eat ourselves into a food coma?"

"I think that sounds amazing." I nod, watching Savannah climb to her feet.

"Why don't you get Netflix fired up, and I'll go down and get the goodies?" She offers.

"Okay."

With that, I watch my friend spin around and quickly exit my room, leaving me with a lot more questions than what I started with.

Savannah has always been my biggest supporter—my cheerleader—the person who pushes me to try new things and not be afraid to take chances. The fact that she felt the need to voice her concerns about Zayden makes me nervous for some reason.

It's not like she knows Zayden. The only things she knows are what I've told her. And while she seemed thrilled the other day, something between then and now has shifted. Maybe because she's had some time to think on it, like she said—or maybe I said something that raised a red flag and put her on alert.

Pushing to my feet, I cross the room and fire up the television mounted on the far wall. As I'm logging into my Netflix account, I catch sight of Oliver exiting his room. At first, I ignore him, thinking nothing of it. But after a couple minutes have passed and Savannah hasn't returned, I start to get a little nervous.

I wouldn't put it past Oliver to start shit with my best friend. The thought has me exiting my room and heading downstairs.

When I near the kitchen, I hear Savannah, but what I hear isn't the normal sweet voice she usually has. I know instantly what that means. I quicken my strides, but then stop dead in my tracks when I hear Savannah's next words.

"Do you really think you can walk in here and flirt with me like I'm some stupid bimbo? That I'll get all giggly over you and forget the hell you've put my best friend through?"

He's flirting with her....

Not that I blame him. She's gorgeous. But that's the last thing I expected him to be doing.

Pressing my back to the wall, I decide to listen for a moment.

"Oh, relax, I was just having a little fun with my dear sister," Oliver says, humor in his voice.

Anger seethes through me. Of course he would think it's funny. Everything is a game to him. I bet he hasn't stopped for one second to consider what his actions have done to me. The embarrassment and humiliation he's caused.

"*Fun*? Are you kidding me? How would you feel if someone did that to you?"

"It's not like I meant for that video to be shown."

"Whether you meant for it or not, the fact still remains that it was. And from what I can tell, you've taken no ownership and haven't even apologized for it."

"I did apologize—not that it's any of your fucking business." Gone is his flirtatious playfulness, replaced by a tone I'm all too familiar with.

"Apologizing because daddy made you isn't apologizing."

"Pretty sure you don't know what the fuck you're talking about."

"Pretty sure I know more than you think," she fires back. "Since you won't tell Rylee what she did to make you hate her so much, perhaps you'd like to enlighten me."

"And why would I do that?"

"I don't know—maybe it would help if you got it off your chest." Her voice softens, but I can still hear the anger lacing her words.

"Doubtful." He snorts. "And if I was going to talk to someone about this, it certainly wouldn't be you."

"Why? Because you're afraid I'll see what a cowardice piece of shit you are? Newsflash—that ship has long since sailed."

"Who the fuck do you think you are coming into *my* house and speaking to me like this?"

"I'm Savannah fucking Reynolds, that's who." I cover my mouth with my hand to contain the laughter threatening to spill from my throat. I've always known V could handle her own, but I never imagined she'd be so ballsy to go toe to toe with Oliver like this. "And in case you've forgotten, but I'm guessing you haven't, this is *my* best friend's house, too," she quickly concludes.

"Like hell it is."

"She lives here, doesn't she?" Her voice has turned sickly sweet, and I know her well enough to know that at this point she's purposely egging him on.

"She wouldn't if I had any say in the matter."

"She wouldn't or her mother wouldn't? Why don't you say the real reason you're so butt hurt? It's because your daddy remarried and you're worried it might cut into your inheritance, isn't it?"

"I won't deny that his new wife is a money hungry slut. Facts are facts."

At this point, I'm not sure if I'm still standing stock still because I'm in shock, or if it's because I know if I move I'll end up doing something I will likely regret.

"Evelyn is not money hungry. Or do I need to remind you that she's a freaking neurosurgeon. You think she doesn't have more than enough money on her own? And she's the furthest thing from a slut. Say that again and you'll find my tolerance of you short lived."

I'm not surprised to hear Savannah stick up for my mom. She's been like a second daughter to her for most of her life.

"Not a slut, huh?" Oliver sneers. "What do you call her fucking my dad behind my mom's back then?"

His words send my heart crashing against my rib cage.

"She would never," Savannah argues.

"She would and she did. They've been fucking each other for well over a year. Did you really think they got married after only dating a few short months? This shit has been going on a lot longer than they've been willing to admit to anyone."

"You're lying. You're grasping at straws, trying to say something that will justify what you're doing to Rylee."

"Am I? Why don't you ask your precious Evelyn? I was home the night my mom confronted him and he didn't deny it. Hell, he all but celebrated the fact that she finally knew. And then you know what he did? He threw my mother out and left her with no choice but to go stay with her sister in Utah. But I'm guessing mommy dearest failed to tell her perfect little daughter this fact."

As much as I don't want to believe what he's saying, a part of me has always wondered.

"And yet, here you are. If you're so angry with your father, why not go live with your mom?"

"You think I don't want to?" His voice echoes through the kitchen. "It's not like either of them gave me a choice in the matter."

"Let's say what you're saying is true—why Rylee? She's an innocent in all of this. Same as you. What could you possibly hope to accomplish by hurting her the way you have?" The two are silent for a long moment before Savannah answers her own question. "You think if you make her miserable enough, you'll drive a wedge between Evelyn and your dad."

"I never said that. You're assuming things. Perhaps you should stick to what you're good at." I step around the corner and see him gesture to the ice cream Savannah is holding.

"Are you calling me fat?" She draws back like she's been physically assaulted.

"Your words." He shrugs indifferently, a slow smile tugging at the corners of his mouth when he eyes me coming into the kitchen.

At this point, I'm ready to explode. It's one thing to throw out false accusations about my mother, it's quite another to personally attack my best friend who hasn't been fat a day in her life.

"Hey, *sis.*" Disdain drips from his voice. "Me and the bestie here were just getting to know each other a little better." His gaze goes back to Savannah.

"You are quite possibly the worst human being I have ever met," I spit at him, balling my fists at my sides.

"Then perhaps you haven't looked in the mirror lately." He lets out a low chuckle, spinning around to grab his drink off the counter.

I open my mouth to say more, but Savannah stops me with a gentle touch to the arm. "Don't," she mouths, shaking her head. "He's not worth it." She glares at him over her shoulder.

"Come to my room later tonight. I bet I could change your mind. Trust me when I say, I'm very, *very* worth it," Oliver calls out as she slides past me toward the hallway.

"Somehow I doubt that." She stops in the doorway, turning to give him the biggest *fuck you* smile I've ever seen. "From what I've seen, you don't have much to work with. Or did you think you were the only one who knew how to operate the record feature on your phone?"

With that, she grabs my arm and together we leave Oliver standing in the middle of the kitchen, speechless for probably the first time in his entire life.

chapter eighteen

ZAYDEN

the heat of rylee's confused stare burns the side of my face.

"Umm… Zayden, you were supposed to turn left back there," she says after I turn in the opposite direction of her house.

I grip her hand, tangle our fingers together, and place them both on my thigh. "I'm not taking you home yet."

"Okaaaay." She slowly draws out the word. "Where are we going then?"

I glance at her. "My place."

She frowns and licks her lips. "Why?"

It's not until I stop at a stop sign, check both ways, and press on the accelerator that I answer. "Because I'm not ready to drop you off yet. You okay with that?"

Her features soften and she gives me a small smile. "Yeah. I'm okay with that."

I put my eyes back on the road. It's been a week since the video fiasco, and except for the pit stop we're making to my place today, we've formed a routine. I pick Rylee up in the mornings, hang with her as much as I can during the school day, then I take her home. I want to claim the only reason I'm doing this is because of the guilt I feel for my part in the shit she's been through, but it'd be a lie, and if there's one thing I hate more than spoiled rich people, it's liars. Guilt may be a small part, but I'm doing it for more selfish reasons. I *like* being around Rylee. She quiets all the bad shit going on in my life.

"When is your next fight?" she asks, breaking the silence.

"Why?"

Her shoulder moves against mine when she shrugs. "I want to come watch."

"That's not a place I want you to be. You don't need to see the shit that goes on there."

"I know." She starts trailing the tip of her finger over the back of my hand, her voice turning quiet. "But I like watching you fight. Or I did the one time I was there."

I glance at her, raising a brow. "You liked seeing a guy beat on my face?"

Her lips quirk. "I liked seeing him try. I liked even more seeing him lose against you."

"So, you're bloodthirsty, then?" I chuckle. This girl surprises the hell out of me.

"Um… I wouldn't really say that, but I don't know…." She trails off.

I stop at another stop sign, and when I see no one behind me, I turn slightly toward her. "What?"

Her face turns a pretty shade of pink and she avoids my eyes. I grip her chin and turn her face toward me. "What is it?"

She chews on her bottom lip. "It uh… kinda turned me on," she admits quietly.

Those words send all the blood in my body south, leaving me mute for a couple of seconds. It doesn't really surprise me, but what does is her admitting it. I've fucked plenty of girls after fights. There are tons who turn into horny fiends from watching the action. Fucking is one of the more satisfying ways to come down from an adrenaline rush.

I knew from Rylee's expression that night at Hart's that she was turned on, but to have her admit it, that shit makes it really fucking hard to concentrate.

"Do you have any clue how much hearing that turns *me* on?"

She dips her eyes away before bringing them back up, smiling shyly. "So, will you let me come to the next one?"

I press my lips into a firm line. Can I say no to her? Do I even want to say no to her? I won't lie and say I don't like the thought of her being there, her pulse racing, her body quivering, getting *wet* while watching me. But I don't like the thought of her being near so many rough people.

"You can go. *But*," I stress the word when she smiles triumphantly, "only if Pierce will be there, and you promise to stick with him from the moment I leave you until I get back to you. I'll also want you right at the front with one of Hart's men, so I can make sure no one fucks with you."

"Hart?"

"The owner."

"Okay." She nods. "I can do that, and I know Pierce will go with me."

Right as I steal a kiss, a horn blares from behind us. Gritting my teeth, I let up on the brake and propel forward. The rest of the trip is made in silence, save the low tune of the rock song playing from the radio.

I haven't seen much of Oliver over the last week. If he wasn't being such an asshole, I would have preferred him to be with Rylee during the fight, but there's no way I'll trust him to protect her. And I'm pretty sure he's been avoiding me; despite his claim he won't let Rylee come between our friendship. If I'm with Rylee, he keeps his distance. If I'm with him and Rylee appears, he makes an excuse to leave. *Whatever.* He'll come around eventually. What counts the most is he's stopped fucking with her.

Pulling to a stop in my driveway, I shut my truck off and climb out. Rylee slides across the seat and exits through my door. I've never been ashamed of where I live—Dad, Danielle, and I make do with what we have—but as I lead Rylee up the sidewalk to the front door, I can't help but wonder what she's thinking. The old, small brick home isn't even a quarter the size of the house she lives in now. And with her mom being a surgeon, I'm sure the house she lived in before was still a hell of a lot bigger and nicer than my small, three-bed, two-bath house. The yard is kept mowed and the inside kept clean, but there's still no comparison.

I stuff my keys into my pocket and kick the door closed behind us the moment we enter. Rylee stands in place and looks around the small living room.

"This is nice," she remarks.

"Yeah," I grunt.

She turns to face me. “I’m serious. It feels like a real home in here.”

I seize her hand and pull her into the kitchen. Grabbing a couple glasses from the cabinet, I fill them both with water and hand her one. As she tips the glass to her lips, she walks to the fridge.

“I assume your sister did these?” She gestures to the pictures hanging by magnets on the fridge door.

“Yeah.” I come up beside her.

“She’s really good.”

“Danielle is good at everything she does, but drawing is her favorite.” I clear my throat of the lump that’s suddenly formed. “She wants to be an artist when she grows up.”

Rylee smiles. “It’s great she already knows what she wants to be. And if these drawings are any indication, she’ll be a damn good artist one day.”

If her fucking lungs last that long. And if the goddamn insurance company will approve her for a transplant. I keep those thoughts to myself and go set my glass in the sink.

“Where are they, by the way? Your dad and sister, I mean.”

“Danielle had an appointment today. They won’t be back until later.”

“Oh.”

She sets her empty glass in the sink beside mine.

“Come on.”

I lead her down the hallway to my room. She takes off her jacket and drops it on my desk chair before she walks around the small space, checking out the shit on my desk, the posters on my walls, and the books on the small bookshelf. She picks up the framed picture I have on my dresser.

“Is this your dad and sister?”

I pull my keys and wallet out of my pockets and dump them on my nightstand, setting my jacket on top of hers. "Yeah. Danielle was three then. It was taken in Florida during the one and only vacation we could afford to take."

I take the frame from her hand and set it back on the dresser. Sitting on the edge of my bed, I pull her down on my lap so her legs straddle me.

She smiles and her eyes dance playfully.

"So, this is the reason you brought me here. You wanna make out?"

I don't smile back at her, just grip her hips and hold her to me. There's so much more I want to do with Rylee than just make out, but I know she's not ready for that. And I haven't earned that right. At least not yet, but I will.

The look in her eyes changes. Going from mischievous to something more sensuous. The look has my dick going from semi-hard to rock hard in seconds. I'm still ramped up from what she revealed in the truck earlier. When her eyes drop to my mouth, I can't hold back anymore.

I slide my hands up her back until my fingers tangle in her hair, and I tug her forward. Our lips meet in a crushing kiss.

Heavy kissing is as far as I've taken it with Rylee, and it's been killer on my control. Tasting her, touching her, feeling her against me, it all puts me closer to the edge than I've ever been before. I've never wanted someone as much as I want her- as much as I have wanted her since the first moment I saw her; even when I hated her.

Her arms lace around my neck and her chest smashes against mine. My hands move to her ass, and I squeeze the plumpness through her jeans, grinding her against my erection. She releases a whimper, the sound vibrating against my mouth.

I nip and suck on her tongue, then swirl my tongue against hers. Her unique sweet flavor explodes in my mouth, and I want more. I want to taste her all over; lick every delectable inch of her.

Leaving her mouth behind, I trail my lips over the underside of her chin and make my way down a few inches. The shirt she has on rises to the base of her neck, and I finger the edge of the material. I look at her, letting her see my need. When she doesn't say anything, and I don't get the sense she wants me to stop, I gently tug the fabric down a little. There's a bit of give, and I drop my eyes down to see her bare flesh. Just a shadow of the hidden valley between her breasts shows, but damn if it isn't enough to make my mouth water.

I kiss the top slopes of her breasts, and her breath hitches. Lifting my head, I lightly rub the stubble on my chin over the tender skin.

"Has anyone ever had their face buried between your gorgeous tits, Rylee?"

She lets out a breathy, "No."

"Hmm… I like that. I like knowing I'm the only one." I dip my chin, scraping my chin firmer against her breasts. I slip my hand between her open thighs. "What about here? Has anyone touched you here?" I grind the heel of my palm against her clit through her jeans.

Her lips part and her eyelids lower. She slowly shakes her head.

"Fuck," I groan. "I like that even more."

I grip her waist and flip her to her back. Her legs fall open, and I settle between them. This can't go much further than it already has—*I know this*—but I want to feel her beneath me for a moment.

Her hands grip my biceps, her nails digging into the muscle. I watch her as I hike her leg up over my hip, opening her up more. I press my hips forward, thrusting against her pussy, letting her feel just how hard I am for her.

"Oh, God," she moans, tipping her head back and closing her eyes.

Dropping my face to her neck, I run my lips up the column until I reach her ear. "Feel me, baby. Feel what you do to me. Feel how hard you make me. I can't fucking wait to slide inside you and see how tight you are."

I pump my hips, wishing there wasn't any clothes between us, imagining her bare flesh against mine. My dick feels like it's going to break off at any second from all the blood filling it. I'm so close to exploding that I know it won't take much more. I need to stop before it gets to that point. I don't want to come in my damn jeans. Fuck, I want to be inside her. What I wouldn't give to be inside her.

I slip my hand between us, forcing myself to not go for the button on her jeans, but instead rub her through the stiff material. I don't trust myself to touch her bare pussy. I may be putting a stop to my own orgasm, but I damn sure want Rylee to have hers. I fucking crave to see her come undone.

Her hips buck against my hand. "That feels so—"

"Zayden! Where are you? Dad and I got some good news!"

I stiffen at the sound of my sister's voice, my head whipping to the door. "Shit," I mutter. "That's Danielle."

Rylee's eyes widen at the same time she tries shoving me off her. "Oh my, God," she whisper yells. "Get off before she comes in here."

I chuckle, enjoying the panic in her eyes. "Relax. I locked the door."

Her eyes narrow to slits. "So? Your sister may not realize what a locked door means, but your dad will. I don't want him thinking we were… doing stuff in here."

"Doing stuff?"

"Yes," she hisses, shoving my shoulder again. "Seriously, Zayden. Will you please get up?"

I decide to take it easy on her, but before I do, I lean down for one more kiss. By the time I pull back, her eyes are back to that lazy look. Using my fists, I hoist myself up. The doorknob jiggles right as I'm pulling Rylee off the bed.

"Zayden? You in there?" comes Danielle's labored voice.

"I'll be out in a minute!" I holler back.

Rylee is nibbling on her thumb nail when I turn back to face her. She looks nervous as she darts her eyes back and forth between the door and me.

I pull her hand down.

"I didn't expect to meet your family today."

"I didn't expect you to either."

She looks over her shoulder. "Umm… I can probably sneak out the window if you want me to."

"Why the hell would I want you to do that?" I don't give her time to answer before I pull her to the door. "I may not have banked on you meeting my dad and Danielle, but that doesn't mean I don't want you to."

She pulls me to a stop when I grab the doorknob. "Wait. Are you sure about this? This is kind of a big deal."

I grab the front of her shirt and pull her to me. "I'm sure."

After a moment, she nods. "Okay."

We follow the sound of Dad's and Danielle's voices into the kitchen. Danielle is being more vocal than usual, indicating she's having a really good day.

They both stop talking when Rylee and I walk through the door. Danielle looks at Rylee curiously, while dad has a slight frown on his face. When Rylee said it was a big deal for her to meet dad and Danielle, she didn't know how true that was. I never bring girls here. Rylee is the first.

"Dad, Danielle, this is my girlfriend, Rylee." Rylee's fingers twitch in my hand at the word *girlfriend.*

Dad steps forward, extending his hand. "It's nice to meet you, Rylee. I must say, I'm surprised to see you here."

Rylee laughs nervously and shakes his hand. "It's nice to meet you, too, Mr. Michaels. Zayden was just showing me around. I'll be out of your hair shortly."

Dad smiles, the look making the wrinkles around his eyes stand out. "No need to rush home. I just meant Zayden never brings girls around. I was starting to think he was embarrassed of us," he jokes.

"Oh." She glances at me for a brief moment before turning to Danielle, who's sitting sideways in one of the kitchen chairs with her oxygen tank tucked under the table. "It's nice to meet you, Danielle. I absolutely love your hair."

Danielle fingers the end of the long thick braid. Dad mentioned cutting it once and she about flipped, claiming she was never cutting her hair. She said she wanted to grow it down to her knees. It's already over halfway down her back.

"Thank you," Danielle says shyly.

"I saw some of the pictures you drew on the fridge. You're really good."

"You really think so?"

Rylee nods, offering a smile. "I do. I love nature. Maybe you could draw me something sometime?"

Danielle grins, her cheeks puffing out. "Nature is my favorite thing to draw."

I walk over and plant a kiss on Danielle's cheek, then ruffle the top of her head. "You'll have to show Rylee your room sometime. I bet you can't guess who her favorite singer is."

Her eyes dart from me to Rylee. "You're a Swiftie?" she asks excitedly.

Rylee grins. "Yep."

She looks to dad next. "Can we keep her here always?"

We all laugh.

"I don't know about that, but she's welcome here anytime," Dad answers.

I pull out a chair for Rylee to sit, and I take the one beside Danielle. "So, tell me about this good news you were hollering about."

"Can I tell him, Dad?"

"Go ahead, sweetie," he says over his shoulder as he pours some juice in a glass. He brings it to the table and sets it in front of Danielle, then takes the seat on her other side.

Danielle's eyes dance with more life than I've seen in a long time.

"I got approved for new lungs."

I'm speechless for a moment. We've been battling the insurance company for almost a year. Danielle's health has declined dramatically during that time, and they didn't seem to care. Hopelessness and helplessness have been the two dominant emotions ruling our lives for so long.

I look to Dad. "Is this serious? They approved her?"

"Yes. Apparently, the company recently fired several of its approval board members for not properly investigating all medical claims. They said that Danielle should have been approved months ago."

"Are you kidding me?" I fist my hands on my thighs in anger. "And they think this is okay? What the hell would have happened had it been too late? What are they going to do to make up for this?"

Dad leans back in his chair, crossing his arms over his chest. "They're offering a settlement for people affected. But even if they hadn't, the most important thing is that Danielle will get on the list to get the lungs she needs."

"This is unbelievable," I mutter. I jackknife out of my chair, the legs scraping across the floor. On one hand, I'm happy Danielle will finally get what she needs to hopefully beat this illness. But on the other, it pisses me off that they didn't catch the neglect before now. How many other people suffered unnecessarily? How many people died because of it? The yearly death rate for emphysema is only five percent, but that's five percent way too fucking much.

"Zayden, sit down," Dad commands, his voice both hard and gentle. This hasn't only affected him. He knows how hard it's been on me, too.

I retake my seat and blow out a harsh breath, calming my frayed nerves and the anger rushing through me. A warm hand slides across mine, and I glance at Rylee. Her concerned gaze meets mine.

"The whole situation is a mess," Dad continues, "but what's important is that it was caught and fixed before it was too late. There's nothing we can do about the past. We can only look to the future."

I nod, relaxing my jaw. "Yeah." I reach over and scoop Danielle out of her chair and pull her onto my lap. She sits sideways, her legs dangling.

"Didn't I tell you everything was going to be okay?" I ask, letting the rest of my anger melt away.

"I already knew it would be." She smirks. "I wasn't worried, you were."

I tweak her nose. "Nah. I knew you were too stubborn to let your little ol' lungs keep you down."

She giggles and throws her arms around my neck. I pull her closer, tightening my grip on her, while silently sending up my thanks to whoever's listening. My eyes meet Rylee's over her head. Her smile is soft as she looks from me to Danielle.

I'm glad she's here. Today has been a damn good day, despite the bullshit that came with it.

Danielle will finally get her lungs.

And I've got a girl that's quickly becoming one of the most important people in my life.

chapter nineteen

RYLEE

"So, what did you think?" I look to where Zayden is sitting next to me, propped up against the headboard of my bed.

When he brought up our English project that's due this Friday, and the fact that he still hadn't watched the movie, I jumped at the chance to invite him over to watch *Twilight* with me—despite the fact that I've already seen it more times than I care to admit.

"People actually enjoy this shit?" His ocean blue eyes slide to mine.

"Oh come on. It's not that bad." I laugh, lightly smacking the side of his leg.

"Not that bad? You can't seriously believe that wasn't the worst movie you've ever watched. I mean, that acting…come the fuck on. As if sparkling vampires weren't enough." He shakes his head. "And I thought the book was bad."

"There wasn't anything you liked about it?"

"Not a single thing." He snorts. "Well, except maybe some of the soundtrack, but I'm not sure that counts."

"Well, look at it this way. At least it's over now and you never have to watch it again." I try to point out the positives. "That is, unless you want to watch the other movies." I grin.

"There's more?" He looks horrified.

"You didn't know that?" I cock my head, thinking someone must be living under a rock to not know there are multiple books and movies.

"Why would I?"

His question is valid. It's not like he strikes me as the kind of guy that follows mainstream pop culture.

"I guess that's a good point," I admit, giggling when he reaches over and gives my side a squeeze.

"What time did you say your mom was going to be home again?" He glances at the clock on my bedside table, and I follow his gaze.

It's almost five o'clock.

"Probably by six at the latest. Her last appointments run up until five, but she usually doesn't leave the office right away. Why? Already planning your escape?"

"Quite the opposite, actually. Do you realize how hard it was for me to lay here next to you for nearly two hours and not touch you?" He grabs my forearm and tugs me toward him. I go willingly, smiling against his mouth as he drops a kiss to my lips.

It starts out innocent enough, but like most things with Zayden, it quickly intensifies. Before I know it, I'm pinned beneath him, his weight pressing me into the mattress as he devours my mouth.

I know I'm inexperienced in a lot of ways, but I find it very hard to believe that most eighteen-year-old guys are as skilled with their mouths as Zayden. I know the very small number of guys I have kissed don't hold a candle to him. I could kiss him all day and never get tired of it. Then again, I don't think we'd make it all day before *more* happened.

And I want more.

God do I want it. More than I think I've ever wanted anything in my life.

But I'm also scared. And not only because I've never done it before. As much as I hate to admit it, a part of me is still hesitant to really trust Zayden. After everything that's happened over the last few days, I know that shouldn't be the case. But there's still this tiny voice in my head planting little seeds of doubt.

"I want to touch you so fucking bad right now," Zayden groans against my lips, and while I don't answer, I think I have a pretty good idea how he feels because all I want is for him to touch me, too.

I don't answer right away, but when my words finally come, I think they shock us both. "Then do it." Zayden pulls back a couple of inches and looks down at me, the hunger in his eyes enough to make me squirm under his gaze.

"Don't tempt me, Rylee. I'm far from a fucking gentleman. And right now I'm hanging on by a very thin thread," he warns.

"I'm not ready for…." I trail off, my cheeks heating. "But I want you to touch me. I want to know what it feels like to…." Again, my words die in my throat as embarrassment seeps in, and I quickly avert my gaze.

"Look at me, Rylee." His soft voice coaxes my eyes back to his. "You don't ever have to be embarrassed to ask for what you want. You got me?" He waits until I nod before continuing, "Did you lock the door? If I'm going to touch you for the first time, I sure as fuck don't want someone barging in and ruining it."

"It's locked." I swallow hard.

"Good girl." He smiles, pushing up off of me. I mourn the loss of his weight instantly, but the thought doesn't linger for long as his hand grazes between my legs.

My entire body stiffens.

"Relax." He smiles, leaning forward to grip the waistband of my leggings. "If you want me to stop, just say the words."

I nod, unable to voice my desire as Zayden shimmies my pants over my hips and down my legs, leaning back so he can remove them completely. My instinct is to cover myself, but before I can move my hand, Zayden stops me, pushing it away.

"I'll leave them on." His eyes dart to my panties before coming back to my face. "This time." He grins wickedly.

"Okay." My is voice barely audible as Zayden shifts, finally settling next to me on his side.

While a part of me is relieved to still have a small barrier between us, the other part wishes he would just strip me bare and make love to me the way I've been dreaming of since the first moment I laid eyes on him. I know all I have to do is ask. I know the power rests solely with me. But I also know that if I let myself make a rash decision in the heat of the moment; I may live to regret it.

Zayden's fingers start at my thigh, slowly swirling the soft skin leading to my center. I swear I forget how to breathe. The anticipation is enough to make me feel like I'm dangling over a cliff, about to plummet to my death at any moment.

When his hand dips inside my panties, I feel like my heart is seconds away from beating out of my chest.

I thought I knew what this would be like—I've touched myself enough to know what it feels like to be touched—but I couldn't have been more wrong. Nothing could have prepared me for the onslaught of pleasure that overtakes me the instant Zayden's fingers are on me.

He slides through my folds with ease—the evidence of my arousal undeniable. I'm not sure if I want to laugh, cry, or scream when he slides a single finger inside of me, quickly followed by another. Several emotions surge through me, but I can't get a grip on a single one.

"Fuck," he hisses, pressing his fingers into me as far as they will go. "You're so fucking tight." He nips at my jaw.

I have no words. I don't think I could speak even if I tried. And while I may be a little timid around Zayden, once his hand starts to move, I move right along with him—shamelessly riding his hand.

I can't help it. It feels too good not to.

When he extends his thumb and presses it against my clit, I nearly come undone. Pleasure rockets through me like tiny fireworks going off, one after the other. I grip the sheets, holding on for dear life. When Zayden pulls my earlobe into his mouth and groans—a deep gritty sound- it brings my orgasm screaming to the surface.

"Zayden," I whimper, knowing I'm seconds away from being past the point of no return.

"Come for me, Rylee." His voice is husky, heavy with lust. "I want to feel you pulse around my fingers."

"Oh God!" The words rip from my throat as an orgasm unlike anything I have ever felt before tears through me.

My body arches and my legs flail as waves of pleasure roll through me one after the other, so intense it's borderline painful.

Zayden's fingers continue to work as he silences me with a kiss. The feeling coursing through me becomes that much more overwhelming. I'm absolute putty in his hands, and I'm positive that he knows it, too.

"You have to be the sexiest thing I've ever laid eyes on," he tells me, pulling back to watch my face as his hand stills and he slowly removes his fingers. Sliding them up and over my clit, he pulls his hand out of my panties.

What he does next nearly knocks me right off the bed. He lifts his hand to his mouth and sucks the desire off of his fingers, one at a time.

"Fuck. Even better than I imagined," he groans, leaning in to kiss me again so that I can taste myself.

It's the single most erotic thing I've ever experienced and instantly has me wanting to do it all over again.

I've heard stories from friends who have been with guys. Everyone swore that having a guy touch you was so much different than touching yourself, but I always had my doubts. How could it really be *that* different?

My God was I wrong. Zayden touching me is nothing like me touching myself. And the orgasm—I don't think I could ever put into words how incredible it was. Mind blowing doesn't even begin to cover what I experienced. More like life changing. Because now that I've felt the power of Zayden's touch, I don't ever want him to stop.

Unfortunately, the perfect moment is broken when Taylor Swift's voice starts blaring from my phone. Because I have assigned ring tones for certain people—like my mom—I usually know who's calling before I look.

"Crap." I let out a frustrated noise. "That's my mom."

"Let it go to voicemail," he murmurs against my mouth, grazing his teeth over my bottom lip.

"She'll just keep calling if I don't answer," I reluctantly tell him. And I mean it honestly—she really will keep calling.

Even though I can tell he doesn't want to, Zayden releases his hold on me and rolls to his back.

"I'm sorry." I say, sitting up before throwing my legs over the side of the bed and snagging my phone off the nightstand.

"It's okay. I should probably get going anyway," he says as he rolls off the bed.

"Why?" I silence the ringer on my phone, deciding that my mom can wait a minute.

"I have to watch Danielle tonight, and I promised her pizza from Perogi's. If I want to get there before my dad has to leave, I've got to hit the road."

"Oh, okay." He slides on his shoes before he crosses to the other side of the bed where I'm sitting.

"Hey." He tips my chin upward at the same time he leans down, putting our faces a couple of inches apart. "You okay?"

"Yeah. Yeah, of course." I try to shake off the disappointment of his abrupt departure.

"I see the wheels turning in that pretty head of yours." A knowing smile graces his full lips. "Today was incredible." He presses a kiss to my mouth. "Better than incredible." Another kiss. "And I can't fucking wait to do it again." When he pulls back and hits me with a sexy smirk, I instantly feel better.

"Me, too," I admit on a shy smile.

"Call me later?"

"I will," I agree, my phone buzzing back to life in my hand as my mom starts calling again.

"I see you weren't lying." He chuckles, straightening his posture as he gestures to my phone.

"She's relentless. I think she forgets that I'm not sitting around with my phone in my hand, ready to answer the instant she calls." I look down at the phone in my hand and realize I'm doing exactly that. "Well, you know what I mean." I laugh at myself.

"Answer it," he tells me, snagging his jacket off the end of the bed. "I'll talk to you later."

"Okay."

Zayden crosses the room and unlocks the door, disappearing into the hallway moments later.

It takes me a couple seconds to realize my phone is still ringing, and once I do, I quickly answer it.

"Hey, Mom." I try to sound as normal as I can given everything that just happened.

"Hey, sweetie. What are you doing?"

"Homework." It's only half of a lie. Technically, I *was* doing homework a few short minutes ago. If you can classify watching a movie I've already seen dozens of times as homework.

"Are you about done? Paul just called me from the office and wants you and Oliver to meet us for dinner."

"I wish I could, Mom, but I really have a lot to get done." A complete lie this time. Truthfully, I don't feel like going anywhere right now. "Maybe next time?"

"Are you sure? I feel like I've barely seen you all week."

Leave it to my mom to throw in a little guilt in hopes of swaying me to do what she wants me to do.

"I'm sure. I really would if I could. Maybe we can make plans to have lunch this weekend—just you and me."

"I'd like that."

I let out a sigh of relief, knowing I've pacified her for now.

"So, Oliver is meeting you guys?" I ask, simply because I want to know if I should be prepared to run into him this evening. I've gotten really good at only leaving my room when absolutely necessary if I know he's home or will be home in the near future.

"I'm not sure yet. Paul was going to call him."

"Okay."

"You sure you don't want to come?"

"I'm sure. I'm gonna go make some Ramen and spend the rest of the evening trying to figure out this calculus homework."

"You work too hard," she tells me.

"I learned from the best," I shoot back.

"Touché." I can hear the smile in her voice. "Well, I won't keep you. Call me if you need anything."

"I will. Love you, Mom."

"Love you, too."

Dropping the device onto the bed next to me, I collapse back onto the mattress.

Today took an unexpected turn, but it wasn't entirely a surprise. Zayden and I have been skirting a very fine line for a few days now. It was only a matter of time before things began to escalate. Even still, I can't wrap my head around all of it.

Daydreaming about what something might be like and actually having it come to fruition are two very different things, and while I'm beside myself with excitement, I'm also in a little bit of disbelief.

If I thought it was hard keeping my thoughts off Zayden before, it's going to be damn near impossible now.

I close my eyes and remember the way it felt when his fingers slid into my panties. The nervousness coupled with a longing I've never felt before. I don't think I have ever wanted something so intensely in my life. And that orgasm… That can't be normal. I've had my fair share of orgasms, and I haven't experienced anything even remotely close to that before. It was like I was a musical instrument and Zayden's fingers were made with the sole purpose of playing me.

And then I think back to what he said before he left. *I can't wait to do that again.* And the only thought I have is… neither can I.

chapter twenty

ZAYDEN

i clasp rylee's hand tightly in mine as we walk down the dark hallway, Charles a few steps behind us. Adrenaline rushes through my veins, and for the first time, it's not only from the upcoming fight.

Part of me hates the idea of Rylee being surrounded by the type of people who are downstairs. Just the thought of something happening to her has my free hand clenching, ready to pummel something.

But I have to admit, a small part of me is looking forward to having her here. Fighting has been a big part of my life for the last couple of years. With Danielle getting the approval to be put on the transplant list, I don't need to fight anymore. I didn't have to come tonight, but I can't leave Hart in a bind. Besides, it's become something I enjoy. It allows me to let out all of the aggression I've felt for years. It's an outlet I need.

Most people would think having Rylee here would be a distraction, but she'll add even more motivation for me to win. There's no fucking way I'd allow her to see me lose.

I stop at the basement door and turn to face her. "Anytime you want to leave, just say the word and we're out," I tell her sternly. "If I'm in the middle of a fight, you tell Charles."

I look at Charles and he nods. "Got it."

"You stay with Charles the whole time, and you both stay with Hart's guy. Got it?" She nods. "Words, Rylee," I bark.

She lets out an exasperated sigh. "I've got it, Zayden. Calm down."

I put my face closer to hers.

"This is no joke. People get hurt here. People who aren't in fights. An accidental shove could land you in the hospital with broken bones or a concussion. Do you have any idea what I would do if that happened to you?" She gnaws on her bottom lip but doesn't say anything. "I'll kill any fuckers who dare touch you."

Her eyes widen and her lips part. I lean down and kiss her. I didn't want to freak her out, but she needs to know how serious the situation can be.

She licks her lips when I pull back. She seems nervous when she says quietly, "I'll stay with Pierce and Hart's guy."

"Thank you."

I dart a glance at Charles to see an amused expression on his face. Ignoring him, I grab Rylee's hand again and open the basement door. Raucous noise greets us as we make our way down the stairs. My muscles tense as we round the corner and I take in the over-packed room. Fight nights are always busy, but it seems even more crowded than usual. There's hardly any walking room.

I spot Hart's shiny bald head through the crowd, standing in the same corner he always stands in before a fight. I pull Rylee behind me as we walk toward him. When he notices our approach, he turns from the guy he's talking to and holds out a fist for me to bump.

"I need a guy tonight," I say, getting down to business. "I need him to stay with her at the front of the ring." I lift my chin at Rylee.

"Done. I'll put Hammer on her." Hart tips his head to the guy he was talking to when we walked up, and he walks off. Hart's eyes then move to Rylee. "Now, how about you introduce me to this gorgeous little lady."

I tug Rylee so she's tucked against my side. "Hart, this is my girlfriend, Rylee." I jerk my chin to Charles. "And her friend, Charles."

Charles holds out his hand and Hart takes it. "It's nice to meet you."

"Same." He looks back to Rylee, his eyes holding curiosity. "So, you're the reason my man Zayden has been off lately." He grins.

"I haven't been off," I grouch.

"Sanders had you pinned down longer than you've ever been pinned before," he reminds me. I don't need him telling me that shit. I remember it well.

"The guy was three hundred fucking pounds and a brute."

He laughs, actually fucking *laughs*. "Big guys always move slower, you know that."

"Whatever," I growl. "It was a one off. I have no plans to let it happen again."

He claps me on the shoulder. "Make sure you don't. I like my undefeated status."

I lift a brow. "You mean *my* undefeated status?"

"That too." He holds his hand out to Rylee. "Anyway, it's nice to finally meet you. He could have picked a better time, like when the store upstairs is open, but it's about damn time Zayden brings a girl around for me to meet."

"It's nice to meet you, too," Rylee says, offering a smile. "I'll have to stop by during the day next time."

"You do that, sweetness." He turns back to me. "So, what's this I hear about Danielle getting approved for a set of lungs?"

"I was actually going to talk to you about that after the fight. The insurance company finally came through. She met with a transplant team a couple of days ago."

"It's about damn time. Took the bastards long enough." He claps a hand on my shoulder. "I'm happy for her."

"Thanks, man." I glance around the crowded room. "It's not normally this packed," I comment. "What gives?"

Hart's expression turns serious. "The guy you're up against is from a couple counties over. Apparently, he's undefeated in his parts."

I nod, not worried about the fight itself, just the tight crowd and the trouble it could cause. Not only for Rylee, but for Hart as well. Things can get out of hand really fast in a group this size.

Hammer, a huge motherfucker Hart normally has moving around the room, keeping an eye on things, walks up to his side. "Sup, boss?"

"I want you glued to this girl's side." He gestures to Rylee. "Not one fucking person touches her, and if they try, break them."

"You got it, boss."

After introductions are made between Rylee, Charles, and Hammer, we leave Hart behind and make our way through the crowd. I have her as close as possible to my side while Charles is on her other. Hammer is in front of us, making a path. People call my name, but I ignore them all. My sole focus is getting Rylee to the front of the crowd, where there are several other men controlling the masses.

Once we're at the front, I turn Rylee by her shoulders to face me.

"Stay here until it's over. I'll come to you."

"Okay."

She rolls to her toes and presses a kiss against my lips. I groan into her mouth, wishing we were alone so I could taste her better. It's been a few of days since I've had my hands on her, and I feel like I'm going through fucking withdrawals.

All too soon, she falls back to her feet, and I almost grab her up and bring her back to my lips. Only the sound of the crowd and Charles' expression I see in my periphery stops me.

"Please be careful," Rylee says with a worried expression. I tuck a piece of loose hair behind her ear. It makes my chest feel warm knowing she's concerned.

"I will be." I kiss her one more time before glancing at Charles. "Take care of my girl."

Lifting his hand to his forehead, he salutes me. "I'll kick anyone's ass who comes close to her."

"Why don't you leave the ass kicking to Hammer and me? I'd hate to have to carry you out of here over my shoulder," I reply, only partially in jest. I'm sure Charles can hold his own in some situations, but he isn't known here. There's no reason for anyone to help him if he needed it.

He looks around at the wild group of people. "Yeah, maybe you're right. Just make sure you don't get *your* ass kicked."

"Not happening."

Reaching back, I yank my shirt over my head, handing it to Rylee. She clutches it to her chest, her eyes briefly raking over my naked chest. I flex my pecs, just to watch her expression. I chuckle when she licks her lips and darts her eyes up to mine.

I lean down until my lips are at her ear. "Be prepared to lose Charles after the fight. I've been fucking dying for another taste of you since I walked out of your room last week." I press a kiss below her ear, then take a step back.

Her cheeks are pink and she looks a little breathless, just the way I want her. To leave her with thoughts of all the ways my tongue will run over her beautiful body.

With one more look, I tip my chin to Hammer, and he steps up beside Rylee. I spin on my heel and walk away before I decide to skip the fight and get her out of this place.

All my good thoughts die away when I step into the center of the open area and spy my opponent off to the side. He has a few inches on me, but our build is the same.

When I notice where his eyes are directed, boiling rage fills my veins. His lips form a slow smirk as he pulls his eyes away from my girl and directs them at me. He's either really fucking stupid or ballsy as fuck. I'm sure he knows of my winning status, just like I know of his. He's got no clue his winning streak is about to end.

I keep my eyes pinned on the motherfucker as Hart steps into the center of the room and begins introducing us and calling out the few rules he expects all fighters to follow.

I stalk forward the moment Hart's out of the way, ready to get this shit over and done with.

His smirk stays on his face as he meets me in the middle.

"That's a nice piece you have there," he taunts. "Looks like she's a little hot and bothered. Maybe once I take your ass out, I'll fix that problem for her."

I clamp my molars together, refusing to let him bait me. That shit may work on some fighters, but I'm smarter than that. It only adds more fuel to the fire raging inside me. I don't get sloppy when I'm angry, it ups my game.

This guy has signed his death warrant.

When he doesn't get the response he was hoping for, he takes his first swing, and I let it connect with my jaw. It fucking hurts like a bitch, but doesn't jar me too bad, and it gives him the sense of the upper hand.

I slowly turn back to face him, to see him still grinning, his white teeth shining in the light. I spit out a mouthful of blood onto the concrete and let my eyes speak of the hell he's about to go through.

When he throws his next punch, I put up an arm and block it, then follow through with an uppercut that has him staggering back and almost falling on his ass. One of the reasons I've stayed undefeated is because my punch packs a shit-ton of weight.

He regains his balance and his head swings my way. His surprised gaze meets mine, and it's my turn to smirk.

Yeah, fucker. It's not going to be as easy as you thought.

The next time he throws his arm forward, aiming for my face, I duck and deliver a hit to his kidney.

While he's hunched over, I land another punch to his jaw. He falls on his ass, then continues down until he's on his back, dazed but still conscious.

But I'm not done with him. I want his ass completely out, so I straddle him and sit on his chest, wailing on his face. Blood splatters out of his nose and mouth with each hit he takes.

By the time I'm pulled off him, his face is covered in blood and his nose looks like it's sideways.

"Enough," someone barks in my ear as I'm dragged off him. I glare down at the bastard, satisfied when he doesn't move and his eyes stay closed.

That was way too fucking easy. The fight was over within minutes. How the hell could he be undefeated? Unless they have pussies fighting over in Wilmot County.

Remembering the way he looked at Rylee, and the words he spoke to me, I sure as fuck wish it had lasted longer.

I'm handed a towel, but before I use it to wipe my face, I look to where I left Rylee. She's sandwiched between Charles and Hammer, her hand at her mouth, her eyes wide. She notices my gaze and slowly lowers her hand, a wide grin stretching across her face.

I barely hear Hart as he announces the winner over the megaphone. After, he walks over to me, says something in my ear that I don't hear, and walks away. The whole time, I've got my eyes pinned on Rylee. Her chest pumps heavily in rhythm with mine and her eyes flare with need. The blood rushing through my body heads straight to my dick.

As I stalk her way, I quickly wipe the towel over my face and chest, then toss it to the floor. People clap me on the back and congratulate me, but I don't stop to talk to them.

Once I'm in front of her, I grab the sides of her head and slam my lips against hers. Her arms lock around my neck and she jumps up, wrapping her legs around me. I palm her ass and pull her center against my hard-on.

I can't hear her moans from the loud crowd, but I feel the vibrations of them against my lips. My cock grows painfully hard.

"It's a good thing I brought my own vehicle," Charles says loudly, interrupting us.

When I pull back, Rylee lets out a throaty laugh and licks her lips.

"Let's get out of here," I grunt just loud enough for her to hear.

She nods, and I let her ass go. I still need to see Hart about my winnings, but I'll do that another day. I'm too anxious to get Rylee the hell out of here and alone.

I pull on my shirt, then fist bump Hammer and thank him for keeping a watch over Rylee. The room is still full, but it's starting to thin out a little, as we make our way out. Most people don't stick around after the fight in case the cops are called.

I force myself to take the stairs one step at a time instead of two or three as we make our way up. I'm tempted to toss her over my shoulder and sprint out of the building, but I don't want to embarrass her.

Once outside in the frigid air, I stop with Rylee at my truck.

"Thanks for coming with me tonight," she tells Charles.

"Anytime you wanna come, let me know. I'm not ashamed to admit I love watching two sexy guys beat on each other." He throws a wink my way and roams his eyes over my body.

She laughs and snuggles up closer to my side, her hand going to my lower stomach. My muscles twitch at the touch. "Well, you're going to have to find your own sexy guy. This one is mine."

Her claiming me turns me on even more.

I'm just about to tell Charles to piss off, when he takes several steps back. "I better get out of here. Your boy looks like he's ready to rip my head off." He gives a little wave and grins. "Have fun."

Before Rylee has a chance to say anything, I've yanked the door open, have both of us inside the truck, and I'm roaring down the road. I usually have Rylee sit in the middle seat, but I purposely pushed her over to the passenger side and buckled her in.

"Is everything okay?" she asks after a few seconds of silence.

I don't answer her, opting to keep my eyes on the road and my foot pressed on the gas. I can feel the anxious vibes coming off her, but I know if I stop to look at her now, I'll pull over and have her on her back before she has a chance to realize what's happening.

I find the road that leads to the outdoor theater, and turn down the dark, overgrown path.

I'm damn near panting and my heart is thumping hard in my chest by the time I stop and put my truck in park.

I grip the steering wheel and take a deep breath, trying to rein in my ramped need. All of my effort is wasted when Rylee takes off her seatbelt and slides closer to me.

Her hand touches my arm. "Zayden, what's—"

I turn to her, grab her hips, and push her down onto the bench seat. I'm leaning over her a split second later, my mouth consuming hers.

The space is cramped as fuck, but I still manage to grip one of her legs and wrap it around my waist. My hips settle between hers and it feels like goddamn heaven when my cock meets her warm center.

She grips my hair, tugging my head closer, just as anxious to taste me as I am to taste her. I rock my hips forward and hiss against her lips when the friction sends delicious pleasure through me.

"Fuck, Rylee, I want you so fucking much right now," I groan, trailing kisses down her neck.

She tilts her head to the side and releases a deep moan. "I want you, too."

Those are words I've been dying to hear… but they come at the worst of times. There's no fucking way I'll allow her to lose her virginity in my truck in a deserted drive-in theater. But I'll be damned if we can't do other stuff.

I lift up enough so I can get my hands between our bodies and start lifting her shirt. I shift my eyes to hers. "I won't take you for the first time in my truck. You deserve something special." Her breathing escalates when I expose her tits covered in a pink bra. "But I promise we're not leaving here until I've given you the release you need and what I've been thinking about giving you all night."

Her chest shudders when she takes a shaky breath. I thank my lucky stars her bra has a front clasp as I pinch the material together and it gives way. Her tits bounce free and my mouth waters. Unable to deny my need, I lean down and take one of her nipples into my mouth. I suck hard and flick the tip with my tongue.

Rylee lets out a small cry and arches her back, shoving her chest in my face. I palm her other breast and tweak her nipple between my fingers.

My cock is so hard it feels like I could hammer nails with it. I want to yank my shorts down, rip her jeans and panties away, and shove myself inside her warm body, but I hold back my need. Right now this is about Rylee.

I switch to her other breast, tugging at the tip with my teeth. Her hands snake into my hair, gripping the strands so tight my scalp burns. I wouldn't care if she yanked out every strand. I fucking love that she's so lost in her pleasure.

An irritating sound comes from my glove box, and it takes me a second to realize it's my phone. I ignore it and continue to devour Rylee's tits. An act of God couldn't pull me away from what I'm doing.

A moment later, the buzzing starts again. I grab Rylee's leg, about to hoist it higher so I can feel her against my cock better, when she tugs my head up by my hair.

"Maybe you should answer that," she pants.

The ringing has already stopped again.

"Just ignore it."

I'm lowering my head back to her breasts when the buzzing begins again. Irritated, I lift myself, yank open my glove box, and pull out my phone to shut the damn thing off. I see my dad's name flash across the screen. Even though Danielle has been put on the transplant list, she's definitely not out of the woods. She won't be until she actually gets her new lungs and they take to her body.

I sit back and bring the phone to my ear.

"Everything okay with Danielle, Dad?"

"Yeah, everything's fine. I just need you to come home. They need me at work."

I lean my head back against the window and close my eyes, releasing a frustrated breath. "When?"

"Now. I need to leave within the next thirty minutes."

Rylee sits up next to me and a moment later, her hand drops to my thigh. I lift my head and look at her. Her bra is snapped back into place and she's righted her shirt. The sun set hours ago, but the moon is in just the right spot to shine in the truck and show off the flushed look on her cheeks.

It pisses me off that I can't enjoy that look and make it more pronounced.

"Okay, I'll be there in twenty." My irritation evident.

"Sorry, son. I know you had plans tonight with Rylee."

"It's alright."

It has to be. I've got no other choice.

"See you at home."

I hang up and toss my phone on the dash before raking my fingers through my hair. It's still damp with sweat from the fight.

"I've got to get home. Dad needs to head into work."

"Okay," Rylee says quietly.

I grip her hand and yank her until she's against my chest. I lean down and kiss her, needing one more taste before I have to give her up for the night. She melts into me, making it damn hard to let her go.

Her eyes are soft when she lifts her head.

"Buckle in, baby."

"Am I allowed to sit here now?" she asks, giving me a sexy grin.

"The passenger seat is off limits to you from now on," I tell her.

She giggles and snaps her seatbelt in place. When I start my truck and begin to drive, her hand moves to my thigh.

chapter twenty-one

RYLEE

"*What are you doing tonight?*" Savannah asks moments after I lift the phone to my ear.

"Hello to you too." I laugh.

"Oh hush." I can hear the smile in her voice. "I'm calling to see if you want to come hang at my house tonight. My parents have been asking about you. I know they'd love to see you. And truthfully, I need some best friend time."

"I thought maybe you were looking for a new best friend after how Oliver treated you the last time you came here," I tease. "It's been almost two weeks since I've heard from you."

"One, screw Oliver. You know I don't scare off that easily. And two, I'm sorry it's been so long since I've called. I've been swamped with student council and cheer, on top of the mountain of schoolwork I'm trying to keep up with. Not to mention I'm in charge of planning the spring formal."

"It's almost time for the spring formal, already?" I think out loud.

"It's February," Savannah reminds me. "The dance is the last weekend in March."

"God, how is it February already?"

"I know, right? In just four months' time, we will be high school graduates. Can you believe it? Time is flying."

"I'm gonna miss not being there with you girls. I can't believe I have to miss the last Spring Formal at Bristol. It feels wrong."

"It feels wrong for me, too. Then again, most things feel strange without you here." She sighs. "But, I do have some happy news to report. You'll never guess who asked me to be his date?"

"Wait, you already have a date to the dance?"

"Yep. Bryan Avers asked me yesterday after Bio. I guess he was afraid I would agree to go with someone else, so he wanted to ask me before anyone else could."

"You're going to the dance with Bryan Avers?" I can't hide the shock in my tone. "I thought you didn't like him."

"I didn't. But then we were forced to work together as lab partners and, I don't know, he's kind of grown on me."

"Wow." I shake my head, ignoring the small pang of sadness in my chest. I hate feeling like I'm missing out on everything. Like my old life evaporated and everyone else's went on like I was never there to begin with. And while I know that's not true, it still feels that way sometimes.

"So tonight? Think you can make it? Maybe we can do some online dress shopping."

I'm just about to answer her when my bedroom door swings open. My eyes dart to the doorway, my heart kicking up speed when I see Zayden prop a shoulder against the doorframe and hit me with a sexy smirk.

"Actually, I don't think I can tonight. I, like you, have a ton of schoolwork right now," I say a little too quickly.

I actually do have quite a lot of homework to get done before Monday, but clearly that's not why I'm declining her invite.

"On a Friday night? Can't you wait and do it on Sunday like most people do?"

"I can't put it off until Sunday. At this rate I'll be lucky if it doesn't take me all weekend. Can I take a raincheck?"

"Fine," she groans. "You officially suck."

"Oh, hush." I chuckle. "Listen, I gotta go. Can I call you later?"

"Yeah, yeah. Love you, Ry."

"Love you, too." I hang up the phone, not able to hide the smile that creeps across my face when my eyes swing back to Zayden.

"Love you, too?" He quirks his head to the side. "Is there something you need to tell me?" I can tell he's teasing, but something in his expression still darkens slightly.

"Well, considering I was talking to Savannah, no, I don't think I do," I fire back at him, pulling my bottom lip between my teeth as I watch him step into my room and close the door behind him.

I don't miss the little flick of his wrist as he locks the knob.

"Savannah, huh?" He stalks toward me.

"She wanted me to come over tonight."

"And you told her no?" He stops at the foot of my bed.

"Pretty sure you heard me do just that. How'd you get in here, anyway?" Last time I checked no one else was home.

"I used my key." He kicks off his shoes, then reaches for the hem of his t-shirt. My stomach swirls nervously as I watch him pull it over his head—revealing his perfectly toned torso.

"You have a key?" I swallow hard.

He nods slowly. "Have since I was like ten."

"And you thought it was okay to walk in like you live here? What if my mom had been home?"

"I knew she wasn't. No one's car is here but yours," he tells me, dropping his shirt on the floor before his hand goes to the waistband of his jeans.

I hold my breath as I watch him pop open the button before slowly sliding down the zipper.

"Um, why are you getting naked?" I ask, a nervous shake in my voice.

"I think the better question is, why aren't you?" He lifts an eyebrow in question. "Considering the last two times we've been alone together, we've been interrupted, I thought maybe we could have a do-over?" He grins, watching my expression as he pushes his jeans over his hips and shoves them to the floor.

My mouth goes dry and every inch of my body tenses as my eyes trail the length of Zayden, standing in front of me wearing only a pair of tight, black boxer briefs.

"A do-over," I repeat slowly, my gaze making its way back up to Zayden's face.

"You're still wearing clothes," he points out, gesturing to my oversized hoodie and pajama shorts.

"So it would seem that I am." I look down at myself and then back up to him. "Perhaps you should do something about that," I say, honestly a bit surprised by my own brazenness.

His nostrils flare as his gaze darkens.

"Perhaps I should." A wicked grin plays on his lips as he steps around the side of the bed and reaches for me. Pulling me to the edge of the bed in one quick tug, he has my sweatshirt over my head before I can even think to react.

When his eyes shoot to my chest, I quickly remember that I don't have a bra on, but before I can attempt to cover myself, Zayden tosses my sweatshirt to the floor and shoves me backward. He climbs on top of me, both of our legs hanging over the edge of the bed as he pins my arms above my head.

"What did I tell you about hiding from me?" He tisks, running his nose between my breasts.

"Zayden," I practically moan his name, jerking when his warm tongue slides over one of my nipples.

"I love your body." He moves to the other nipple, pulling it into his mouth on a hard suck. "I love how good you taste." He trails kisses upward—across my collarbone to the soft spot at the base of my neck. "I love how you smell." He inhales deeply and goosebumps erupt across my skin. "You're all I can think about." He presses a kiss to my jaw. "I go to bed thinking about you." His lips graze mine. "I wake up thinking about you." He gives me a soft, closed mouth kiss. "You have completely fucking consumed me, Rylee Harper."

"Zayden." I arch into him when he grinds his erection into my center.

"Do you have any fucking idea how badly I want you?" He slides his tongue along the seam of my lips. "How badly I want to feel you tight around me?" He dips his tongue into my mouth, and I'm instantly lost to the sensation.

When I'm with Zayden, it's like the rest of the world falls away. I suddenly no longer care about anything or anyone else—only him. I want to be with him.

"I want that, too," I admit, my voice thick with desire.

He pulls back slightly and stares down at me for a long moment.

"I would never ask you to do something you're not ready to do. You know that, right?" His voice is soft, almost hesitant, and is a complete contradiction to everything I know about this man.

"I know." I slide my hands into his hair, fisting the smooth strands between my fingers. "But I want to," I admit truthfully. "I want this. I want you. I'm ready."

"Are you sure?" He doesn't seem convinced.

"I am." I pull him back to me, kissing him slow and deep as I press upward, rubbing my center against his erection.

If there's one thing I've learned about Zayden over the last few weeks, it's that he's not one to ease into anything. He's aggressive and takes what he wants without apology. Because of this, I'm surprised he doesn't rip the rest of my clothes off and take me right here and now. But that's not what he does.

Instead, he takes his time.

He studies me.

His hands roam my body lazily, like we have all the time in the world.

And he kisses me… *everywhere.*

He makes me feel cherished and cared for. He makes me feel special. So much so that by the time he's settled between my thighs with his condom covered erection nudging at my entrance, I don't feel an ounce of fear. Nervous, most definitely. So nervous that my heart pounds so hard against my chest, I'm fairly certain it's going to beat right through my ribcage. But there's no fear.

I feel safe with Zayden in a way I've never felt with any other person in my life. The way he looks at me, is like he would kill anyone who dared hurt me. And in some weird way I know the feeling, because I feel just as protective of him. Not that a guy like Zayden Michaels would ever need me to protect him, but even still, I want to. I want to make him feel the way he makes me feel. I want to take every fear and silence it. I want to kiss every wound and heal it. I want to guard him as if he were the most precious and rare gem in the world, because truthfully, he just might be.

I suck in a sharp breath, my body tensing as Zayden slowly eases inside of me. His eyes stay fixed on my face, gauging my reaction as he enters me. I stretch and pull around him, the pressure so intense that tears prick the backs of my eyes—but no part of me wants him to stop.

Once he's planted completely inside of me, Zayden stills, brushing my hair away from my sweat dampened forehead.

"I'm okay," I reassure him. "Keep going."

His lips brush mine as he slowly begins to move. At first, I feel like I might rip apart from the inside, but before long my body starts to adjust and my natural instincts take over. Eventually, I start to move with him. Pressing up to meet him, thrust for thrust as we push each other higher and higher.

The build starts slow—like a little voice that keeps getting louder and louder until it can't possibly be ignored a second longer. My body shakes under the intensity—every cell feeling the effects of Zayden's movements.

And while I recognize the familiar swirl of pleasure as it builds in my core, there's something so different about it. It's like my body is being pulled in a million different directions and my mind can't seem to keep up with the sensation.

The pleasure is blinding. The intensity is overwhelming. And when Zayden groans against my lips—a deep, gritty noise that tells me he feels it too—everything peaks, and I go tumbling over the edge seconds later, Zayden falling right along with me.

Time seems to slow down around me. I experience an array of emotions that all hit me like rapid fire—one after the other until I feel like I can't catch my breath. And I have no idea if it's from the physical, the emotional, or a combination of the two.

All I know is that when Zayden presses up on his elbow and looks down at me, I feel like I'm seconds away from bursting into tears. Not sad tears, though. Actually, what I'm feeling is the furthest thing from sad I think a person can feel.

I'm elated. I'm overjoyed.

I think I'm in love....

"i wish i could stay." Zayden presses a kiss to the top of my head as he hugs me tightly.

The last two hours have been indescribable, and while I know Zayden has to leave, I'm not ready to let him go just yet.

"Me, too," I whine, my arms wrapped around his middle.

"Look at me." His hand slides under my chin seconds before he lifts my face upward. "Tonight was probably the best night of my fucking life." He smiles, leaning down to kiss my lips. "And I can't wait to do it again." He kisses me again. "And again." Another kiss. "And again." He smiles when I laugh against his mouth.

If you had told me a month ago that this version of Zayden existed, I never would have believed you. Don't get me wrong, he's still unapologetically Zayden—domineering, abrasive, an asshole. But he's also so much more than that.

He's sweet and funny. Caring and compassionate. And when he looks at me the way he's looking at me right now, I forget why everyone is so damn afraid of him.

"Can I see you tomorrow after I get off work?" he asks, taking a step backward so that he's got one foot still on the porch and the other on the top step.

"Call me when you get off." I nod, placing both of my hands on the sides of his face as I lay one more lingering kiss to his lips.

Seconds later, he's jogging across the front lawn. The faint interior light of his truck comes on as he pulls open the door and climbs inside. He fires up the engine and moments later, I watch his taillights disappear down the street.

Not able to contain the smile that I'm pretty certain is now permanently attached to my face, I make my way back inside and head for the kitchen. I haven't eaten anything since lunch at school earlier today, and I am downright famished.

The kitchen is dark when I enter. I flip on a light, screaming when I catch sight of someone sitting at the table.

"Oliver! What the hell?" I flatten my palm to my chest. "You scared the hell out of me. Why are you sitting here in the dark?"

I take in his disheveled appearance. His wrinkled t-shirt. His messy hair. The dark circles under his eyes. I also don't miss the glass in his hand that's about half full of an amber liquid.

I can't help but wonder what's going on with him. He seems even more out of sorts than usual.

I try to remember if he looked this bad at school today, but truthfully, I can't remember seeing him. Was he even at school?

"So he actually pulled it off." His head bobs as he nods, an almost impressed look on his face.

"Huh?"

"You know, the sad thing is I was actually rooting for you." He leans back further into the chair—his gaze locked on me as he swirls the liquid in his glass. "I didn't think you'd go down quite so easy."

"What are you talking about, Oliver?" My confusion quickly morphs into irritation.

"After all the shit we've pulled—Zayden and I—did you really think this was anything other than a game?" He empties his glass in one long pull before slamming it down on the table as he pushes to a stand. "You didn't really believe that one minute he hated you and then suddenly," he snaps his fingers, "Z has a thing for you?"

"I don't…," I start, but Oliver doesn't let me finish.

"He said he could do it. But I gotta say, I didn't think he could. Especially not this fast. I knew you were a virgin, after all. I figured it would take him at least a couple months to get into your pants, not a couple weeks. I guess what they say *is* true. Like mother, like daughter."

"Am I supposed to know what the hell you're talking about?" My pulse is thrumming rapidly against the side of my neck.

"I guess not." He snorts. "You would think after everything you'd be a little more careful. But alas, you let Z right on in. You let him fuck you for sport and clearly you had no idea that he's been playing you this entire time."

"Seriously?" Anger surges through me. "You expect me to believe that?"

"You don't believe it?" He snickers. "How else do you think I would know that you were a virgin? Or that you two had sex for the first time tonight?"

"Well, considering you have zero boundaries or respect for other peoples' privacy, I think there's a few ways you could have known that information," I fire back, refusing to let him ruin this night for me.

And even though I'm not willing to entertain what he's saying, a part of me has always wondered why Zayden went from hating me to liking me, seemingly overnight.

"And what about this?" Oliver pulls his phone from his pocket and unlocks it, turning the screen to face me. On it is a single text message from Zayden.

I told you I could do it. Easiest bet I've ever won.

"That could mean anything." My voice goes up an octave as doubt starts to creep in.

"Look at the time stamp."

I lean in, looking closer.

"The message came through right as you were walking into the house," he points out. "He didn't even make it to the end of our street before letting me know of his conquest."

"No." The single word falls from my lips as disbelief and uncertainty starts to take hold.

"Yes." Oliver smiles. "I bet my best friend that he couldn't score your V card. He bet that he could. Looks like I lost. The sad thing is, you really thought this was real, didn't you? You thought he actually cared about you." He lets out a throaty laugh and it takes everything in me not to rear back and punch him in his smug face.

"He wouldn't…."

"He wouldn't do this to you?" He cuts me off. "Sorry to tell you, sis, but he already did." His phone vibrates in his hand. "Oh, and there he is again." His eyes scan the phone, his smile widening.

"What? What is he saying?" I rip the phone out of Oliver's hand, a thick knot lodging itself in my throat.

The floor sways beneath me as I read the text Zayden just sent Oliver.

It was easier than I thought. She ate up every fucking word I said. Too bad she wasn't a better lay.

Tears prick the backs of my eyes as my stomach turns over on itself.

He couldn't. He wouldn't.

Would he?

"I told you." Oliver snags his phone out of my hand, locking the screen before shoving it back into his pocket.

"Why?" I croak out. "Why would he do that? Why would he pretend?" I'm still clinging to the possibility that Oliver is lying, but my grip is slipping with every second that passes.

"Because that's who he is. Zayden is out for only one person. Himself. It's all about what he stands to gain. And in this case, he got laid, helped his best friend out, and earned himself an easy thousand bucks. And thanks to your eagerness to jump on his dick, it only took him a couple weeks to accomplish it all."

"I don't believe you." My voice shakes as I fight the tears threatening to spill.

"No? Why don't you call him then? See what he has to say?"

"Fine. I will." I pull my phone out of the front pocket of my hoodie and quickly pull up Zayden's number. It only rings once before it goes to voicemail.

My heart drops.

Hitting his number again, the same thing happens. One ring and then voicemail.

"Not answering your calls I see?" Oliver chuckles. "Wonder why that is. Oh wait." He taps the side of his head. "I know why. Because he got what he was after and now he's done with you. Poor, Rylee." He pouts out his bottom lip dramatically.

I want to lash out. I want to scream. I want to lunge at Oliver and punch him over and over until he feels even an ounce of the pain that's tearing through me right now—like a wild animal trying to claw its way from the inside out.

I want to tell him how much I hate him. How much I hate Zayden. How much I wish I had never met either of them. But the words get clogged somewhere in my throat and never make their way to the surface.

Without even realizing what I'm doing, I turn, snagging my car keys off the counter as I head for the front door. I throw it open, leaving it flapping in the wind as I take the front porch steps two at a time.

I don't care that it's thirty degrees outside and that I'm in shorts with no shoes. I don't care that I have no idea where I'm going or what I'm doing. All I know is that I have to get away from here. I have to get away from this house, from Oliver, from Zayden, from everything.

And I have to do it right now.

chapter twenty-two

ZAYDEN

"i'm headed out, benny!" I call to the boss man, pulling my keys from my pocket as I head out of the bay. "I'll see you Monday."

"Later," he yells without removing his head from the Jeep he's working on.

Benny always keeps the shop open until eight on Friday and Saturdays for people who work and need to drop off their cars for the weekend.

I reach toward my back pocket when I remember I don't have my phone with me. I was supposed to call Rylee when I got off work, but it looks like I'll be stopping by her house instead since I must have left my phone there last night when I left. You'll not hear a lick of complaints from me though.

Memories of last night filter through my head, and I'm forced to adjust my hardening dick as I climb into my truck. I've had numerous girls since the first time

I had sex at fourteen, but not a single one of them felt as good as Rylee did last night. She, as girly as it sounds, rocked my fucking world.

I hated leaving her after, but my dad needed me at home to watch Danielle. Besides, I have many, *many* plans of repeats. Just as I feared, once I had Rylee, and knew what she felt like from the inside, it's going to be a very long time before I've gotten my fill. *If* I ever get my fill.

I pull up to the curb in front of her house a few minutes later. Disappointment hits when I don't see her car in the driveway. Last I heard, we were supposed to see each other when I got off work. Of course, she had no way of getting in touch with me if something came up.

There's a black Beemer in the driveway, and I know it's not Oliver's or his dad's, so it must be Rylee's mom's. I haven't met her mother yet, but it looks like I'm going to now.

I rap my knuckles against the door and wait for it to open. The woman before me is an exact replica of Rylee. While her looks are more mature, she doesn't look old enough to be Rylee's mom, maybe an older sister.

"Mrs. Conley?" I ask, just to be on the safe side.

"Yes." She smiles and holds out her hand. "But please call me Evelyn. And you're Zayden, right?"

I shake her hand. "Yes, ma'am."

"Well, it's about time I met you. I've heard so much about you from Paul, but it always seems like our schedules never mesh for us to meet."

Paul and Rylee's mom have been married for a little over two months. Normally, I'm at Oliver's house more, but since winter break ended, I haven't been over as much, or when I have, neither Paul nor Evelyn have been around.

"It's nice to meet you." I shove my hands in my pockets and rock back on my heels. "I was over last night, and I think I left my phone and jacket here. You mind if I come in and look?"

"Not at all. Come on in."

She steps back from the door and gestures with her hand for me to enter. I immediately spot my jacket lying over a chair by the stairs. After I snatch it up, I turn to face Evelyn.

She has her arms crossed over her chest, a curious glint in her eyes. "I didn't realize Oliver was home last night. He told Paul he was out with some friends."

I have no idea if Rylee's told her mother about us, but there's no way of getting out of telling her the truth. I already told her I was here last night; my jacket proved it.

"I wasn't here with Oliver," I say, holding her eyes.

It only takes a moment for her to register what my words mean. "Oh." She says the word slowly, her mouth forming a circle. "Rylee. You were here with Rylee." She frowns. "I didn't realize you two were friends."

"More than friends, actually."

She frowns, lacing her fingers together in front of her. "Oh, well, I haven't seen much of her lately. I'm sure that's why she hasn't told me."

I don't comment on that. Rylee hasn't said much about her mom, but I get the sense things are a little tense between the two since they made the move to Paul's house.

"Do you happen to know where Rylee is? We were supposed to meet after I got off work."

"No, I haven't spoken to her since I got home. She was rushing out the door when I was coming downstairs after changing my clothes. She was on the phone with one of her friends. Someone named Pierce, I think. She mentioned something about a party."

There's only one party going on tonight that I know of. Why the hell would Rylee want to go to Regina's party? She has to know she's part of Tiffany's bitchy little squad. Rylee's brave, strong, and tenacious, but I don't see her purposely putting herself in Tiffany's crosshairs. Not to mention, we were supposed to meet up. She knew I got off at seven, so why the hell did she leave?

I pull out my phone, turn my screen on, and see several missed calls from Rylee that came in last night, right after I left. I also have a couple of missed calls from Oliver from thirty minutes ago.

"Do you know where Oliver is?" I ask Evelyn.

She shakes her head, her dark hair, so much like Rylee's, swaying over her shoulders. "I'm sorry, I don't. He doesn't keep us in the loop much on where he's going."

I jerk my chin up in a nod, my jaw clenching with sudden irritation. I need to get out of here and find Rylee before something happens. And if she's at Regina's house, I have no doubt Tiffany is, too; therefore, shit will definitely happen. Tiffany may have been quiet recently, but I know damn good and well she's not over her snit with Rylee.

I thank Evelyn for letting me in to grab my phone before leaving. As I walk to my truck, I pull Rylee's name up and try to call her. It rings until her voicemail picks up. I smash the End Call button and try again. Getting the same results, I toss my phone on the dash, start my truck, and haul ass out of the neighborhood.

Oliver will have to wait until later for me to call him back. My only thought is of getting to Rylee.

A bad feeling forms in the pit of my stomach. Something isn't right. Rylee wouldn't up and leave to go to a party when we were supposed to meet up. And she certainly wouldn't do it without calling me first. The only missed calls I have from her are the ones from last night. None today and no text messages.

I stop behind a line of cars a couple houses down from Regina's. When I get out of my truck, I can already hear the thump of loud music. This neighborhood is one of the richer ones, so you'd think the neighbors would call the cops with a noise complaint. But then again, I'm sure most know each other and wouldn't dare call the cops for fear of insulting the other. Appearances and reputations are everything to these people.

Although it's still kind of early, people already litter the yard; some are so drunk they sway and fall over, some make out in the shadows, while some simply stand around and talk to others. When I walk in the house, I can barely hear myself think because the music is so fucking loud. And the amount of people is ridiculous. You can't move without bumping into someone.

I head for the kitchen first. It's ironic because the kitchen is usually where the booze is kept, but it's normally the least crowded part of the house during these things.

I keep my eyes peeled for Rylee, but instead of finding her, I spot Tiffany leaning against the wall down one of the hallways right outside the kitchen. Her skirt is so short, that I have no doubt if it wasn't so dark, I'd be able to see her panties. Her shirt isn't much better with one side hanging off her shoulder so low, the tops of her breasts are on full display. Lifting my gaze to hers, she's wearing a smile I really don't fucking like. It's the type that says she knows something I don't, and whatever it is, it's something she's enjoying immensely.

That bad feeling I had in my truck triples in strength.

When I don't find Rylee in the kitchen, I head out to the backyard. While the party is very much going on out here as well, it's not nearly as loud. Most people are circled around several fancy fire pits that line the end of the stone patio.

Again, there's no Rylee.

Maybe there was another party she went to. Maybe it was one with her friends from her old school. It still doesn't explain why she didn't shoot me a text telling me she was going.

The thought occurs to me that she could be upstairs, but just as quickly, I dismiss it. Upstairs is usually reserved for fucking.

I turn to go back inside to look around again, thinking I should call Charles to see if he knows where she is, but I'm waylaid by Tiffany right outside the door. She stares up at me with seductive eyes. Or eyes she *thinks* are seductive. To me, they're just a plain shit brown. Not like the warm caramel that Rylee's are.

"I didn't expect to see you here, Z. You haven't been to any parties lately," she purrs.

"I'm looking for Rylee," I state. "Have you seen her?"

Instead of answering, she dances her fingers up my abs. Before she makes it past my belly button, I grab her wrist, pull her hand off me, and shove it away.

"Tiffany," I warn, my voice hard and unforgiving. "Have you seen Rylee?"

"Maybe." She tilts her head to the side and juts out her tits, as if the bitch thinks that would entice me.

"No more fucking games, Tiffany," I growl impatiently. "Where is she?"

"Why are you so hard up on her? What does she have that I don't?"

"I don't have enough time to go through all the things she has that you don't. The list is fucking endless. Now, tell me where the hell she is."

She tosses me a scathing look, but it doesn't last long as a slow smile creeps across her face. I ball my hands into fists to keep from wrapping them around her throat. I don't like her look. It holds secrets.

"She's upstairs," she says, her grin widening.

I take a threatening step toward her. "If you've done something to her, Tiffany, I swear to Christ I'll make your life fucking hell."

"Oh, *I* haven't done anything to her." Her tone a saccharine sweet.

I leave her in the backyard, afraid if I stay in her presence much longer I may do something I'll regret. Heading inside, I shove people out of the way and go for the stairs leading to the second floor. Charles hits the bottom step right as I do. He looks surprised to see me. I'm damn surprised to see him, too. He and Rylee are usually stuck together like glue when they're out together.

"Why aren't you with Rylee?" I demand.

His brows jump up then narrow, his expression changing from surprise to anger.

What the fuck?

"I was, but then I lost her. I'm looking for her now. Question is," he leans closer, "why are you here looking for her? Haven't you done enough?"

"What the hell does that mean?" I grit my teeth. "You know what? I don't have time for this. We need to find her."

Without waiting for a response, I take the stairs two at a time and stalk toward the first door I see. I've been to this house plenty of times for parties, so I know there are six bedrooms up here.

The first one has a couple going at it on the bed, the guy's white ass in the air as he pumps away, while another couple is on the loveseat in the corner. I don't bother to close the door before I move onto the next room. This one is surprisingly empty. I check two more rooms and find them both occupied, but no Rylee.

I move to the fifth door and spy Charles going for the last one. The door is cracked open a couple of inches. I push it open and it taps against the wall. The room is dark, the only light coming from a bedside lamp.

"Leave. This room is taken," the guy grunts from the bed as his hips rock back and forth against the girl underneath him. He's still dressed, but I'm sure that'll change within the next few minutes. The girl's face and body are hidden, the only thing showing is one of her bare legs the guy has propped around his waist.

I'm about to leave when the glint of metal catches my eye. Taking a couple of steps closer, I zero in on the silver bracelet wrapped around the girl's ankle. Pain hits me square in the chest, followed closely by red-hot anger. Just a few days ago, I fiddled with that bracelet when Rylee had her feet propped up in my lap.

"Shit, Rylee," Charles mutters behind me.

I don't know if the guy heard or sensed we hadn't left the room, but he turns his head. I briefly register that I know him before my eyes lock on Rylee's face. Her head is tilted to the side, her hands resting on the mattress on either side of her face, and her eyes are hooded from the alcohol she must have consumed. Her gaze briefly glances over me before she twists her head to look up at the ceiling.

Betrayal and blinding rage fill my system, making my body quake. Before I know what I'm doing, I'm across the room and have the guy's throat in my hands as I haul him off Rylee.

"Shit, Zayden, I didn't—" Bryant manages to wheeze out before I tighten my grip. His eyes bulge and his hands claw at my fingers.

I release his neck, but don't give him time to recover before my fist lands on his face. He falls to the floor, and I fall with him. Straddling his chest, I lock his arms at his sides and use one hand to hold him down by his chest. I rear back my other and clock him across the nose. There's a loud crunch, followed by a gush of blood.

"Zayden!" someone barks, but I'm too far into my rage to pay attention. My only concern is destroying this motherfucker. He touched what is mine, even if the bitch was lying there with her legs spread, letting him have his way with her.

I clock him in the jaw and his head slams to the side, blood spraying from his mouth all over the white carpet. I rear back to land another punch, when my arm is grabbed, and I'm suddenly pulled off of him. Oliver stands in front of me, blocking me from getting back at Bryant.

"Get the fuck out of my way," I snarl and take a step to my right. Oliver follows.

"Calm the hell down," he growls. "You've made your point. The guy has had enough."

I grind my molars. "He wasn't about to fuck your girl. Until that happens, you don't get to say when he's had enough."

"Unless you want him dead, then *yes*, he's had e-fucking-nough."

I look at the prone body on the floor. Seeing the bloody mess of Bryant sobers me enough to clear my head of the murderous rage. I'm not nearly done with him, but he's not worth a prison sentence.

"You calm?" he asks.

No, I'm not fucking calm. I just caught my girlfriend in the mist of cheating on me. What the fuck is there to be calm about?

I nod anyway.

I look back at Rylee, my anger mounting again, and find Charles sitting on the bed beside her. They're both facing away from me. She's leaning against his side, his arm wrapped around her shoulders. Oliver walks over to them and sits on the other side of the bed, his face a mask of concern. The way they're treating her, especially Oliver, the guy who can't stand the sight of her, pisses me off. They're acting like she's the one who was wronged.

"Fuck this shit," I mutter and stalk to the door.

"Zayden, wait!" Oliver calls from behind me, but I keep going.

Several people are outside the room looking in. I bare my teeth and shoot them all glares as I pass by. Wisely, they scurry their little asses out of my way. No one intercepts me as I leave the house, but I'm sure the look on my face warns them not to. I climb in my truck and roar away from the curb.

Fucking Rylee. She was the very last person I thought would do something like this. The girl practically had me wrapped around her deceiving little finger.

Is this her way of paying me back for my part in Oliver's pranks? If so, I have to hand it to her, she's a damn good actress, and I was the fucking fool who fell for her tricks.

I punch the steering wheel, then curse and pull my truck back on the road when it swerves.

The last place I want to be is at home, so I text dad to tell him I'll be gone for a few days and he'll need to ask the neighbor to watch Danielle while he's at work.

My head pounds an unbearable beat, my skin feels hot, and my hands swell and ache from using them against Bryant's face.

I should stop and calm down, instead I hit the gas and head east.

chapter twenty-three

RYLEE

i pry one eye open and then the other, my head thudding so hard it feels like there's something inside it, pounding against my skull like it's trying to escape. Rolling to the side, bright light hits my face from the open blinds, and I quickly look away.

Groaning, I roll to the other side, my stomach feeling like I swallowed a bucket of nails. *What the hell happened last night?* I don't remember drinking anything beyond the two beers I had shortly after I arrived at the party. Truthfully, I don't remember much of anything after that.

I attempt to sit up, but only make it a few inches before I decide against it. Resting my head against the pillow, I look up at the ceiling, willing my eyes to adjust to the light.

Eventually they do, but my vision still seems a little blurry.

Did I drink more than I realized?

Did I get so drunk that I can't even remember how I got home?

Is this what a hangover feels like?

Question after question pops into my head, but I can't definitively answer a single one.

Certainly if I had so much to drink that I blacked out, I would at least remember drinking more than two beers, wouldn't I? Then again, my experience with alcohol is pretty limited, so how would I really know.

A light knock sounds against my bedroom door, and I groan again. The last person I need to see right now is my mother.

I force myself into an upright position, propping my back against the headboard of my bed, trying to tame my hair as I do my best to sound as normal as possible.

"Yeah?" I finally answer, the words dragging across my throat like sandpaper.

The door tentatively swings open and Oliver appears in the doorway. He has a glass of juice in one hand and a plate with a muffin on it in the other.

What the hell?

"Can I come in?" he asks, holding up what appears to be his attempt at a peace offering. Given everything, I hate to tell him it's *way* too little, *way* too late.

"I'm really not feeling well, Oliver," I admit, too weak and out if it to attempt to give him the attitude I normally would.

"I figured as much. That's why I brought you these." He enters my room anyway, kicking the door closed behind him before making his way to the side of my bed. He sets the muffin on my bedside table before turning to face me. "I was wondering when you'd wake up. After last night, I was worried about you."

"I'm sorry, but did I miss something? Since when do you worry about me? Last time I checked, you hate me." I quirk a brow. Despite my irritation and confusion, I take the glass of juice when he extends it to me.

Lifting it to my lips, I drink half the contents in one long gulp. The cold liquid feels incredible on my dry throat.

"I don't hate you," he starts, his voice uncharacteristically soft.

"Yeah, okay." I snort, setting the glass on my nightstand next to the muffin.

"I need to talk to you about what happened last night." He ignores my comment as he turns and grabs the accent chair that sits in the corner of my room. He pulls it over next to the bed before taking a seat.

"What do you mean? What happened last night?"

The confusion on my face must answer at least one question that he has, because he nods like he understands.

"That's what I thought."

"What's what you thought? What the hell is going on, Oliver?"

"Can you tell me what you remember from the party?" He leans back, crossing one leg over the other.

"Not much, truthfully," I admit. "I remember getting there. I remember being with Pierce. I remember having a couple beers. I remember at one point I left to go to the bathroom. Everything gets a little fuzzy after that."

"Fuzzy how?"

"Fuzzy as in I have no idea what happened. I left to go to the bathroom and then woke up here." I gesture around the room. "But I'm guessing by the way you're looking at me, you're not surprised by this information. What's going on, Oliver?"

As much as I can't stand my stepbrother, right now he seems to be the only one who may have the answers to the questions I woke up asking myself.

"This isn't going to be easy to hear." He gives me an apologetic look.

"Just say it," I insist when he pauses way too long for my liking.

"We think you were drugged."

My stomach knots so tightly I have to lean forward in an attempt to quell the sudden uneasiness I feel.

"You mean *you* drugged me," I accuse.

"It wasn't me." He holds his hands up in front of himself. "But I understand why you would think that. After everything I've done, trust me, I get it. But I promise you, I had nothing to do with it."

"Then who?" My voice shakes.

"I can't prove it, but I'm ninety-nine percent sure it was Tiffany."

"Tiffany?" I draw back. "I wasn't anywhere near Tiffany last night."

"That doesn't mean anything and you know it. She's been out for you since the start. And while I will admit it was my fault in the beginning, she's gone rogue, no doubt fueled by her jealousy over you and Z."

"She's jealous, so she drugged me?" I repeat, hoping it will sound less crazy than it does in my head. Unfortunately, that's not the case.

"Tiffany is… well, let's just say she doesn't like to lose."

"What are we, living in some kind of television drama? People actually drug people like this?"

I can't wrap my head around it. I knew Parkview was different than Bristol, but this is insanity. It's like living in two completely different worlds.

"I wish I could say that was the worst part." He cringes slightly and my stomach completely bottoms out. A nervous jittery feeling starts at the base of my spine and quickly spreads through my entire body. "Z showed up looking for you."

"Why?" I blurt, having no idea why he would come looking for me after everything he's done.

"Maybe I should rewind for a second so you can fully grasp the magnitude of what I'm about to tell you." He sucks in a deep breath and slowly blows it out, nervously knotting his hands in front of himself.

I've never seen this side of Oliver. Right now, sitting in front of me, his posture tight, his expression uncertain, he seems almost… *human*.

"Zayden didn't send those text messages. Julia did."

"Wait, what?"

"The text messages about him playing you, the ones I showed you Friday night, those weren't from Z. He was never playing you and he had no idea that I had convinced you that he was. When I came home and heard you two upstairs together, I don't know, I guess I just lost it. Zayden has been my best friend forever. I already lost my mom because of yours, and the thought that I was losing him because of you. I don't know, I just snapped. When I heard Z's phone ringing in the hallway, I took it out of his jacket and that's when the idea hit me. I gave his phone to Julia and told her what to say when the moment arrived. She was hiding in the pantry, listening to us the entire time we were talking."

"He wasn't playing me?" I say slowly, almost fearful to believe it. And while what Oliver did is despicable, I'm so relieved to learn that this wasn't just some game that a part of me doesn't even care. "Why are you telling me this now?" I ask after a long moment of silence has stretched between us.

"Because I realized last night how much Zayden cares about you. I had convinced myself that you were just another conquest for him, but seeing him last night, seeing how hurt he was, I knew it was real for him. And I knew right then and there that I'd made a horrible mistake. I did it because I knew it would hurt you. But I never knew that in turn it would be hurting the one person who has stood beside me through everything."

"Wait, what do you mean how hurt he was? What happened last night, Oliver?"

"Someone drugged you. That much I'm sure of. My money is on Tiffany. What Bryant's involvement in it was, I'm not sure. Maybe he was in on it, maybe he was just the unlucky son of a bitch that got caught in the crossfire, either way—he's the one who paid the price." He uncrosses his leg and shifts forward. "I'm not sure how Z knew you were at the party, because he didn't have his phone, but when I saw him head upstairs, I knew something was up. I followed him, got into the room just in time to pull him off Bryant before he killed the bastard."

"I'm not following. Who is Bryant and what does he have to do with any of this?"

"Bryant is a friend of mine, and a friend of Tiffany's. He's also the guy Zayden caught you with last night."

"Wait." I can feel the juice I drank turning in my stomach and for a moment, I'm quite certain it's about to come back up. "What do you mean *caught me with*?"

"Z found you in bed with Bryant. I don't know the specifics, but he was on top of you and things appeared to be escalating quickly."

"Oh my God." My hand goes to my mouth.

"You were still dressed, so nothing had happened, yet. But there's no doubt it would have had Z not gotten there when he did."

"I didn't know." Tears sting the backs of my eyes.

"I know that. But Z didn't. He thought you were cheating on him. After I pulled him off of Bryant, he didn't stick around long enough to find out otherwise."

"Where is he now?" I throw the covers off of me and swing my legs over the side of the bed. "I have to see him. I have to explain what happened."

"He's gone." Oliver leans forward, resting his elbows on his legs. "He took off last night, told his dad he'd be gone a few days. No one has heard from him or been able to get a hold of him since." He blows out a hard breath.

"This isn't happening." I drop my face into my hands for a brief moment, not able to fully digest everything Oliver just said.

"After I got my first real look at you, I knew someone had given you something. Charles helped me get you out of there. You were completely passed out by the time we got home. I had to carry you upstairs." He sits upright, reaching around to squeeze the back of his neck.

"Why?" My question seems to catch Oliver off guard.

"Why?"

"Why bring me home? Why even try to help me? Why not just leave me there?"

"Listen, I know what I've done is horrible but I'm not a monster."

"Yes, you are." I point my finger at his face. "You did this. All of this." I gesture to nothing in particular. "If it wasn't for you making me believe that Zayden had slept with me for sport, I never would have been at that party. I never would have been drugged. And Zayden wouldn't be off God knows where doing God knows what, believing that I willingly went into the arms of another guy less than twenty-four hours after we slept together for the first time!" My temper flares in my voice.

"It's not like I knew this would happen," he argues.

"It doesn't matter if you knew it would or wouldn't. This is what happens when you play games. When you lie. When you turn people's lives upside down for your own sick amusement. This. This is on you," I tell him, pushing out of bed. I sway slightly when my feet hit the floor but I don't let that deter me. Straightening my spine, I look down and see that I'm still wearing the same outfit I wore to the party last night.

"I get why you're angry. You have every right to be," he starts, his words cutting off when I spin toward him.

"Do not tell me what I have the right to feel! Don't say another fucking word to me!" I scream, my hands shaking so badly I can barely keep them from flailing all around.

"Rylee…." He stands.

Before he can say anything else, my hands connect with his chest, shoving him backward. He stumbles against the chair, barely able to keep himself upright.

"You are easily the worst person I have ever met." I shove him again right as he's recovered from the first push. "I hate you." My hands connect with his chest again. "I hate you!" I shove harder. "I hate you!" I scream in his face, pure rage igniting through my entire body.

I draw back to hit him, but Oliver catches my hand mid-air. I try again with the other hand, but again, he's able to deflect with ease—securing my wrists, one in each hand.

"Let go of me," I seethe.

"Not until you stop swinging at me," he fires back.

"You deserve it. You deserve to be hit and kicked and, and, and, ran over with my car," I stutter, spitting out the first thing that pops into my head. "Why do you hate me so much? What did I do to you? Why are you ruining my life?" The last question comes out on a sob and my shoulders go limp.

Oliver releases my hands and they fall to my sides as I stumble backward, doing everything in my power not to completely break down.

"I don't hate you," he admits, defeat the most prominent thing in his voice. "I've never hated you. I just wanted you to leave."

"Why?" I cross my arms in front of my chest to shield myself from him.

"Because I blamed your mom for breaking up my parent's marriage. I blamed her for my mom leaving. I blamed her for ripping apart my life. And I wanted her gone. You were the easy target. You are the thing she loves the most. I thought if I could make you miserable enough that eventually it would start to wear on their marriage. I knew that if it came down to you or my father, she would choose you."

"So all of this has been to try to drive a wedge between our parents?" I ask, even though I already know the answer.

Oliver had said something of this nature before when I overheard him and Savannah talking, but hearing him say it now, seeing the vulnerability on his face as he opens up to me, it's a complete game changer. It doesn't make a single thing he's done okay. But for the first time I'm seeing him more as a wounded child that's acting out of hurt, than I am as an evil bully that gets some sick thrill out of hurting other people.

"Your mom and my dad had an affair. That's why my mom left."

"But they didn't." My voice softens. "My mom would never sleep with a married man, ever."

"You can't know that."

"I can and I do. And even if they did, why would you think terrorizing me would get you what you wanted? Did you ever stop to consider that I wouldn't go to my mom? That I wouldn't tell her what's going on *because* I don't want to cause problems between her and Paul? I haven't seen my mom this happy in a very long time. As hard as you were trying to sabotage this whole thing, I was fighting just as hard to make everything seem fine. So essentially, you've done all this and accomplished nothing."

"I guess I'm starting to see that," he admits, switching his weight from one foot to the other.

"Have you ever sat down with your dad and asked him point blank? You're so busy assuming everything, maybe if you get his side you'll see things in a new light."

"My dad isn't the easiest person to talk to. And I don't have to ask him, I heard it all from my mom."

"What parent is easy to talk to? And did you ever stop to think that maybe your mom spoke to you out of anger and hurt that her marriage was ending?"

"She wouldn't do that."

"Maybe she would, maybe she wouldn't. But is it really worth all this, just to avoid having a simple conversation with someone to clear the air and get to the truth? And now, because for whatever reason you thought it would be easier to take your shit out on me, you've not only hurt me, but you've hurt someone you claim is like a brother to you."

"He *is* my brother."

"Given everything you've put me through, I shouldn't be surprised that you would treat your *brother* that way then, should I? Because now it's not just me you've hurt, but Zayden as well."

"I know that. And it makes me sick." He grimaces. "For what it's worth, I am sorry. I'm sorry for how far things went. I'm sorry for all the immature schemes. For invading your privacy. For going out of my way to humiliate you. I know it doesn't mean much now, but I want you to know it's over. All of it."

"I really hope you mean that."

"I do. And I'm going to fix this with Zayden. You have my word. I'll come clean and tell him everything I did."

"He's never going to forgive me, is he?" I ask in a moment of weakness.

Even though I know what happened last night isn't my fault, it doesn't make what happened any less real. I was still there. I was still in bed with another man—whether things had gotten very far or not. I still betrayed him—or at least I feel like I did.

"He will. I know Zayden—sometimes a little too well." He chuckles to himself. "He doesn't forgive easily, but it's not you he needs to forgive, it's me." His lips turn downward. "I've known Z for years and I've never seen him tore up over a girl the way he was over you last night. Not ever. And that tells me that you're really special to him. Zayden is hard to get close to, but if you can break past the barrier and get him to let you in, he's one of the greatest people you will ever know. He's fiercely loyal and protective. There isn't a thing he won't do for the people he loves. And if I had to guess, I'd say you're among those people now."

I don't know how to react to that statement.

Oliver takes a step toward me, reaching out to lay a tentative hand on my shoulder. "I hope one day we can move past all this. If you're going to be in Zayden's life, then you're going to be in mine."

"Our parents are married. Pretty sure I'm in your life whether you like it or not," I point out.

"This is true." He smiles, dropping his hand. "But you know what I mean."

"I do."

"I guess I should give you some time alone. I know I've given you a lot to process and honestly, I've got a few things I need to work through myself."

"Okay."

"I'll track down Z and set everything straight. I know it's not easy but be patient. This isn't the first time he's disappeared, and he never stays gone long. He'll come back, and when he does, I'll fix this. I promise." He waits until I nod before stepping past me, pulling open my bedroom door moments later. "Oh, and you may want to give Charles a call. He was pretty worried about you last night," he adds as he steps into the hallway, pulling the door shut behind him.

chapter twenty-four

ZAYDEN

i cruise down the interstate, the radio on low, as I head back toward home. I have no desire to go back, but I know I need to. Not only for Dad and Danielle, but also because I can't afford to miss more school. Today's Tuesday, and while it's only a couple of days of missed schoolwork, I refuse to let Rylee fuck up my life any more than she has.

My blood heats as my anger comes back. I refuse to acknowledge the incessant pain in my chest, choosing instead to focus on the rage. I still can't believe how much of a fool I was. How easy it was for her to get to me. I'm usually a good judge of character, but with her, my attraction blinded me. I should have stuck with my original assessment. Spoiled rich bitch.

I grip the steering wheel so tight my fingers cramp. The rest of the school year is going to be hell. While I could pull an Oliver and pay her back in kind, I'm done with the games. Fuck Rylee. Fuck Oliver. Fuck the entire fucking school. There's only a few more months left before graduation. With Danielle on the transplant list, there's no dire need for me to be around as much. I've got enough money saved up to get an apartment close to campus, no matter where I decide to go, and to still help dad out financially. I'll come back as much as I can, but as soon as school lets out, I'm out of here.

When I walk through the front door an hour later, I'm immediately accosted by a nine-year-old hurricane.

"I missed you," she mumbles against my chest, tightening her arms around my waist.

I smooth her hair from her cheeks and tip her head back so she's looking at me. Her breathing is labored, so I pick her up and carry her to the couch where her oxygen tank is. Guilt eats at me when she takes the mask and settles it over her mouth and nose, pulling in several deep breaths.

"I'm sorry I left without saying goodbye. I just needed a bit of time away."

She pulls the mask away. "Please don't do that again. I was scared you weren't coming back."

Her words break my heart. "I'll always come back, Danielle. You never have to worry about that. Never, you hear me?"

Her lip trembles slightly. "Okay." She nods. "Where did you go?"

"To Aunt Teresa's house. She actually gave me something to give you."

I get up to grab the bag I dropped when Danielle barreled into me and hand it to her.

"What is it?"

"Open it and see," I tell her and sit back down.

Grabbing one handle in each hand, she pulls the bag open. The knot in my chest loosens when she smiles.

"Art supplies." She beams up at me. "A whole bunch of them."

"Aunt Teresa said she's going to come visit soon and she expects a couple of pictures from you."

"I can make her a hundred with everything she sent."

I laugh. "I'm sure two or three will do just fine. Save some for me and Dad."

She lifts her head from peeking in the bag of goodies, her expression turning serious once again. "Are you okay now?"

I tug her toward me and place a kiss against her forehead. "I will be soon."

Just as soon as I get out of this godforsaken town and away from the girl who so callously wrecked me.

Getting to my feet, movement out of the corner of my eye has me looking over at dad. Concern draws down his brows as he leans against the wall watching Danielle and me. I've ignored all phone calls and texts over the last couple of days, including his. He knew I was at Aunt Teresa's house. If he needed me for anything important all he had to do was call his sister.

"Danielle, why don't you go find a place in your room for your new supplies?" Dad suggests, and I know it's so he can talk to me in private. I really don't want to talk about what happened, but I've got to give him something to explain my disappearance.

After Danielle leaves the room, he walks over to the couch and sits. He tips his chin to the other end. "Take a seat."

I'm exhausted and want nothing more than a shower and to sleep, but I walk over and take a seat anyway.

"You wanna tell me what happened to make you up and leave like that?" he asks, getting comfortable with one arm stretched out on the back of the couch.

"Just some shit that happened with Rylee." I lean forward, rest my elbows on my knees, and clasp my hands together. "It's over between us."

"What happened?"

I sigh. "Dad, I really don't want to get into details right now. I just drove eight hours and I'm tired."

I feel his eyes on me for several long seconds, but he thankfully doesn't force the issue. "It's a shame. I really liked the girl."

I grunt. "I did, too, but apparently she didn't feel the same."

"You sure about that? You sure it's not something you can't work out?"

I bark out a harsh laugh. "I'm pretty damn sure. Even more sure that it's certainly not something we can work out."

Just then, there's a loud knock on the door.

"That's probably Oliver," Dad comments. "He's come by the last two days looking for you."

Why the hell is Oliver looking for me? All he's done is avoid me as much as possible since Rylee and I got together. Although, he was there the night I caught Rylee on the verge of fucking Bryant, so maybe he's come to renew our friendship now that we aren't together anymore. But then I think of the way he acted right before I walked out the door. He sat on that fucking bed, looking like he was trying to comfort her. Like he actually cared and was worried about her. All the while his supposed best friend stood by feeling like his heart was being ripped from his chest.

I get up from the couch, stomp over to the door, and yank it open. I open my mouth to tell him to fuck off, and that I'll talk to him later, but the haggard look on his face forestalls the words. He looks like shit warmed over. His hair, which is normally styled, looks like he's raked his hands through it a couple hundred times, and his eyes look tired and wary. His clothes are wrinkled, something Oliver wouldn't normally allow.

"We need to talk," he grunts.

Not waiting on an invitation, he shoulders past me. I shoot his back a glare and slam the door shut.

"What do you want, Oliver?" I ask, following him into the living room where dad is still sitting comfortably on the couch.

"Hey, Allen," he says, ignoring my question.

"How have you been, Oliver? It's been a while since I've seen you."

He shrugs. "Been busy."

"Oliver!" I bark.

He turns to face me. "There are things you need to know." He looks back at my dad. "With all due respect, sir, your son and I need to speak in private."

"Have at it. Maybe you can talk some sense into him about whatever's going on between him and that girl."

Oliver gives him a jerky nod, then tips his chin toward the hallway. "Bedroom," he says to me.

I bite back a retort and follow him to my room. I leave the door open, but he walks over and shuts it.

"Take a seat," he orders, like he's my father or some shit, and my patience crumbles.

"Just spit out what you have to say and get the fuck out. I want to be alone," I growl.

"Take a seat, Z," he repeats firmly. "You're gonna need the support after you hear what I have to say."

I cross my arms over my chest, silently giving him a fuck you.

"Fine," he grates out.

He crosses to the desk chair, takes a seat, and leans his elbows on his knees. He looks tired and worn out.

"There are things that went down Friday and Saturday night that you don't know about. What you saw with Rylee wasn't what it appeared to be."

A harsh laugh escapes me. "My eyes work just fine, Oliver. I know what I saw."

"No, you *think* you know what you saw, but it was wrong."

"What? Rylee has a twin none of us knew about and she magically happened to appear at the same party we were all at?" I ask sarcastically.

The notion is ridiculous, but it's the only possible explanation he could give.

"I need to back up to Friday before I get into Saturday night's events." He pauses long enough to slash his fingers through his hair a couple of times. When he lifts his head again, his eyes are glazed over in a mountain full of regret. "I heard the two of you that night." His voice is quiet. "I knew you had sex with Rylee, and it pissed me off. I was fucking jealous, because I thought I was going to lose you to her, just like I lost my mom because of Rylee's mom. I had a girl over, Julia, and when I heard your phone ringing in your jacket, an idea formed in my head. I sent myself text messages from your phone, faking a conversation between the two of us. They basically said you were playing Rylee the whole time, that it was all a joke between us. After you left I showed her the fake messages."

I'm shaking by the time he stops talking. My nerves are completely shot and iron-hot lava forms in my veins. Taking out his resentment against his parent's divorce on Rylee, I understood. But this? I was his best fucking friend. We've known each other for years. I considered him a brother.

"I know you want to hit me, and you have every right. I deserve every punch you'll inevitably throw, but there's more you need to hear first."

There's fucking more?

What more could there be after finding out my best friend betrayed me?

It takes every ounce of will power I possess to not beat the shit out of him this moment. Walking over to the bed, I take a seat on the end, rest my fists on my thighs, and give him a tight nod to continue.

He blows out a long breath.

"After showing Rylee the text messages Friday night, she was devastated. Which is exactly what I wanted. I didn't see or hear anything from her after that. From what Charles told me after the fact, Rylee called him Saturday evening and asked him to go with her to Regina's party. Apparently, she wanted to get out of the house and blow off some steam. He somehow lost track of her. He was looking for her when you met him at the stairs. After you beat the shit out of Bryant, you left, so you didn't see what we saw. By the way Rylee was acting, Charles and I came to the same conclusion."

He stops and his eyes take on a hard look. His hands mimic mine, turning into fists between his knees.

"What?" I snarl, dreading what I already know he's going to say.

"Something was slipped into her drink."

I explode out of my chair and pick up the first thing I come across. The lamp on my desk goes sailing across the room and shatters against the wall. I release a roar of rage and pick up a statue dad got me a couple years ago and it receives the same treatment as the lamp.

A wave of dizziness hits me, and I realize my breathing has become erratic and uncontrolled.

A red haze fills my vision as I begin to shake. I bend and put my hands on my knees, trying to catch my breath.

The vision of Rylee lying on that bed, drugged and out of her mind, defenseless and alone, fills my head. I fucking left her there. I fucking left her there and was gone for days. I didn't help her. I didn't stick around to ask questions. I just believed she was cheating on me. It fucking destroyed me to see her like that, to think she was capable of that type of betrayal. I should have stayed and demanded answers.

I knew in my gut that wasn't something Rylee would do, but my heart was being torn to shreds at the time, so I ran. I ran because I couldn't handle the truth. Or what I thought was the truth. That Rylee didn't love me like I love her. That I was just a means to an end; to get back at me.

I squeeze my eyes shut and pull in several deep lungful's of air, until the dizziness begins to fade. I slowly stand up and lock eyes with Dad over Oliver's shoulder. I can't hear what Oliver tells him, but dad looks back at him and gives a tight nod before turning and walking away, closing the door behind him.

I lace my fingers on top of my head and regard Oliver. "Is she okay?" I ask hoarsely.

"She's fine now. Sunday morning she had a hell of a hangover and doesn't remember much about the night before, but the drug had no lasting effects."

I drop my arms and stand rigidly. "What happened to Bryant?"

If I had my way, he'd be six feet under. I've never wished death on anyone before, but damn it if I don't wish it on the person who almost raped Rylee.

"He had a busted jaw and a broken nose. He was forced to spend the night in the hospital. I went to see him the next day. He confirmed the assumptions that she'd been drugged. He didn't give it to her; he was only meant to take advantage of the situation. He claims he wouldn't have taken it all the way."

I narrow my eyes. "Who spiked her drink?"

His eyes turn glacial. "Tiffany."

I let out a string of curses and spin around. My fist meets the wall and chunks of plaster fall to the floor.

"I'm going to fucking kill that bitch," I growl darkly.

"She's gone."

I spin back around and pin him with a glare. "What the hell do you mean she's gone?"

He stuffs his hands in his pockets.

"Sunday, after I left Bryant, I paid a visit to Tiffany. I told her parents what Bryant said. She'd promised him a week's worth of blow jobs to get Rylee upstairs in that room. I was going to threaten her parents with going to the cops if they didn't ship her off somewhere, but there was no need. Apparently, they've been having issues with her the last couple of years. She was sent to live with her aunt in Alaska for the last few months of the school year. They're also giving her no choice but to attend college there or be cut off."

Thank Christ for that. I'm not sure how much self-control I'd have if I ran into her again.

"I also advised Bryant to not try and press charges against you. It'd be fucking stupid on his part. We may not be able to prove he knew Rylee was drugged, but if word got out, his family would suffer. We both know how important reputation is around here."

I grunt. Last I heard, Bryant's dad was running for Mayor. If word got out that his son was involved in something like this, he could kiss his chance of winning goodbye. The public doesn't take kindly to scandal, especially when it's of the sexual variety.

I'd still like to get my hands on the bastard again.

"Zayden," Oliver calls my name, pulling me from my thoughts. "I know it doesn't mean much, but I'm sorry."

His apology doesn't mean shit to me. He may not have orchestrated Rylee getting drugged, but she was at that party because of what he did.

"You say you didn't know at first that she was drugged?" He nods. "Then why did it look like you were trying to care for her? Before I left, I saw you sitting on the bed and you looked concerned."

He drops his head for a moment before lifting tormented eyes to me. "I knew something was off. I never wanted her to get hurt like that. I swear, Zayden. I would never wish that on any woman. I knew Rylee wasn't that type of girl, and I knew she was only there because of what I did. I felt like shit for my part in it. But when I saw how much it hurt you when you thought she cheated on you, it made me see how much you actually care for her. I thought she was just some girl you were using to pass the time, but she isn't. I felt like the lowest bastard for hurting you like that and for almost getting her raped."

That last word has my blood boiling again. Bryant said he wouldn't have taken it all the way, but he could have just been saying that to save his own ass. The thought of it being a possibility makes me want to find the bastard and finish what I was forced to stop that night.

As calmly as I can, I walk over to Oliver. He stiffens and stands, but he doesn't move away from my advance. Once I'm in front of him, I take a good look at my best friend. I don't even know if I want to label him as a friend at all anymore.

The Oliver I know can be a bastard and sometimes mean, but I believe him when he says he's sorry and that he never meant for it to go this route. But it's hard for me to look past his role in all of this. Knowing that it was his selfishness that hurt Rylee in such a cruel way, albeit unintentionally, is something I'm not sure I can get over.

Without warning, I rear back and clock him in the jaw. He stumbles back a step and bumps into the desk chair, losing his balance. He falls to his ass, then slumps back until he's lying down. He holds his nose, as blood trickles out from between his fingers.

I stand over him.

"I don't know if I can ever forgive you for what you did. But if I ever find out you so much as say one bad word about Rylee ever again, I'll take you out. You got me?"

With his hand still covering his nose, he looks right at me, no anger, only understanding, and gives me a single nod.

I leave him on the floor and walk out of my room.

chapter twenty-five

RYLEE

"rylee," mom says seconds before she appears in my doorway. She's dressed in blue scrubs, her hair twisted into a tight bun at the back of her head.

"Hey, Mom." I close the textbook in front of me. It's not like I've retained anything I've attempted to read over the last thirty minutes—or the entire day for that matter. My mind has been consumed with thoughts of Zayden. I've replayed the events from this past weekend over and over again in my head. It's all I can think about.

I still haven't been able to fully digest how quickly things changed. I went from my highest high to my lowest low in the matter of minutes on Friday. Then to tack on what happened Saturday, accompanied with what Oliver told me Sunday, and then Zayden's absence at school the last two days, I swear I've never felt more off kilter than I do right now. The last few days have been absolute torture.

"You got a minute?" Mom asks, stepping into my room.

"Yeah, of course. What's up?" I tuck my legs Indian style, shoving my schoolwork to the side to make room for my mom to sit. She takes a seat on the edge of the mattress, angling her body toward me.

"I know this move has been difficult for you. And I know you've been doing your best to make the best of a less than ideal situation. But I wanted to check and make sure you're okay. I feel like we haven't talked much recently. At least not like we used to."

"Yeah, I'm fine," I lie, not wanting to get into the ridiculous drama that has taken over my life. Mom has enough on her plate as it is.

"I know our situation has changed, but I'm still your mom. You know you can tell me anything, right?"

"Of course I do." I study her expression, trying to figure out what she's getting at.

"So is that why you didn't tell me about you and Zayden?" She doesn't try to hide the hurt that tugs at her expression.

"What?" I stutter, a little caught off guard.

Up to this point, I haven't really said anything to her about Zayden. Mainly because we were still so new, and I wasn't sure where it was going. But also because a small part of me worried that she wouldn't approve. It's not like Zayden is the kind of guy a mother would pick for her daughter. He's actually the exact opposite. No mother wants her daughter to end up with the bad boy. And Zayden is the epitome of a bad boy.

But he's also so much more. I just didn't know how to convince her of that.

"Zayden stopped by on Saturday. Apparently, he left his phone here on Friday night after he had been visiting you." She gives me a pointed look.

"We got partnered up together for an English project. He's stopped over a couple of times to work on it with me."

"And the fact that you two are dating has nothing to do with why he was here?" She gives me the look only a mother can give. The one that says, *I was a teenager once—do you really think I'm that stupid?*

"Mom, I…."

"Don't even bother denying it. Zayden was all too happy to tell me that you two are seeing each other. He seems quite smitten with you, I must say."

"He did what?"

On one hand, I'm instantly irritated. Telling my mother wasn't his place. On the other, I can't deny the way my heart does a little flip inside my chest that she thinks he's smitten. Not that any of that really matters now. It's not like he's talking to me anymore. Hell, no one has heard a word out of him since Saturday night—not even Oliver.

"It was really kind of cute actually." Mom smiles to herself. "Though, my feelings are a little hurt that I had to hear it from him and not you."

"I had been meaning to talk to you, but it seems like we're never in the same room longer than a few minutes at a time, and more often times than not, we're not alone. Besides, I'm not sure how serious it is or if it's even still a thing for that matter."

"What happened?" Concern clouds her face as she clearly picks up on more than I intend for her to.

"Just drama with Oliver." I wave my hand around, trying to blow it off.

"Is he giving you a hard time for seeing his best friend? I can't imagine that's easy for him. Out of everyone, I think he's having the hardest time with this entire transition."

"How do you know that?"

"A mother just knows." She shrugs. "Tell me what happened."

"I really don't want to get into it."

"Honey, if Oliver has done something…."

"He hasn't," I cut her off, not sure why I'm jumping to defend him after everything he's done. "It's just complicated between me and Zayden and having Oliver as part of the equation has made things a little hard to maneuver. That's all. Everything will work itself out. Or it won't." I try to act indifferent. "But speaking of Oliver, I do have something I want to ask you."

"Okay." She nods, waiting for me to continue.

"I don't really know how to ask this, so I'm just going to be as blunt as I can be." I take a deep breath. "Did you and Paul start seeing each other while he was still married to his wife?"

I can tell my question catches her off guard, but she quickly recovers, her expression smoothing.

"Why would you ask me something like that?" she questions, shifting her weight on the bed.

"Just something Oliver said."

"Which was?"

"He said that he overheard his parents' arguing just before they split. His mom apparently mentioned the affair his dad was having. Then, after you two started dating, I guess his mom told him you were the woman that his father was sleeping with while they were married and that you were the reason they divorced."

"I guess I shouldn't be surprised. Maria Conley would say or do anything to make herself the victim."

"Wait." Her comment makes me pause. "You know her?"

"Not well, but yes, we've met."

"So then it's true?" I ask hesitantly.

"Yes and no." She lets out a heavy breath. "When Paul and I met, he *was* married to Maria, and we were just friends. And while I'll admit, our feelings were bordering on more than platonic, we never acted on them. Paul and Maria had been having problems for years. In fact, when we met, Paul had just found out about her second affair. He was trying to keep things together for Oliver—hoping he could make it work until he was out of the house, but that second affair really took a toll on him. I was there for him, as a friend."

"So you didn't…."

"I won't lie to you and say that nothing happened between Paul and me before they divorced. But I can promise you that *I* was not the reason that they did. Maria had done damage that couldn't be undone. It wasn't until Paul told her that he wanted a divorce and they officially separated that our relationship began to move into a more intimate direction. But I don't think you want all the details where that's concerned." She smiles when I cringe.

"No, no details." I shake my head, causing her to giggle.

"I didn't realize that Oliver was struggling with this. I'll talk to Paul and make sure he sits down with his son. Sounds like they need to have a conversation that's a bit overdo." She leans over, patting the top of my leg. "Let's keep what I just told you between you and me for now. I think this is something that needs to be handled between the two of them."

I nod in agreement, hoping for all of our sakes that they have this conversation sooner rather than later. While Oliver has played nice the last couple of days, that doesn't mean it will last. Maybe if he learns the truth about his mother, this vendetta he has against my mom, which has bled over onto me, will be over, once and for all.

My attention is pulled away from my mom when my phone pings on the bed next to me. Glancing down, my heart nearly leaps right out of my chest when I see Zayden's name pop up on the screen, followed by a text that reads *I'm outside.*

"I'm sorry, Mom." I jump up off the bed like someone just lit the bedding on fire. "But can we finish this conversation later?"

"Um, okay." She seems surprised by my abrupt movement.

"Zayden's here," I tell her in a way of explanation. And even though she has no idea what's been going on these past few days, something about my expression must tell her that this is important.

"Okay." She smiles as she stands. "Just don't leave without letting me know."

"I won't." I lean in, pressing a kiss to her cheek. "Thanks, Mom." With that, I take off out of my room, running down the stairs so fast it's a wonder I don't end up on my face at some point.

When I push my way outside, I spot Zayden's truck out front, parked on the curb. A brisk wind blows across my face, stealing my breath, but I don't let it deter me. I jog across the front lawn, no jacket, no shoes, with a trillion butterflies flapping wildly in my stomach.

When I pull open the passenger side door and catch sight of him for the first time in days, it takes everything in me not to burst into tears. I didn't realize how much I needed this, how much I needed to see him, until this very second.

"Hey." He gives me a tentative smile. "Get in."

I do as he says, hoisting myself up into his truck before pulling the door closed.

I angle my body toward him, honestly not really sure what to say or do.

"Oliver came to see me," Zayden confesses after a long moment of silence passes between us. He grips the steering wheel so tight that his knuckles turn white. Even though he's speaking to me, his eyes remain forward. "He told me what happened." He blows out a heavy breath through his nose, his jaw locked tight.

"Zayden…." I start, feeling like I owe him an explanation of some kind.

"Don't." He cuts me off. "Just let me say this, okay?" When his eyes finally look at me, there's so much regret etched on his face that it nearly knocks the wind right out of me.

I nod, suddenly feeling even more uncertainty than I did just moments ago.

"I fucked up." He releases the steering wheel. "What happened Saturday…. I have no excuse. You needed me, and I fucking left you there." The words catch in his throat as he looks down at his hands that are now knotted in his lap.

"Don't do that." I scoot across the bench seat, not stopping until my leg is resting against his. "You didn't know." I slide my hand against his cheek before gently coaxing his eyes back to me.

"But I should have known. I thought… I thought you were cheating on me. After everything I put you through, you opened your heart to me, you gave me your body, and that's how I repay you—by believing the absolute worst of you. Had something worse happened to you, had you been… raped." He swallows hard. "I don't think I could have lived with that."

"Nothing happened. Look at me. You stopped it. You showed up and *you* stopped it. And I'm okay." I reach up and push his hair away from his forehead. "You read the situation as you saw it. I don't know what I would have done had the roles been reversed. I probably would have done the exact same thing." I give him a reassuring smile. "This isn't on you, Zayden. This is on me. I let Oliver get to me. I let him make *me* believe the worst in *you.* And because of that, I put myself in a really bad situation. This isn't on you," I repeat.

"Looks like Oliver played us both," he grunts, his shoulders relaxing slightly.

"He did." I blow out a small sigh. "But what he did doesn't change how I feel about you. No matter how messed up everything has been over the past few days."

"It doesn't change the way I feel about you either. If anything, this whole thing has made me realize just how much you really do mean to me." He shifts, turning so that we're facing each other. "My whole life has been a parade of users and abusers. Full of people who only care about themselves. I learned from very early on to keep people at arm's length, but then you came along, and for the first time in my life, I found myself wanting to be close to someone. Wanting to let someone in. I've never felt that way about a girl before." He smiles. "Fuck, I sound like a pussy."

"You do not." I shove at his shoulder. He snags my hand and lifts it to his mouth, pressing a gentle kiss to my palm.

"I do. But I don't fucking care." His ocean blue eyes bore into mine. "Just tell me I haven't lost you." His words are almost pleading, bringing every emotion that has been brewing in my chest straight to the surface.

"You haven't lost me," I croak, tears stinging the backs of my eyes. "You are the only thing I want, Zayden. The only thing in this world that feels right to me."

"I'm in love with you, Rylee." The words fall from his lips so effortlessly that it's almost like he's said them a hundred times before.

The tears I've been holding at bay for days break free. All the devastation and uncertainty I've been lost in for the last few days evaporates in an instant. And when Zayden looks at me the way he's looking at me right now, it's hard to remember ever feeling them.

My chest swells and my hands tremble.

"I'm in love with you, too," I admit. No sentence has ever held more weight or more truth. Because I'm not just admitting to him how I feel, I'm also giving him a power that I can't take back.

"Thank fuck." He blows out a breath, his shoulders sagging forward as he pulls me into his lap.

The steering wheel bites into my lower back, but I don't care.

Zayden's fingers slide against my scalp, tangling in my hair as he tugs my face down to his.

"You're mine, Rylee." He kisses me slow and deep, like he's relishing his first drink of cold water after spending days on a hot desert. He kisses me until there's nowhere I can't feel him. Until there's no part of my body that isn't affected. "Say it. Say that you're mine."

I've never been happier to oblige.

"I'm yours." I smile against his lips. "I'll always be yours."

"I fucking love you." He slides his tongue against mine.

"I fucking love you, too." I giggle when he pulls back and hits me with an amused look. "What?" I cock my head to the side, draping my arms around his neck.

"I love that word even more when you say it."

"What word?" I nibble on my bottom lip. The way he's looking at me makes me feel all kinds of ways.

"Fuck." His eyes go dark as his hands slide around my back.

"Fuck. Fuck. Fuck," I repeat, laughter rumbling through my words. I've never been one to use much profanity but being around Zayden has definitely loosened my tongue where that's concerned.

"Keep talking like that and Friday will seem like a warmup for what I've got planned for you."

I lean forward and press a kiss to his mouth before seductively whispering against his lips, "That's what I'm counting on."

chapter twenty-six

ZAYDEN
THREE WEEKS LATER

i tuck my girl against my side as we walk out of the door. Normally I can't wait for spring and the warmer weather, but I have to admit, I'm liking the cold more and more. It gives me a damn good excuse to have Rylee snuggled up to me. Not that I need an excuse. I've never been the affectionate type, with the exception of Danielle, but I'm realizing it was because I hadn't found the right girl to be affectionate with. If Rylee is near, I have to be touching her in some way. Thank fuck, she's totally down with my clingy ass.

Three weeks ago, I damn near lost her. While the thought still incites my anger, I refuse to let the greediness and mistakes of others dampen mine and Rylee's relationship.

"Hey, Z!" someone calls my name. "You and Rylee coming to the game tonight?"

"We'll see," I answer back.

Opening my truck door, I toss both of our books behind the seat. After, I get in Rylee's space until she bumps into the back fender with nowhere else to go. I curl my fingers around the bed of the truck over her shoulder. "What are our plans for tonight, baby?"

She tips her head back to look up at me. "Hmm… I was thinking we could watch *New Moon*."

I wrack my brain, trying to think of what movie she's talking about, but come up with nothing.

"I don't remember that one. What's it about?"

Her eyes take on a mischievous sparkle and she grins. "It's the second movie in The Twilight Saga."

"Lee!" I yell, still holding her eyes. "What time does the game start? Looks like I'm going solo."

Rylee giggles and slams my stomach with the back of her hand. "I'm just kidding." She leans up and presses a kiss to my lips, her delicious flavor enticing me to further the intimate contact. "Actually, Paul and Mom are going away for the weekend. Savannah was supposed to come visit Saturday and spend the night, but she came down with the flu. I heard Oliver tell his dad he'll be gone for the weekend, too." Her eyes take on a sensual look. "Looks like I'll have the house all to myself. I'll be alone all weekend."

She pouts playfully, and it makes me want to lick the look off her face.

"Well, I guess we'll have to rectify that."

My dick instantly hardens. I fucking love the idea of having Rylee all to myself for an entire weekend. I groan when I think of all the different ways I can take her.

"You're being naughty in that head of yours, aren't you?"

Leaning forward, I bury my face in her neck and take a deep breath. I nip at her skin, then tug her earlobe between my teeth.

"Very fucking naughty, baby," I admit huskily.

"Alright, you two, knock it off," Charles says, interrupting our moment.

I lift my head and shoot him a glare. "Bad timing. Leave and come back later."

He chuckles and throws his book bag in the bed of my truck. "No can do. You're my ride home."

"What the hell? Since when?"

His eyes move to Rylee. "Since she said you'd give me a ride because I'm getting new tires on my car."

I turn to Rylee and lift a brow. She shrugs her slender shoulders. "I forgot to tell you."

I look back at Charles. "How did you get to school this morning?"

"A friend dropped me off."

"Then get a ride home with them."

"Can't. They had to leave early." He grins wickedly. "Besides, it's much more fun cramping your style with my girl, Rylee."

I tip my head back and pray for patience.

"Fine," I grumble.

Rylee kisses me under the chin. "Thank you."

If it makes her happy, I'd do anything.

I look to the left and lock eyes with Oliver as he steps up to his car a few spaces over. I haven't spoken to him much in the three weeks since everything went to shit. I'm still a long way from forgiving him, but I think we'll eventually get back a resemblance of our friendship.

He tips his chin to me, and I do the same before he gets into his car and drives off. Rylee said she and Oliver have spoken several times. I know she's still wary of him, but she's much more forgiving than I am. It's hard to imagine her having a tighter bond with my former best friend than I do. As much as it irks me that she's forced to see him almost daily at home, it helps to know he seems to be genuinely remorseful and is working on making it up to her.

Rylee follows my line of sight as I watch Oliver's car drive out of the parking lot.

"He misses you," she says softly.

I bring my eyes back to hers. "He should have thought of that before the shit he pulled," I say, my voice stony.

She nods and slides her hands up my chest, stopping right below my collarbone. "You're right, but he had no way of knowing it would lead to what it did. I think he holds a lot of guilt."

"He should. He damn near got you…." I stop and close my eyes. Even thinking that word steals my breath.

"Hey. Look at me." I open my eyes and peer into her warm brown ones. "He deserves every bit of your anger. And quite frankly, I'm still pissed at him, too. But everyone deserves forgiveness and a second chance."

I grunt. That may be so, but I'm not ready to give it yet.

"When do your parents head out?" I ask, changing the subject.

She looks at her watch. "They actually left about an hour ago."

A slow grin creeps across my face, as I slide my hand down to cup her ass, giving it a squeeze. "How about we drop this yahoo off." I tip my head to Charles. "So I can get you alone and do wicked things to your amazing body."

"I heard that," Charles calls without looking up from his phone.

"You were supposed to," I deadpan.

He lifts one hand and sticks his middle finger in the air, again without looking away from his phone.

Rylee laughs, pushing against my chest until I'm forced back a couple of feet. "Let's go."

Charles walks to the other side of the truck, and I open the driver side door. I pinch my girl's ass as she climbs in from my side. She shoots me a glare over her shoulder, and I give her a cheeky grin.

Once we hit the road, Charles fumbles with the radio until he finds a rock station.

"Fuck my life," he grumbles a few minutes later, looking down at Rylee's hand on my thigh. "Y'all are going to be the type of couple who can't keep their hands off each other, aren't you?"

"I could always move her hand a little higher. Would you like that, Charles?"

"Seriously, Zayden?" Rylee gasps.

"Fuck no. I may be into chicks and dicks, but it's a hard pass watching one friend getting another friend off." He flicks a piece of lint off his knee. "And also, since we're officially friends and all, it's probably about time you called me Pierce."

"Fine." I pull to a stop outside his house. "Pierce, get the fuck out of my truck."

He laughs as he opens his door.

"Later, lovebirds." Just before he closes the door, he peeks his head back in. "Word of advice, Rylee. Fucking against the washing machine is hella hot. Those extra vibrations do wonders." Before Rylee can say anything, he shoots her a wink and slams the door shut.

I expect her to be embarrassed, so her next words both shock me and send a good amount of my blood rushing to my dick.

"Is that true?"

I shrug. "No clue. I haven't fucked in the laundry room before."

"I think we should try it," she says nonchalantly, like she's talking about trying some new food or something.

"Killing me here, woman," I grumble and adjust my hard cock.

She giggles and nuzzles her face into my neck, kissing me just below my jaw.

"Just drive and I'll kill you even better at home."

I groan and put the truck in drive, but before I press the gas pedal, I turn to look at her. "I love you."

Her smile is sweet and beautiful- her eyes soft and mesmerizing. "I love you, too."

They say love comes when you least expect it. It sure as hell smacked me in the face when I wasn't looking. I'm only eighteen, and I've already found the woman of my dreams; the one I know I want to spend the rest of my life with. The one I'll love until my dying breath.

Our relationship may have had an ugly and treacherous beginning. It may have grown in the midst of anger, hate, and betrayal. But our future will be beautiful, happy, and full of love. Of this much I am certain.

epilogue

RYLEE
SIX MONTHS LATER

"hey babe, where do you want this?" Zayden appears in the open doorway of my apartment, a large moving box in his arms.

I can't believe moving day is finally upon us. And even though this is technically day two in me and Savannah's new apartment, it still feels so unreal.

"You can set it in here." I nod to the counter next to me where I'm sorting out plates and cups. "How many more boxes are in your truck?" I ask when he slides up next to me.

"A lot." He gives me a knowing look. "How the hell did you girls end up with so much shit?"

"Talk to Savannah. She's the one who's been planning this day since we were twelve." I laugh, leaning into his touch when he leans down to kiss the side of my head.

"Well, she's lucky my scholarship also covers housing, otherwise she'd be moving into this apartment alone and you'd be living with me."

Savannah and I both got into Seattle University. It was my top pick to begin with, but knowing Zayden got a full scholarship to the University of Washington, it made the whole thing that much sweeter. Who knew my bad boy fighter was also a straight A scholar? He's a man who's full of surprises.

Zayden's dorm is less than twenty minutes from my apartment and we're still close enough to home that he's able to see Danielle whenever he wants, so it works out really well. After receiving her lung transplant in June, Dani's been doing really well, but I know Zayden still worries about her. It gives him peace of mind being so close.

"Don't tell her this, but I think I'd much rather live with you," I tell him, crinkling my nose as I knock my hip into his.

"Probably better that you don't—I don't think we'd ever leave our bedroom." He wraps an arm around me and squeezes my hip.

He's not wrong. Six months together and we still can't keep our hands off each other.

"Speaking of which." I turn, wrapping my arms around his neck. "My bed is finally up." I lean up, trailing kisses from his jaw all the way to his mouth. "I think I've earned a break," I mumble against his lips.

Leaning forward, Zayden grabs my backside, hoisting me up moments later. My legs wrap around his waist, pressing down onto his already rock-hard erection.

"You definitely deserve a break," he agrees, sliding his tongue against mine.

Like it does every time Zayden kisses me, my entire body ignites. Heat starts at my neck and slowly creeps down my torso, warming me from the inside out.

One of Zayden's hands tangles in my hair, while the other presses to the small of my back, holding me in place as he devours my mouth.

Unfortunately, before we can go any further, we hear a throat clear behind us. Zayden groans against my lips before pulling back to look over my shoulder.

"You realize the fucking door is open," Oliver says, laughter in his voice.

"That doesn't give you permission to just walk the fuck in," Zayden fires back. "Asshole."

"Yeah, hello to you, too." Oliver throws Zayden a playful middle finger. "Hey, sis." He nods when we lock gazes.

"Oliver." I nod, not nearly as embarrassed as I should be having been caught in such a compromising position. Oliver has seen worse. He's also exploited worse. Thank goodness those days are far behind us.

It's been a long and rocky road, but Zayden and Oliver have finally gotten back to a version of normalcy. Zayden still hasn't fully forgiven Oliver, but he's trying to move past it. We all are.

I tap Zayden and wiggle, indicating I want him to put me down. He gives me a dissatisfied look, like it's the last thing he wants to do, but he eventually lowers me to my feet.

"I brought the rest of your stuff from the house. Your mom also sent a couple boxes of kitchen stuff she thought you might need."

"More boxes," Zayden grumbles, giving me an exasperated look. "At this rate you won't have room to move around. This apartment isn't that big."

"Oh stop." I swat playfully at his chest as I step past him. "Thank you for bringing them," I tell Oliver.

"No big deal. I've got some shit to run to my dorm while I'm at it. Figured I'd just swing this stuff by on my way."

Oliver is also attending Seattle University, but unlike Savannah and me, he decided to live on campus in the dorms. Honestly, I think it's the best thing for him. Oliver thrives in that type of environment. I have no doubt he's going to have the time of his life living in a co-ed dorm.

"I'll help you bring it up." Zayden steps past me, his hand purposely brushing my ass.

I smile at him but don't comment.

"Be right back." He winks, sauntering off toward the door, Oliver right on his heels.

I shake my head and laugh. That man….

It's crazy to think how much things have changed over the last few months. After everything Oliver did to me, you'd think I wouldn't be able to stand to be in the same room with him. But something changed between us after the night Tiffany drugged me.

I wouldn't say all is forgiven, and it definitely has not been forgotten, but little by little we've moved into a semblance of a friendship. He still drives me crazy most days and always insists on calling me *sis* because he knows how much I hate it, but for the most part, we've learned to co-exist quite well. Of course, part of that is probably because Zayden has threatened to beat him within an inch of his life if he ever does anything to hurt me again.

And while my senior year was nothing like I'd planned it would be, in the end, it turned out better than I could have ever dreamed. Because at the end of it all, I walked away on top—with Zayden by my side.

Not to mention, I also found a forever friend in Charles Pierce. He's only been gone for a week and I already miss him like crazy. Zayden and I have plans to visit New York for a week over the holiday break. I've always wanted to visit the East Coast, so having one of my best friends attending NYU isn't the worst thing in the world.

"Please tell me that's not Oliver I just passed in the parking lot." Savannah sighs as she walks into our apartment and spots me in the kitchen.

"He brought some stuff from the house." I meet her halfway, relieving her of two of the fountain drinks she has wedged between her side and her arm.

"Of course he did. He can't really believe any of us buy this good guy act he's got going on." She huffs, setting the third drink and a bag of food on top of the stove as she turns toward me.

"Savannah." I give her a knowing look.

"Why is it that after everything he's done to you, you still insist on giving him the benefit of the doubt?"

"Because he's my brother."

"*Step*brother," she corrects. "And not a very good one, I might add." She rolls her eyes, turning back toward the stove. "I didn't get him anything, and I'm not sharing," she tells me as she empties the bag of sandwiches in front of her.

When Zayden mentioned he was hungry earlier, Savannah jumped at the chance to go get us lunch. I think it was her way of getting out of carrying up anymore boxes.

"I don't think he's staying. He said he's on his way to his dorm room and just came by to drop off some stuff from the house."

"Well, thank goodness for that. I am not in the mood to deal with him today."

I think it's safe to say that while everyone has done their best to move on from what happened in the past, Savannah has not. She harbors a lot of hatred toward Oliver for everything he put me through—and rightfully so. If the roles were reversed, I know I would probably feel the same way. Best friend code and all.

I'm curious to see how this year is going to go with all three of us at the same school. Then again, Seattle University isn't small by any means. Savannah or I don't have any of the same classes our first semester—mainly because our majors are completely different—and it's unlikely that we'll share any with Oliver, either. So, other than maybe a group setting, I can't see where Oliver and Savannah will be forced to share much interaction. It's not like I'm betting on him stopping by to visit on a regular basis or anything.

Things did get better after Oliver settled things with his dad, but he still isn't going to be winning any stepbrother of the year awards anytime soon. I may no longer be the object of his cruelty, but that doesn't mean he's some kind of angel all of the sudden. Oliver is still Oliver. Arrogant. Selfish. Beyond full of himself.... The list goes on and on.

"What the fuck, dude." Zayden barks out a laugh as he and Oliver make their way back into the apartment, both carrying large boxes. They drop them right inside the door.

"Do I even want to know?" My gaze bounces between the two men. Thanks to the open floor plan of our apartment, I have a clear view of both of them from the kitchen.

"Fucking Oliver just about tripped me up the stairs." Zayden throws him a sideways glance.

"Not my fault you walk like a grandpa," Oliver fires back.

"Men," I grumble under my breath to Savannah, who sets my sandwich in front of me.

"Z, I have your sandwich here whenever you want it," Savannah tells him, holding it up so he can see it before setting it next to mine.

"Thanks, Savannah." He smiles and nods at her before turning. "I'm going to head back down and get the rest of the boxes. There's only a couple left. I'll eat after I get them up here."

"K." I smile, loving the way his eyes do a quick sweep of me before he turns and disappears back into the hallway.

"Are you not going to help him?" Savannah crosses her arms over her chest and pins her gaze on Oliver.

"I don't know. I think now that you're here I might just hang out up here." He winks and smiles, clearly messing with her.

He pulls out a box of Red Hots and tosses a few in his mouth.

She has not made her dislike of him a secret. In fact, I can't think of a single time that these two were in the same room together that they didn't share some sort of altercation. Oddly enough, it doesn't seem to bother Oliver one bit. In fact, I think he rather enjoys getting her riled up.

"You might want to think again," she challenges. "I may have been forced to be civil to you when you were living at home, but this is my house. I will not tip toe around you here."

"Civil." He snorts. "Is that what you call it?"

"Stick around and you'll see just how civil I was being," she warns, the look on her face compelling me to step in.

"Okay, you two, that's enough." I laugh, trying to make light of the situation. "Oliver, will you please go help Zayden with the last boxes."

"Only because you asked nicely." He smirks at Savannah before spinning on his heel, disappearing from the apartment moments later.

"God! I cannot stand him!" Savannah throws her hands up in frustration.

"I don't know why you do that." I shake my head at her. "Just ignore him. You know he only says stuff to get you all worked up."

"Oh, I'm worked up alright." Her nostrils flare.

"Tell you what." I pick up her sandwich and hand it to her. "Why don't you go eat this in your room and relax for a little bit? I've got things under control out here, and I'll let you know when the coast is clear. Deal?"

"Fine." She takes the sandwich, snagging her drink off the counter before she spins on her heel and stomps off toward the back of the apartment where our bedrooms are located.

Zayden reappears just in time to hear her door slam shut.

"Let me guess.... Oliver?" He gives me a knowing look.

"How ever did you know?" I joke, rolling my eyes.

He drops the two smaller boxes he just brought up on top of a larger one right inside the front door.

"If those two didn't look at each other like they wanted to fucking kill the other, I might think they actually had a thing for one another."

I bark out a laugh.

"I think you're way off base." I shake my head at him.

"I didn't say I did. I said I might." He chuckles.

"You might what?" Oliver reappears, dropping another box next to the growing stacks that are taking over my living room.

"Nothing." Zayden shakes his head, trying to mask his smile.

"Okay, well, I've got some stupid orientation thing with the RA I have to get to. As long as you guys are good?" His gaze darts from Zayden to me.

"Yeah, I think we've got it covered. Thank you again for bringing that stuff by." I gesture to the boxes next to him.

"No problem. Just call if you think of anything else you might need from the house. I've got a few more trips to make, so it won't be a problem to bring it by."

"Okay. Thank you."

He nods, turning his attention to Zayden.

"I'll see you later, man." They bump fists.

"Yeah, later." Zayden waits until Oliver is in the hallway before closing the front door and sliding the dead bolt in place. "Now." He turns, stalking toward me. He doesn't stop until he has me firmly pinned between him and the kitchen counter. "Where were we?" he murmurs against my lips before kissing me.

"Well, I think we were just about here." I slide my arms around his neck and deepen the kiss, loving the way he groans into my mouth. "But," I pull back slightly, "we should probably eat first." I smile, slowly sliding my hand down his stomach. "You need your energy." I cup his heavy erection in my hands, loving the power I seem to have over his body.

He practically whimpers at my touch.

"Fuck food." He hoists me back up in the same position, my legs going around his waist as he takes off in the direction of my room. "What I want right now, only you can satisfy."

"Well, when you put it like that." I grin, pressing my lips on his.

"That was…" I smile into Zayden's bare chest, not really even sure how to describe what that just was.

Mind blowing doesn't begin to cover it. Then again, it usually never does.

"Yeah." His lips press to the top of my head. "Kind of makes me wish we had moved in together instead of agreeing to live separately for the first year."

"Me too," I admit.

"I hope you know I'm going to be here every night that you're not at my dorm."

"I hope you know I'm not staying in some stinky dorm that you share with another dude," I tease.

"Such a spoiled princess." He squeezes my side playfully.

"I am not a princess." I pop my head up and give him a pointed look.

"Yes you are." He grins, tucking my hair over my shoulder. He leans in so his lips are a beat away from mine. "Don't worry, I still love you."

"Is that so?"

"It is. And you want to know why?" He's talking so quietly his voice is almost a whisper.

"Why?"

"Because I love every part of you."

"I love every part of you, too." I close the small gap between us and lay a light kiss to his lips.

"I mean it, Rylee. You have changed my life in unimaginable ways. You've made me realize things I never thought I wanted. You've made me believe in myself in ways I never did before. You took me from a selfish, lost boy, and turned me into a man I'm proud to be."

"Zayden." His name barely escapes my lips. As much as I love dirty talking, tough guy Zayden, I love the sweet, gentle side of him even more.

"I'm serious. You are everything to me. Everything," he reiterates. "I need you to know that."

"I do know that. Because you tell me every day." I kiss him again. "My closet sweetheart."

"Just don't tell anyone. It would ruin my reputation." He chuckles, rolling us so that I'm pinned beneath him.

"Your secret is safe with me," I promise.

"I love you." He leans down, resting his forehead against mine.

"And I love you," I whisper back.

Things with Zayden haven't always been easy, but it's always been worth it. From the moment I first opened the door to find him standing on my front porch, I knew there was something there. Something that doesn't come along very often. And while we may have started off on the wrong foot, eventually we both found our way to each other. And I'd do it all over again if it meant that we would end up right back here.

We're far from perfect and nothing is without hardship, but when two people love each other as fiercely and deeply as Zayden and I do, there isn't a thing you can't overcome.

I don't know what the future holds for us next. But I do know that as I branch out on this new adventure, there's no one I'd rather have by my side than Zayden Michaels.

He started out as my bully. Then he became my protector. And now, he is the love of my life.

And I wouldn't have it any other way….

The End

other books by alex grayson

The Jaded Series

Shatter Me
Reclaim Me
Unveil Me
Awaken Me
The Jaded Series: The Complete Collection

The Consumed Series

Always Wanting
Bare Yourself
Watching Mine

Hell Night Series

Trouble in Hell
Bitter Sweet Hell
Judge of Hell
Key to Hell

Standalones

Endless Obsession
Whispered Prayers of a Girl
Pitch Dark
The Sinister Silhouette

other books by melissa toppen

ALL THAT WE ARE
VIOLETS ARE NOT BLUE
LOVE ME LIKE YOU WON'T LET GO
HOW WE FALL
WHERE THE NIGHT ENDS
TEQUILA HAZE
TEN HOURS
THE ROAD TO YOU
CRAZY STUPID LOVE
FORCE OF NATURE

about alex grayson

Alex Grayson is the bestselling author of heart pounding, emotionally gripping contemporary romances including the Jaded Series, the Consumed Series, and three standalone novels. Her passion for books was reignited by a gift from her sister-in-law. After spending several years as a devoted reader and blogger, Alex decided to write and independently publish her first novel in 2014 (an endeavor that took a little longer than expected). The rest, as they say, is history.

Originally a southern girl, Alex now lives in Ohio with her husband, two children, two cats and dog. She loves the color blue, homemade lasagna, casually browsing real estate, and interacting with her readers. Visit her website, www.alexgraysonbooks.com, or find her on social media!

Facebook
BookBub
Twitter
Instagram
Pinterest
Newsletter
Email

about melissa toppen

Melissa Toppen is a Bestselling Author specializing in New Adult and Contemporary Romance. She is a lover of books and enjoys nothing more than losing herself in a good novel. She has a soft spot for Romance and focuses her writing in that direction; writing what she loves to read.

Melissa resides in Cincinnati Ohio with her husband and two children, where she writes full time.

Website
Facebook
Goodreads
Twitter
Instagram
Pinterest
Amazon
BookBub
Book and Main

Made in USA - Kendallville, IN
1060365_9781704836638
03.20.2020 2332